GABRIELLE AND THE REBELS

WINDS OF CHANGE: BOOK 1

MAUREEN ULRICH

Copyright © 2022, 2024 by Maureen Ulrich

All rights reserved.

No part of this book may be reproduced in any form or by any electronic or mechanical means, including information storage and retrieval systems, without written permission from the author, except for the use of brief quotations in a book review.

First edition published in 2022. Second edition published in 2024 with new ISBN.

ISBN: 978-1-7782965-3-6 (paperback)

ISBN: 978-1-7782965-4-3 (electronic book)

All characters are fictitious products of the writer's fertile imagination.

Cover Artwork: Awan Designer

Map: Wild Rose Printing

Young Adult/Historical Fantasy/Coming of Age

After her father is murdered, sixteen-year-old Gabrielle March finds herself alone in a city of the verge of revolution. Her older brother appears to be involved with the rebels. Will she be able to save him from the hangman's noose?

Cover Image: A young woman with flowing red hair and a grey cape sits astride a brown horse. The background is a seventeenth century Belgian city.

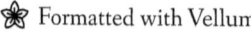 Formatted with Vellum

For lovers of history.
I ask your pardon for this alternative version of the evolution of certain inventions as well as Pilgrim's Progress.

For non-lovers, please check the glossary at the back for some archaic (and invented) words.

REVIEWS

"***Gabrielle and the Rebels*** is a well-crafted fantasy with just the right amount of realism, a touch of romance and a fearless female lead whom we cheer for at every turn. A map at the beginning and a glossary at the back of archaic and invented words assist (although likely unnecessary) readers in this romp. Gabrielle and the Rebels would be a great addition to any YA public or school library collection. Highly Recommended." - **Canadian Review of Materials:**

"I love the premise of ***Gabrielle and the Rebels***, the first book in the Winds of Change series. Travel back to a time a few centuries ago, throw technology in the mix, and see what happens. From page one, this was a fun read. I found it categorized in many ways - fiction, urban fantasy, historical fantasy, and alternate history, among others - but for me the only important category is 'must read.' Ulrich's writing is my favourite kind in a work of fiction—pared down. She doesn't feel a need for flowery prose, instead opting for tight language where every word is carefully chosen to keep the action and storyline constantly moving forward. Don't get me wrong—Ulrich still describes things, she just does so in a proactive way. I have a love/hate relationship with dialogue. I love it when it is done right and struggle to finish books that have weak dialogue. Luckily for us readers, the dialogue in **Gabrielle and the Rebels** is spot on and keeps the flow of the book on track. This is a great thing as the book is heavy on the dialogue, in all the best ways!" - **Toby Welch**, **Sask Books Review**

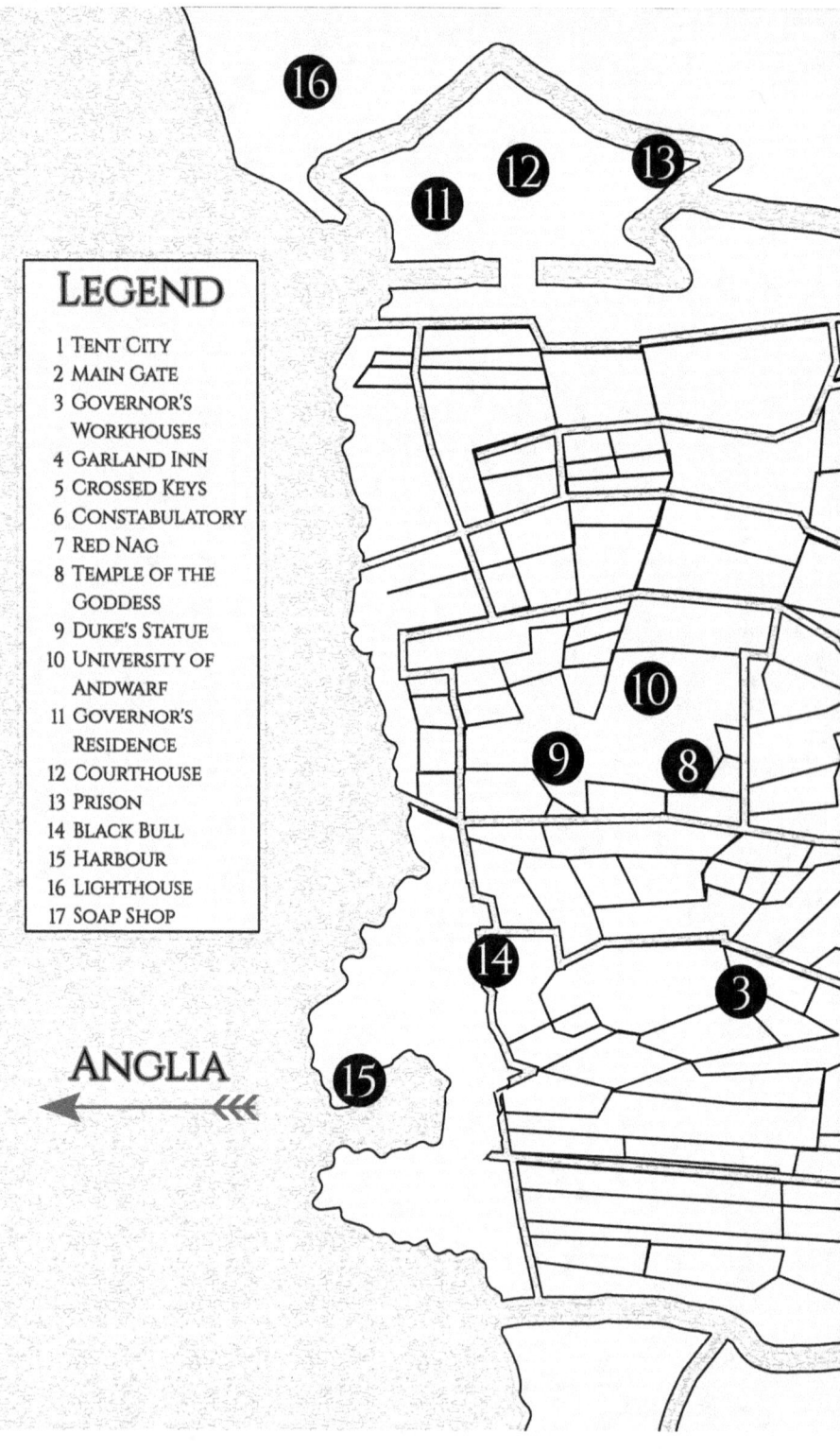

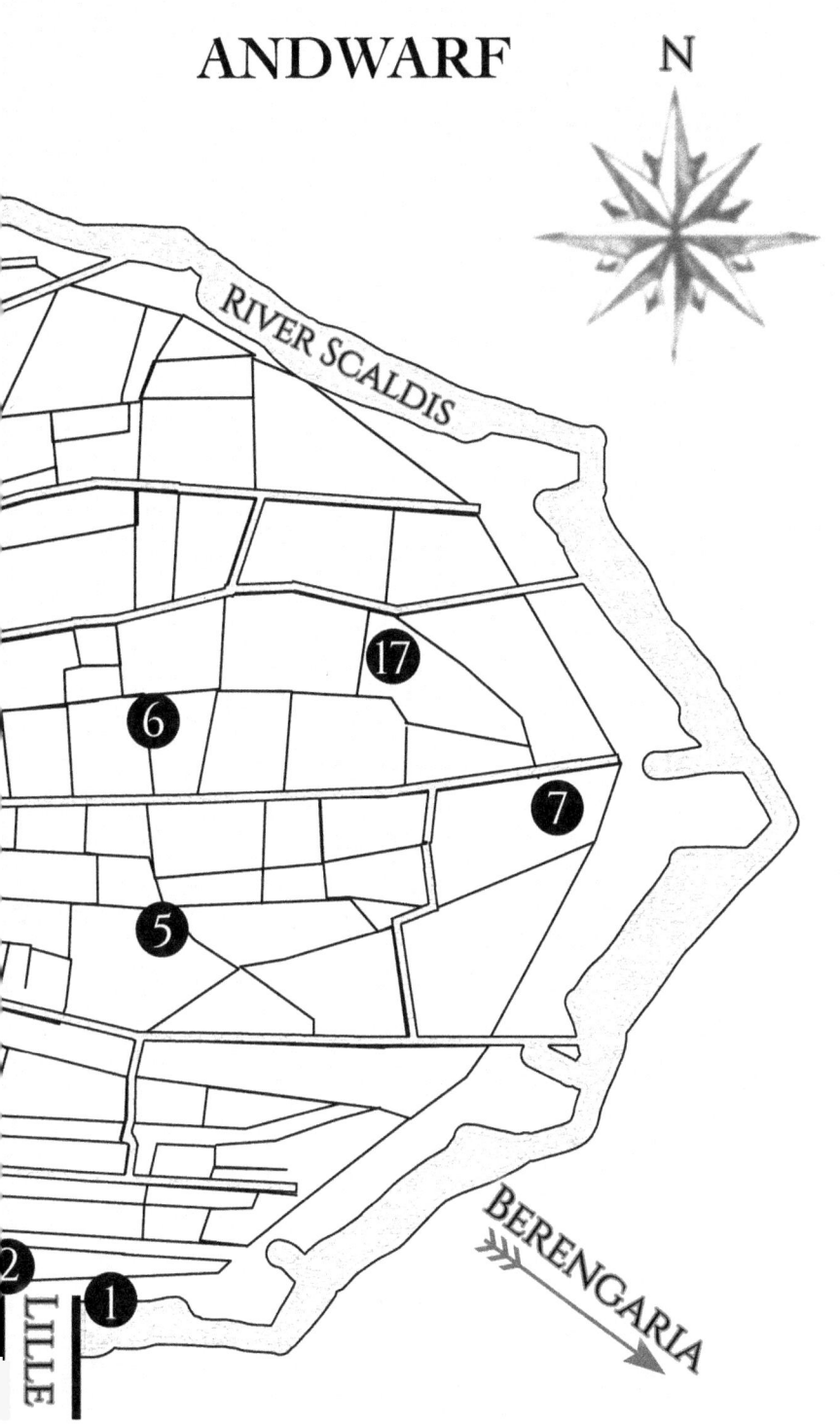

CONTENTS

Chapter 1 *Welcome to Andwarf*	1
Chapter 2 *An Old Friend*	8
Chapter 3 *The Garland*	13
Chapter 4 *Portents*	19
Chapter 5 *Crossroads*	26
Chapter 6 *The Red Nag*	31
Chapter 7 *The Best Meat Pies in Andwarf*	38
Chapter 8 *The Great Gonzalo*	43
Chapter 9 *The Governor of Andwarf*	50
Chapter 10 *Chaos in the Courtyard*	59
Chapter 11 *The Black Bull*	62
Chapter 12 *Ale and a Tale*	65
Chapter 13 *The Leetle Prince*	71
Chapter 14 *Discovery*	80
Chapter 15 *Breakfast at the Black Bull*	84
Chapter 16 *Disguise*	91

Chapter 17 *The Prison Gates*	94
Chapter 18 *The Wheels of Justice*	99
Chapter 19 *The Temple of the Goddess*	111
Chapter 20 *Night Visitor*	116
Chapter 21 *Missions*	122
Chapter 22 *The Quest for Knowledge*	132
Chapter 23 *A Bargain*	135
Chapter 24 *The Temple Roof*	139
Chapter 25 *Confrontation*	147
Chapter 26 *Under Siege*	151
Chapter 27 *The Walnut Tree*	156
Chapter 28 *Meeting of Minds*	159
Chapter 29 *Ironfist*	168
Chapter 30 *The Redemption*	174
Chapter 31 *The Green-eyed Monster*	184
Chapter 32 *The Soap Makers' Shop*	188
Chapter 33 *Change in Plans*	196
Chapter 34 *The Governor's Perch*	199
Chapter 35 *His Greatest Performance*	206

Chapter 36 *Retribution*	211
Chapter 37 *Sanctuary*	216
Chapter 38 *From the Ashes*	223
Chapter 39 *Forgiveness*	228
Chapter 40 *Bitter Fruit*	233
Chapter 41 *The Mob*	240
Chapter 42 *Parting*	247
Afterword	253
Glossary of Archaic and Invented Words	255
Discussion Questions	259
Acknowledgments	261
About the Author	263
Also by Maureen Ulrich	265

1

WELCOME TO ANDWARF

As we wait our turn at the entrance to the city, the sea breeze cools the sweat patches beneath my arms and between my breasts. Minx, my bay mare, snorts and fidgets beneath me. I shade my eyes from the bright August sun and crane my neck to get a better look at the object mounted on top of the gatehouse.

Before I can ask my father or Jack what it is, the cart ahead rattles under the portcullis and drives onto the bridge. A young man in a black uniform beckons imperiously at my father, who trots his grey horse towards the gatehouse. I urge Minx to catch up while Jack's ox cart trundles behind us.

The young official twitches his straggly brown mustache and purses his lips as he stares at my father.

"Name?" the official demands.

My father removes his hat and uses his sleeve to wipe the sweat from his brow. "Lord Simon March of Lille."

The official doesn't react. Perhaps he's too young to link my father's name to the history of this city.

"How long do you intend to remain in Andwarf?" The official's chest is puffed with his own self-importance.

Why doesn't Papa put him in his place?

"A few days," my father replies instead.

The official walks a slow, haughty circuit of Papa and Ghost. He seems unimpressed by my father's dusty coat and sweat-soaked hat, but his eyes rest for a moment on the broadsword slung behind Papa's hip.

He may not look like it right now, but my father is a war hero. Twenty years ago, he led the Duke's triumphant army over this same bridge.

Not that I was there to see it. I was born four years later. Papa is reluctant to talk about his years as the Duke's most-decorated warrior, but I've wheedled a few tales out of Jack, who served under my father.

I stiffen as the official, thumbs thrust in his belt, turns his disdainful gaze on me.

"This is Lady Gabrielle March—my daughter," Papa explains.

The young man studies the breeches that poke from beneath my frock. When he shakes his head and smirks, I raise my chin.

He turns away and gestures at Jack, demanding, "Who's driving the cart?"

"Jack Shepherd. One of my crofters," my father explains. "He's brought wool for the Governor's looms."

"Check the cart, guardsman." The official waves at a hulking man-at-arms who lounges in the shade of the gatehouse.

The guardsman jabs his pike into the wool sacks piled high on the ox cart while Jack digs a stubby forefinger in his ear. The sheep farmer and I exchange looks of annoyance.

What do these officials hope Jack is hiding? A chest full of pirate treasure?

"The tax is twenty marks," the young official announces. "Five for each person, one for each animal, and two for the cart."

While my father pays him, something plops on my hat. I look up as a seagull lights on top of the gatehouse. Even the birds in this city seem disposed to insult us.

That's when I realize that the object mounted on a spike is a man's head. Nearly all the flesh has been torn from the cheekbones. I've never seen anything so horrible.

"Look away, Gabby." My father's jaw is rigid as he stares between Ghost's grey ears.

He's seen the head too. I resist the urge to vomit as my eyes are drawn back to the grisly sight.

Who was he? What did he do? Why would the authorities put his *head* up there?

"Are you done?" Papa says to the official, who examines each coin with elaborate care. "I've business to conduct, and this is taking longer than necessary."

"I'll decide what's necessary, Lord Simon," the official snaps. "The Governor has authorized me to make certain no undesirable persons enter this city."

Who would come here by *choice?*

At last, the official tosses the coins in a wooden box, clears his throat, and waves us on.

On the other side of the gatehouse, the red roofs of Andwarf rise to meet the cloudless sky. Though I dread what tomorrow will bring, I can't wait to get to our lodging and wash away two days of road dirt—and put that hideous sight behind us.

When we reach the bridge's highest point, I can see the top of a lighthouse and bright blue water that stretches to the edge of the world. My pulse skips at my first view of the Great Sea. I want to ask my father if we can visit the harbour tomorrow, but I already know the answer.

He is far too preoccupied with the business at hand—delivering first the wool, then my older brother and me to our respective fates. Damon is betrothed to the daughter of Conrad Visser, a wealthy merchant and the Governor of Andwarf. Whilst I—

"Do you see it, Gabby?" My father has turned Ghost sideways. He points to a white building, topped by a shining glass dome, which soars above the red roofs. "The Temple of the Goddess!"

I nod and smile, but all I feel is despair. Tomorrow, life as I know it will be over.

To avoid looking at the Temple, I rein Minx closer to the side of the bridge and stare into the pale green water, which stinks of sewage and decay. Dead fish, vegetable scraps, and dirty rags bob near the surface.

How I miss the smells of home: damp earth after a rain, freshly harvested wheat, my mother's hyacinth soap.

Will I ever see Maman again?

"The workhouse labourers live down there," Jack says behind me. "Too poor to sleep anywhere else."

At the base of the city wall, tents and lean-tos crowd the bank of the River Scaldis. A waif squats beside a campfire and stirs a pot. The poor little thing can't be more than six. She stops stirring and boldly returns my gaze. I wish I had a few coins to toss her.

"By the Goddess' eyes! Hurry up, Gabby!" my father shouts.

I hadn't realized he'd ridden ahead. I kick Minx and trot after him. Guardsmen armed with crossbows patrol the city walls. Two more sneer at us from either side of the arch as we pass between them.

A wide cobblestone avenue lined with shops stretches before us, and my curiosity takes over. I trail my father through districts busy with tanners, weavers, tailors, hat-makers, jewellers, and silversmiths. We ride alongside a canal where a man rows a slender boat laden with goods. We pass by an open-air market, and though I'd like to take a closer look at the stalls and displays, Papa doesn't stop until we reach two tall buildings. A rhythmic pounding resonates through the open windows.

"What's that noise?" I yell at Jack.

His ox pulls up next to Minx. "The governor's looms!"

The sheep farmer guides his cart into the shadows between the two buildings while my father gives instructions to a sullen man in an apron. Papa then tosses a handful of coins at the dirty children who huddle in the doorway. As the children squabble and claw each other for the money, I recall the skinny girl on the riverbank and wonder why her parents would choose to work here.

Coming down the street towards us is a noisy throng, led by two men with arms slung around each other's shoulders. Behind them, women gossip and laugh as baskets swing from their forearms. Perhaps there's a festival today.

A gaggle of youngsters caper around a stocky boy who tugs on a rope. To my dismay, the other end is knotted loosely about a small boy's scrawny neck.

"Over here, Gabby!" my father beckons.

Before I can turn Minx into the passage, the crowd spills around me. My mare snorts and sidesteps as a man presses against my left leg.

"Good sir, please tell me what's the occasion," I say to the man.

"Were you not at the hangings?" His eyes are bloodshot, and the bulb of his nose is just as red. "They strung up four today. They're bringing two to the bridge." He jerks his thumb over his shoulder.

I look up the street. At the back of the crowd, a pair of heads hover on pikes.

"Who were they?" I ask, though I'm not sure I want to know.

"Students from that bleeding university." The man spews a clump of phlegm on the cobblestones at Minx's feet. "Good riddance to them."

My mind flies to Damon, who was also a student before the university closed. Did my brother know these poor lads?

My unpleasant companion wipes his forehead with his grimy sleeve. "Every rat should be flushed from his hidey hole and exterminated."

"You should be ashamed to say such things," I tell him.

"You're a fine one to speak to me of shame." He glowers at me from beneath thick black brows. "Riding a horse like a man. It's not natural."

Ghost's broad chest propels the man backwards. "Mind your manners around my daughter," my father threatens.

"Or you'll *what?*" the man retorts.

Papa's hand rests on the hilt of his sword. Those closest shuffle away though the nasty man tries to stare my father down.

My pulse quickens when I see Papa's grim expression.

"Step away now," he says quietly.

The nasty man opens his mouth then shuts it. To my relief, he turns and shoulders his way into the crowd.

"Gabby, haven't I begged you to stay close?" My father's brown eyes are furious.

I open my mouth to explain, but a voice shouts, "Listen! Rise up!"

In the middle of the crowd, a fist waves a pamphlet. Behind it, a larger fist brandishes a baton.

"You there!" the man with the baton cries. "Stop!"

Still clutching the pamphlet, a youth in a grey cowl swims sideways through the river of people, then levers himself into the doorway of the workhouse to our left. "Hear me, citizens! Stir from slumber and take back your city!"

Doesn't he see those *heads*?

The burly guardsman shoves people aside in his haste to reach the lad.

"Read about our cause! The truth is at your fingertips!" the fugitive cries as he urges passersby to take the pamphlet.

No one does.

The guardsman will reach him in a moment.

"Run!" I shout at the lad.

Indeed he runs—straight at me. He ducks under Minx's neck and flashes me a cocky grin. His cowl slips, exposing a riot of brown curls, as he darts into the passage behind me. I hope it doesn't lead to a dead end.

"Stop him!" the guardsman orders as he bears down on us. A whistle bounces on a cord about his neck.

To my surprise, my father reins Ghost into the guardsman's path to prevent him from following the lad.

"Out of my way!" the guardsman shouts. "You just let that rebel escape!"

Rebel?

The guardsman rams the whistle between his lips and tweets a sharp blast. Metal scrapes as my father draws his sword and aims the blade at the guardsman's throat.

By the Goddess' eyes. What is Papa doing?

2

AN OLD FRIEND

Ghost advances, and the burly guardsman retreats. Curious citizens press closer.

Do they find this standoff entertaining?

"I'll throw you in prison for aiding a rebel," the guardsman threatens Papa.

"I'm to dine with the Governor tonight," my father replies calmly. "What will he think if I fail to appear?"

To my relief, uncertainty steals over the guardsman's face, and he lowers his baton.

"As I live and breathe—Simon March."

A man with long yellow hair guides his mount through the crowd. Behind him, men-at-arms hold the pikes bearing the two severed heads. The man stops his horse in front of Papa and leans on his pommel. A scar slashes his nose and cheek, and a crossbow is strapped to his back.

Who is he?

"It's been a long time, Simon." He smiles, exposing a broken tooth.

"Nigh twenty years, Rolf," Papa says.

Papa must have known Rolf from the Imperial War. My father rarely speaks of that time. Any information I *do* have has been weaselled from Jack and Andrew, our blacksmith.

Rolf turns to the guardsman. "I'll take care of this."

The guardsman hesitates—as if he'd like to argue—but he returns his baton to his belt and badgers the crowd to move along.

Papa slides his sword back in its scabbard. "I heard you were in the Governor's employ, but I didn't believe it till now."

Rolf's laugh is harsh. "Sniffing out rebels is hardly my usual line of work." His gaze swings towards me. "Your daughter, I assume? She's got your red hair. Apple trees make apples."

What does he mean by that?

"You assume correctly," Papa says. "This is Lady Gabrielle."

Rolf removes his sweat-stained hat. "Good day to you, milady."

I nod a greeting.

"Peace has brought you prosperity," Rolf says to Papa. "Not so for this old mercenary. There's nothing I'd like better than a good, long war."

What an awful thing to say.

"I've seen too many men die," Papa contends. "Fighting for causes that wouldn't have improved their lives a whit had they lived."

Though they speak in familiar terms, I can tell my father doesn't care for Rolf. Papa's face and voice are tight, as they are when he addresses our neighbour Lord Hector, a thoroughly despicable man.

Rolf straightens in the saddle and cranes his neck. "Is that Jack the Steady unloading the cart?"

"It is." Papa flicks at a fly on Ghost's withers. "He raises sheep now. He hasn't stretched a bow in years."

"No wonder. His belly's grown big," Rolf observes. "Are many of the old lads about?"

"Just Andrew," Papa says. "He's my blacksmith now."

"He was a fine gunner. Strange he didn't go home after the War." Rolf cocks his head as he studies Papa. "Who would have guessed that Simon Rouge would one day bear the soil of his fief under his fingernails. Peace has made you soft."

Papa says nothing, but his shoulders tense. I wonder if Rolf knows how close he has come to the truth. Not about Papa being soft. Papa is as tough and weathered as the saddle beneath him. But he has grasped the handles of a plough when a crofter proved unequal to the task and shouldered wheat sheaves when a late frost threatened. I suspect Papa led his men into battle in much the same way—through personal example.

"Best you be wary, Simon. Those are fine horses," Rolf warns, "and there are scoundrels aplenty in this city."

Papa points at the heads on pikes. "Like those lads? They weren't old enough to be dangerous."

"The danger is in their ideas." Rolf shifts in his saddle. "And the Governor pays me to make sure those ideas don't spread. Keep your wits about you, so no harm befalls your pretty daughter."

No one has ever called me pretty. Is Rolf making fun of me?

"I can look after myself and my daughter," Papa says.

I have no doubt of that.

Rolf puts on his hat and gives Papa a bland smile. "You'll be staying at the Garland. We should lift a pint while you're there."

"I have enough tasks to fill my time." Papa rubs the grey bristles he's neglected to shave since we left home. "My daughter is to become a vestal at the Temple of the Goddess."

Ah. The Temple.

Due to the excitement of our brushes with the rebel and the City Guard, I'd forgotten my misery. My flesh itches under Rolf's heavy-lidded gaze. I'm certain I can read his thoughts.

No man wants her, so she'll spend the rest of her life serving the Goddess.

How humiliating.

Rolf bows his head to me. "I'd ask you to say a prayer for me, milady, but there wouldn't be much point. My sins are too numerous." He nods at Papa. "Till we meet again, Simon. Let it be soon."

Rolf guides his horse towards the gates while citizens jostle to get closer to the hideous heads bobbing in his wake.

And I am to spend the rest of my life in this terrible place?

"I never liked Rolf."

I didn't realize that Jack has backed his empty cart out of the passage.

The sheep farmer rubs his round belly as he stares up at my father. "He's a vile one."

My assessment exactly.

"Don't speak ill of a former brother-in-arms. Besides that, he proved useful just now," Papa replies.

Jack glances over his shoulder. "That cocky lad vaulted over my cart and jumped in the canal. What was his crime, Lord Simon?"

"Never mind that now." Papa looks impatient. "How much was the tax on the wool?"

"Two tenths," Jack replies, scratching his neck. "Highway robbery couldn't be worse. If I had my way, I'd string up the ruddy wool merchants instead of young lads."

"You should keep such opinions to yourself," Papa replies. "This is where we part ways, Jack."

"As you wish, milord." Jack holds out his hand, and Papa

clasps it. "I'll spend the night with my wife's family in the weavers' district." The sheep farmer turns to me. "I'll bid you farewell and good luck, milady. I don't imagine I'll see you again."

I blink away tears, for sorrow has stolen my voice. Bit by bit, my old life sifts like golden grains of wheat through my fingers.

3

THE GARLAND

The Garland is a tired old inn on a quiet street. When Papa asks the plump innkeeper about Damon, the man shakes his head.

"I'm sorry, milord. I haven't seen your son for a fortnight." He wrings his puffy hands. "As a matter of fact, he left without paying his bill."

Papa scowls and settles the account.

Where could Damon be?

After the innkeeper shows Papa and me to our rooms, I unpack and smooth out the wrinkles in my best frock—the green one with ivory lace on the bodice. I'll wear it tomorrow. I use the basin and pitcher to wash away dust and sweat while next door, Papa splashes and sings in his low rich voice. I know the song well, for he often teases my mother with it.

The lass was the fairest
With eyes blue as rain
Her hair in a love knot,
She strolled down the lane.

Tu lar tu lee
Tu lar lee a lee
A great lord came riding,
The lass he did see.
Ah, his poor heart was stolen
By one so pretty.
Tu lar tu lee
Tu lar lee a lee

I sit on the bed to unbraid and brush out my hair. Maman used to do this for me when I was little. My longing for home is a powerful ache. I close my eyes and picture the yellow roses fanning the windows of our manor. I already miss my corner bedroom which faces the fishpond and garden to the south and the old keep to the west.

A week ago, Papa informed me that he'd made arrangements for me to be installed at the Temple of the Goddess in Andwarf. I was shattered.

Although I've never wanted to leave home, I assumed one day Papa would procure a strong and generous husband for me —a landowner who wouldn't mind having a wife more at home in the saddle than supervising a busy household.

But I'm destined to never marry or bear children. Even worse, based on the way Maman clung to me when we said our goodbyes, I will likely never see her or Papa again after tomorrow.

A rap disturbs my thoughts. I open the door to a servant girl with a tray.

"I've brought your supper, milady." The girl bobs a curtsey and sets the tray on a small table near the hearth.

The smell of the savoury stew is tantalizing, and despite my anxiety about what tomorrow will bring, I'm famished. I dig in immediately, scarcely noting the girl's departure.

"I take it the meal appeals to you."

Papa stands in the doorway. He wears his brown velvet surcoat. It's the finest item of clothing he owns, though the cuffs and elbows are worn.

I chew and swallow. "It does. Are you leaving for the Governor's?"

Papa nods.

I'm curious about Visser's daughter Katarina, who will soon become my brother's wife.

"Can I please come with you?"

Papa runs a large hand through his reddish hair, which is streaked with silver. "I have much to discuss with Visser, and it would be better if you remained here."

Is he afraid I'll ask silly questions or forget my place?

I put down my fork. "But Papa—"

"You will stay in your room and keep the door bolted." His face is stern. "Don't wait up for me either. In the morning, I'll take you to the Temple."

"But why must I go there? You know I'd rather stay with you and Maman. If I'm not to marry eventually, then what difference will a few more years make?"

"Your mother insists I've already ruined you." Papa folds his arms over his chest. "Too many days in the saddle and not enough time on your studies—or your faith. On this, I am in agreement—though I must bear much of the blame."

I open my mouth, but words will not come. There's no moving Papa when his mind is set.

"I hope the Governor will know where Damon is staying," Papa continues, altering the subject. "If he doesn't, I'll speak to Thomas Smithson."

My heart quickens. Andrew's son Thomas and my brother were boyhood friends, despite the differences in their years and stations. I haven't seen Thomas for six years, but I remember well his broad shoulders and handsome smile.

"Thomas would be twenty-two by now." Papa leans on the mantle above the hearth. "Well on his way to becoming a master blacksmith. Meanwhile, my own son has yet to show signs of maturity."

"It's strange that Damon left the inn so suddenly," I observe. "Do you think he had a falling out with the Governor?"

Papa laughs. "Not likely. Visser is deeply in my debt, and I have agreed to offset some of that debt as part of his daughter's dowry." He removes a book from under his coat. "While I'm gone tonight, I'd like you to read this. Damon gave it to me."

I take the slender volume, hoping for a subject related to animal husbandry. "*Everyman's Journey.* By Adelaide Fierelli. Never heard of him. What's it about?"

Papa picks up a poker and stirs the ashes in the cold hearth. "It's an allegory. Everyman travels from his home to the Celestial City, just as each of us journey from birth to death to life beyond death. Hopefully, Fierelli will help deepen your convictions, as he did mine."

Everyman's Journey doesn't sound very interesting, but at least it isn't thick.

Papa continues stirring the ashes. "Fierelli has some profound ideas, not that Damon's taken any of them to heart. If he had, he might understand a thing or two about his responsibility towards his family."

"Are you referring to Damon's infatuation with the miller's daughter?" I place the book on the small table beside me. "Is that why you sent him to Andwarf and married Fanny off to John Angusson?"

Papa shoots me a glance. "I'll not discuss that with you. It's not fitting."

I rise and slip my arm through his. "I'm sorry, Papa."

He leans the poker against the fireplace and turns towards me. Do his eyes look sad because he will miss me as much as I will miss him?

I place a hand over his, my forefinger tracing the dolphin on the Duke's ring. "Does Rolf have one of these?"

Papa's brow wrinkles. "No. Why do you ask?"

"I think he envies you."

"As he should." Papa kisses my forehead. "I have the most beautiful wife and daughter in the duchy."

Tears smart behind my eyes at his unexpected compliment. "I love you, Papa."

"And I love you, Gabby." He draws his handkerchief from his sleeve and dabs my face. His voice is hoarse when he continues. "I have no idea how I will give you to the Temple, but I must. You are too tall, too outspoken, and too rough around the edges." He pauses and swallows. "The Goddess alone understands why you were born second—and a girl. You are more suited to overseeing a fief than any man I know."

Though his words echo my unspoken desire, they shock me just the same. I had no notion Papa felt this way.

Love shines in his brown eyes. "Better I should send you to the Temple than marry you to a stranger who would never appreciate your courage or wit. Who would only strive to break your spirit. If that should come to pass, I couldn't bear it." He clears his throat and tucks his handkerchief back in his sleeve. "Sleep well, my daughter."

Later, I clutch my own handkerchief and watch from my window as Papa mounts Ghost in the inn yard. Papa holds up a hand to me, and I wave. I turn away and blow my nose and resolve to enjoy my last few hours with him tomorrow.

I finish my supper and settle into a chair with *Everyman's Journey*. I'll read a few chapters so I can discuss them with

Papa while we have our last breakfast together. I reach for my handkerchief again as tears blur the words on the first page. I wipe my eyes and read:

An Apology

When at first, I took my quill in hand,
To write this book, little did I understand
The power of words to instruct
Or impair the souls of man.

After the emotional hills and valleys of the past week, I don't need verses that tax my mind. I close the book.

My gaze falls on the neat yellow stitches in each corner of my handkerchief. Goldenrod is the flower of the Goddess. Maman pressed the handkerchief into my hand when she bade me farewell:

"I shall miss you every day, Gabby. You're good and wise beyond your years. The Goddess has blessed us, and it's fitting we should give you to Her. Imagine. You could rise to Guardian one day."

As I envision a future bound within the thick walls of the Temple and the tedious drone and drag of days spent in endless ritual, Maman's hopes offer no comfort at all.

4

PORTENTS

The next morning, I dress and wait for Papa's knock —the signal that my transformation from landowner's daughter to vestal will soon be fulfilled. When a distant bell chimes seven times, I leave my room and rap on Papa's door.

Nothing.

I press my ear against the wooden panel and listen. "Papa, are you awake?"

Still nothing.

Papa never sleeps this late.

I rattle the knob, but his door is locked. Confused, I go downstairs.

"He didn't come back last night, milady." The plump innkeeper scuttles from behind the counter. "His horse isn't in the stable either. Most unusual. I've sent the kitchen maid to fetch the City Guard. That's why she never brought your breakfast."

Concern for Papa hammers in my ears. "I don't give a ram's bollocks about my breakfast. Why didn't *you* wake me?"

His round face reddens. "I didn't want to disturb you, milady."

"I'll go look for him. Tell your stable boy to saddle my horse."

"But it's not safe for you to go into the streets alone," the innkeeper sputters. "If your father should return and not find you here, he will be furious." The possibility appears to terrify him.

I start back up the stairs. Papa is not a hard drinker, but perhaps—just this once—he took a glass too many and spent the night at the Governor's.

"Furthermore, there's the matter of his bill." I can tell the innkeeper chooses his words carefully. "Should Lord Simon not return—"

"You'll get your money. My father never had a debt in his life." My cheeks are hot, but not because of the warm summer morning.

"At least take the stable boy with you," the innkeeper pleads.

He lingers at the bottom of the stairs while I hesitate at the top. Is he worried about me or his money?

I return to my room where I pin on my hat. I ponder packing up my things, then rule against it. I will come back for them later—after I find Papa.

I pace the inn yard while the stable lad, who is close to my own age, outfits Minx and a mount for himself. When he finally leads the horses out, I check Minx's girth and tighten the cinch. I should have saddled her myself.

"If my father returns, tell him I've gone to search for him at the Governor's residence," I call to the innkeeper, who frets in the doorway.

The innkeeper blinks. "But you can't just go there and demand admittance."

Stupid man. Has he forgotten how important Papa is?

I jam my foot in the stirrup and swing onto Minx's back. "Do you know where the Governor lives?" I ask the stable lad.

He nods.

As I trot Minx out of the yard after him, my mood is as acrid as the smoke spilling over the rooftops and stealing between shops.

I pull up beside the lad. "That smoke isn't from cooking fires, is it?"

"No, milady." His face is serious.

I drop back and shadow him up the narrow, nearly deserted street. The smoke grows thicker, irritating my eyes and throat. Just ahead, a man with a measuring tape draped about his neck locks the door to his shop.

"Do you know what's burning?" I call to the tailor.

"One of the Governor's workhouses, miss." The tailor pockets his key. "Going up like a tinderbox, I hear. There's also been a stabbing at the Crossed Keys." He hurries away.

Apparently the citizens of Andwarf are attracted to all sorts of horrific events.

A crone in a tattered shawl flutters out of a doorway, startling Minx. I tighten my reins to stop my mare from bolting.

"Be careful!" I shout at the woman while Minx plunges beneath me.

"*You* be careful!" she croaks. "The city is doomed! Signs are everywhere! Watch for them! Watch!"

Hooves clatter on cobblestones. A riderless grey horse, reins dangling, turns the corner and trots towards us. I'd recognize Ghost's white blaze from a league away.

What's become of Papa?

Ghost neighs and quickens his step. Minx does the same. When we reach him, I lean over to snatch his reins. Papa's sword and scabbard still hang from their loop. There are streaks of dried blood on the saddle.

"Your father must have come to harm, milady," the stable lad says.

"It's not possible." I struggle to reconcile the blood on the saddle with the certainty that Papa is indestructible. "Simon March was the most decorated warrior of the Imperial War." I hand the lad Ghost's reins. "Trust me. He won't be the one who was hurt."

I kick Minx and ride ahead. Around the corner, I come upon a throng gathered in front of a tavern.

"What's happened?" I call out.

A stocky man swaddled in a nightcap and dressing gown faces me. "A man's been stabbed to death. Robbed too, it seems. He's got no wallet."

Not Papa. Surely not Papa.

I slide off Minx's back and shoulder my way into the crowd. On the other side, Papa is slumped against the building, his long legs outstretched. His head is turned towards the street, but neither his face nor his eyes move as I approach. His bloody right hand cradles his side. Blood also soaks his coat and breeches. A rat scuttles into a hole under the tavern wall.

I touch my father's stiff hand. He's been dead for hours. His fourth finger has been cut off, and the Duke's ring is missing. Recalling the rat, I try not to imagine where Papa's finger has gone. I shut his glazed eyes and kiss his cold cheek.

The smoke hanging in the air makes my eyes water and my nose run. When I wipe them on my sleeve, I notice blood on my hand. Where's my handkerchief? Did I leave it at the inn?

Someone taps my shoulder.

"I'm sorry, miss. Is he known to you?"

When I nod, my head feels disconnected from my body.

Two guardsmen loom over me. One is young with a bright

red beard. His older companion has a thick neck that bulges above his tight uniform collar. I beat back the urge to unfasten the top button.

Red Beard spreads his hands on his thighs and leans closer. "We need you to come to the constabulary and answer some questions." His blue eyes are pools of sympathy.

"Who is he?" Thick Neck demands.

It takes me a moment to realize whom he means.

"My father." My voice sounds peculiar. "Lord Simon March of Lille. Perhaps you've heard of him."

Thick Neck shrugs, obviously unimpressed.

Red Beard drops on one knee. "Do you have family here, milady?"

"The Governor." When Red Beard raises an eyebrow, I add, "His daughter is betrothed to my brother."

A memory of Papa waving farewell clouds my brain. How can he be dead?

"You'll want to take your father back to Lille for burial," Red Beard suggests.

"And with this heat, I'd do it right away." Thick Neck unfastens the top button on his collar.

Thank goodness.

Red Beard examines Papa's chest and abdomen. The gashes are long and jagged, wide and deep—very like the ones Papa left in the wild boar that ravaged the town last winter. Papa's knife, which he used to sever a calf from its afterbirth or geld a pig, is still in its sheath.

"My father didn't have a chance to defend himself." My fingers move of their own accord as I draw the knife. I'm certain the blood crusting the blade does not belong to a beast.

Red Beard's lips are moving again.

I wipe each side of the blade on my bodice before returning the knife to the sheath. "What did you say?"

"I said—is there anyone I should send for, milady?"

I unbuckle Papa's belt—too long for my waist—and remove the sheath. "My brother Damon March. *Lord* March," I add, correcting myself.

Damon is Lord of Lille now.

Gripping the sheath, I rise and step back, my mind and gaze frozen on Papa's mutilated hand. Who did this?

"Come help with the body," Thick Neck orders.

Two churlish fellows lift Papa, wrap him in a coarse wool blanket, and bind the ends. They sling him across Ghost's back.

"This isn't the treatment my father deserves," I tell Red Beard.

"I apologize, milady, but we've no time for niceties," he says gently. "Where might I find your brother?"

"I don't know where he's staying. Perhaps the Governor does. I must . . . inform him." My thoughts begin to thaw. "And Jack—one of my father's tenants—is staying in the weavers' district. I'll speak to him as well." I jam the knife and sheath in my boot.

"Of course," Red Beard says patiently. "But first you must go to the constabulary so a report can be written up."

"No. *First* I must find out who did this." I face the throng. "Did anyone see anything?"

Every face turns to the stocky man in the nightcap. He must own the tavern.

"Was my father inside your establishment last night?" I ask him.

He flits a glance left and right then wobbles his head in denial. He's lying. Before I can ask why, he turns his back and disappears inside the inn.

"This is a robbery gone bad, milady, and you'll never know who did it." Thick Neck gives me a surly look and addresses the crowd. "Nothing more to see here. Move along now."

The crowd disperses, flowing in the direction of the black smoke which billows over the rooftops.

"Please go to the constabulary, milady," Red Beard urges. "Let me take care of the rest."

Thick Neck jerks Ghost's reins, and the horse throws up his head. I grab his mane and place my palm on his nose.

"There now," I soothe him. "You must bear your master with dignity." When the horse calms, I slide the reins from Thick Neck's grasp. "I'm ready," I tell him. "Lead the way."

5

CROSSROADS

At the constabulary, the scrawny clerk who questions me seems to have drawn his own conclusions.

"I'll mark the time of death as undetermined." He dips his quill in an ink pot. "As well as the cause."

"The *cause* was murder." I unpin and remove my hat, then fan myself with it. "My father was stabbed."

"And robbed. Happens all the time." The clerk scratches a word on the ledger in front of him.

I look to the window. Outside, Minx and Ghost are tied to a post. Papa's body is still draped across Ghost's back. The Garland's stable lad has vanished.

Will Red Beard return with any information? The Governor hasn't even sent a servant to advise me. Has the workhouse fire distracted him as it has everyone else?

"Funny the thief didn't take the horse," the clerk remarks.

What did Rolf say to Papa?

"*Those are fine horses, and there are scoundrels aplenty in this city.*"

Rolf. Yes.

Could my father's former brother-in-arms have a hand in this? Is fear of Rolf the reason the tavern owner wouldn't tell the truth?

"It wasn't thieves," I say.

The clerk mops his brow with a grubby handkerchief.

Did he even hear me?

"We encountered an acquaintance of my father's yesterday." I pull my chair closer to the clerk's untidy desk and set down my hat. "He knew where we were staying, and he wanted to meet my father for a drink. His name was Rolf."

"Rolf Von Haugen?" The clerk sets down his quill, and his lower lip quivers. "It's unlikely he would have anything to do with it. He's far too busy with the Governor's business."

"My father served the Duke during the War." I raise my voice since the clerk refuses to look me in the eye. "Lord March was trained to fight. His killer must have been someone he knew."

Someone who wanted the Duke's ring.

Minx neighs, and my attention is drawn back to the window. A woman in a white bonnet plucks at the twine binding Papa's body. Meanwhile, her gaunt companion clasps his hands behind his back and glances apprehensively over his shoulder.

What do these people want?

Ghost jerks his head and sidles away from the woman. Minx neighs again.

I rise and lean on the window sill. "Who are those people?"

"Just the Levers." The clerk seems relieved by the interruption. "Since our business is concluded, milady, I'll ask you to leave."

"Since *when* is it concluded?" I rap on the window to get the woman's attention.

She glares at me and makes a crude gesture. I don't know what it means, but I know I don't like it.

I fling open the door and stride into the yard. "Get away from them!"

The woman has beady eyes and a sharp nose, very much like a rat's. "How much?" she asks.

I step between her and Ghost. "These horses aren't for sale!"

"I don't want to buy *them*," she states. "How much for the *body*?"

The question smacks me between the eyes. "That's not a body." I pronounce each word carefully. "That's my father."

I draw Papa's sword. I need both hands to keep it raised. The woman scuttles backwards, bumping into Minx—who snorts and shakes her head in umbrage.

"Leave now before I cut off your nose," I threaten.

"No need to get huffy, milady," the woman replies. "I meant no disrespect."

The couple quickly retreat to their mule cart and bounce out of the yard.

I slide Papa's sword back in the scabbard and lean against Ghost's rump. The door to the constabulary is now closed and the curtains drawn. That clerk is another coward afraid to cross Rolf Von Haugen.

"Papa, what happens now?" I whisper.

Minx whickers, and I look into her soft, intelligent brown eyes.

A memory flickers of Papa and Damon leaving for Andwarf four years ago. I was devastated as I waved goodbye to my older brother, my weaver of stories and adventures. Maman assured me that he would return one day—though not before he was educated and married—and that Papa would be back within a week. The sun rose and set on seven days with no sign of him, but long after supper, Papa rode up to the manor, leading a spirited bay mare.

"Sorry I've been so long," he said as he slid off Ghost. "The minx got away from me twice on the road, and I had to chase her down. She's too clever for her own good." He placed the mare's halter rope in my hand. "Your legs are too long for that fat pony of yours, so I bought her for you. I know you'll care for her, as you care for all that's mine."

I reach over to stroke Minx's nose, centering myself in the realization that from this moment forward, I must do what Papa would do.

By the time Jack the sheep farmer appears, I have a plan.

"You will take Lord Simon and Ghost back to Lille," I tell him. "But first you need to retrieve my father's things from the Garland. Can you also settle the bill?"

The farmer's eyes are red and watery. He served Papa as an archer for ten years before he started raising sheep. He's bereft at the news of my father's death.

"I can, but what of you, milady?" Jack's voice is rough.

I place a hand on his furry forearm. "I'll go to the blacksmith district and speak with Andrew's son. Papa thought Thomas would know where Damon is."

"Thomas works at the Red Nag," Jack says. "But I should go with you."

"No, you must take care of my father's affairs." I'm impatient to be on my way now that I know the name of the blacksmith shop.

Jack scowls and scratches his ear. "This is a dangerous city, milady."

"I'll take a guardsman with me," I lie. "The pair who dealt with Papa this morning were very helpful."

Jack looks relieved. "Very well, milady. Thomas is a good lad—a man by now, I expect—and loyal to your family. He'll find your brother, and then you'll go to the Temple, as your father intended."

"Of course."

I say this only to appease Jack. The Temple is the last place I plan to visit now that my life has been upended.

"I never met any man worthy to walk in Lord Simon's boots." Suspicion sneaks across Jack's homely face. "Were the authorities certain it was thieves that killed him? Did anyone *see* what happened?"

"They're certain," I say quickly. "There must have been witnesses."

It's not fear of Rolf that prompts this falsehood, but fear Jack will contrive a way to drag me to the Temple, leaving Damon unfound and unaware of what's happened.

Jack rubs his jaw. "And what shall I tell Lady Violet?"

What indeed. I banish the image of Maman weeping over Papa's body.

"Tell her what I've told you. And tell her I love her and will write to her soon." I hope I will remember that promise.

"As you wish, Lady Gabrielle." Jack takes hold of Ghost's bridle. He appears to notice for the first time that Papa's sword is now tied to Minx's saddle, and he gives me a long look. Still, he doesn't question my actions. He leads Ghost to the ox cart.

Despite my determination to appear confident, doubt batters me as Jack maneuvers the ox cart—Papa's grey horse trotting behind—into the busy street. Still, as I swing onto Minx's back, the pressure of Papa's sword behind my hip brings a measure of comfort.

I may be alone, but someone must know where the Red Nag is. I only have to ask.

6

THE RED NAG

A RED HORSE WITH ROLLING WHITE EYES IS PAINTED ON the door of the ramshackle brick building. The ring of metal on metal soars through the open window.

I tie Minx to the post and unfasten the straps holding the scabbard. Struggling under the sword's weight, I open the door to the smithy.

Fire crackles in the forge built into the brick wall. A giant wearing a sleeveless shirt and long apron towers over the anvil bolted to a wooden pedestal. With a clang, his mallet strikes the horseshoe.

"Excuse me!" I call out.

The huge man sets down his mallet and tongs. A leather patch conceals his left eye. His dark hair has retreated from his wide forehead. "How can I help you, miss?"

My ears are still ringing as I wrestle the sword into the shop and close the door behind me. "I'm looking for Thomas Smithson."

The blacksmith leans both fists on the anvil. "He's out, but he'll be back soon. Why'd you bring that?" His one eye rolls from the sword to my face.

"I intend to sell it."

The blacksmith gestures at the rack of swords, shields, and pikes in the corner. "I don't buy them. I repair them. But there's a swordsmith near here who might be interested."

The sword is getting heavier by the second. "Could you please tell me its worth? I don't want to be cheated."

The man wipes his huge, sooty hands on his apron. "Bring it here then."

"My father used it in the Imperial War," I explain as I place the scabbard on the anvil.

The blacksmith draws Papa's sword and wrists it this way and that, testing its weight. The sunbeam exposes the pits and gouges in the blade. "This weapon has a history. And a pedigree." He traces the hilt with a large forefinger. "See these three thistles? That's the trademark of Leopold Wulgram, the master of the Duke's foundry. Thomas apprenticed under him."

"I know," I reply. "My father arranged the apprenticeship."

The giant looks surprised. "Who did you say your father is?"

"Was." I rally the courage to say Papa's name. "Lord Simon March."

The eyebrow above the leather patch arches. "Simon March is *dead?*"

Here at last is someone who knows my father.

I lower my eyes as they well with tears. "He was robbed and murdered last night."

The blacksmith clears his throat. "I'm sorry to hear it, milady." He reaches across the anvil, as if he intends to pat my forearm then withdraws his hand, remembering the difference in our stations. "Might I get you a sip of cider?"

"Please don't fuss," I tell him.

"'Tis no fuss. And you shouldn't part with his sword. You'll never get its worth. Not much demand for this style of blade anymore."

I need lodging tonight—perhaps for several nights. Will I be forced to sell Minx?

My nose drips, and I wipe it on my sleeve. I won't grovel before this man.

"I'll give you a talen for the sword," he offers. "And we won't concern ourselves with the Governor's tax."

I doubt a talen reflects the weapon's true value, but my options are limited.

"A talen it is." I extend my hand, as I've seen Papa do so often to his people. "Will you shake on the bargain?"

The blacksmith's eye widens, but he encloses my fingers in his damp clasp. "My name's George."

"Gabrielle."

I concentrate on his curious eye. Have I earned George's respect?

He smiles as he releases my hand. "Pleased to make your acquaintance, Lady Gabrielle." He removes a pouch from his apron pocket and extracts a large gold coin.

I've never seen a talen before. I hold it up to the sunbeam streaming through the window. The coin bears the profile of a nobleman on one side while a dolphin leaps on the other.

"This is the Duke of Anglia?" I ask, pointing to the head on the coin.

"It is indeed," George affirms, returning the pouch to his apron. "When he was considerably younger." His gaze returns to the weapon, and he whistles softly. "The sword of Simon Rouge."

My memory tweaks. Rolf called Papa that.

"Simon *Rouge?*" I repeat. "Did people call him that because of his hair?"

"Partly. But more because of his bloody reputation." George rubs his broad forehead. "Emperor Maximillian's men turned and ran when they saw Simon Rouge's banner. He was a fierce warrior, milady."

"So I've heard." I tuck the talen in my bodice, having no other place to keep it. "George, did *you* fight in the War?"

The blacksmith doesn't answer. His face is still, and his eye glistens. I sense that he's lost in a swirl of armoured knights and impatient steeds. He hears only the rattle of swords, clash of shields, and boom of cannons.

The door creaks, drawing me back to the present.

The young man who enters the shop is tall, slim-hipped, and broad-shouldered. Though his unruly dark hair and beard are much longer than I remember, I know this is Thomas. My quickened pulse has little to do with the prospect of finding my brother.

"Is that *your* horse tied outside, miss?" Thomas asks, tucking his shirt into his tan breeches. "If so, I hired a boy to keep an eye on her. She's too fine a filly to be left unattended." He reaches for the apron hanging on a hook.

"Thomas, this is Lady Gabrielle March," George says.

The younger blacksmith lowers his arm. "Lady Gabrielle?" He comes straight over. "What brings you to the city? Is Lord Simon here?"

His questions punch me in the gut.

"Lord Simon is dead," George says. "Murdered. Just last night."

I'm thankful for George's intervention since Thomas' arrival appears to have turned me to stone. Why do the walls of the smithy seem to be drawing closer?

"I'm sorry to hear it, Lady Gabrielle." Thomas' voice is gentle. "Come out in the sunshine. There's a quiet place we can sit behind the shop, and you can tell me how this came to pass."

"A peaceful place would suit me well," I say, finding my voice.

George slides Papa's sword into the scabbard. "I'll take good care of this, milady. Go with Thomas."

Thomas pours two tankards of cider from a keg and precedes me into a small, walled yard furnished with a table and two benches. A white horse munches hay in a stall next to a privy. I have a desperate urge to use the latter. Cheeks flaming, I don't even ask. I go inside, hoist the hem of my frock, and pull down my breeches.

When I came out, I rinse my hands under a water spigot, avoiding Thomas' gaze. His beard and sleeves are wet, so I gather he washed up as well. He hands me a clean rag. I dry my hands and dab at the stains on my bodice. The sight of Papa's blood soaking the white cloth fills me with such despair I decide to leave them be.

As I sink down on a bench, Thomas slides a tankard in front of me and produces a clean handkerchief. Surely, he's a fortune-teller as well as a blacksmith, for he's read my mind from the moment he stepped in the shop.

I blow my nose. "Thank you."

The bright sun assaults my eyes, and I realize I no longer have my hat. Where did I leave it?

Thomas sits across from me. "I'm sorry to ask, milady, but will you tell me what happened?"

I take a deep breath and plunge, beginning with the reasons for the journey to Andwarf. When I come to Papa's murder, I can't stop the tears, and Thomas puts a warm hand over mine. The gesture startles me, and I stop in mid-sentence.

A memory surfaces of the time my pony refused to jump a

stone wall, and I hurtled over his head like a cannon ball. Thomas dried my tears then set me on the stubborn brute and led me—wrist sprained and pride bruised—back to the manor. He scarcely said a word, yet his silence was a comfort, as it is now.

I relate to him the details of this morning's tragedy. When I'm done, Thomas squeezes my hand before releasing it.

"A sad story, lass, to be sure. That's much for you to bear." He sips his cider. "And you think Rolf Von Haugen might have something to do with it?"

"Yes." I blow my nose again. "Do you know him?"

"I know *of* him." Thomas straightens and folds his arms across his chest. "Lately the Governor has surrounded himself with some questionable types. But never mind that now. Your mother will be sore vexed when she finds out what's happened. You should've gone home with Jack, rather than come here."

I fold Thomas' handkerchief and place it on the table while I consider my response. "I thought it more important to get the news to Damon and bring him back to Lille."

"Leave that to me," Thomas says. "It's not safe for you to wander about the city alone. Isn't your father's death proof of that?"

He's missing the point entirely. *I* must be the one to inform my brother. Papa would want it that way.

I raise the tankard to my lips, and the cool, crisp taste of the cider freshens my resolve. "Please help me find Damon. Do you have any notion where he might be? All I know is he left the Garland a fortnight ago."

Thomas strokes his dark beard. His gaze moves to the horse in the stall.

"That's Damon's horse," I say.

"It is," Thomas admits.

"Please tell me why you have him."

Thomas clears his throat. "I gather you don't know much

about your brother's actions and . . . associates. It's better if I say nothing."

Anger sparks. "If you know where he is, enlighten me. I must speak with him as soon as possible."

Thomas heaves a sigh. "Have you considered going to the Temple? 'Tis the safest place for you, and it's where your father intended you to be. I should take you there."

"No." I slam my tankard, spilling cider on the table. "I don't want to be walled up inside the Temple. Am I the only person who cares about Papa's murder?"

"Not at all," Thomas demurs. "Lord Simon gave me an opportunity I'd never dreamed of when he sent me to Marianas. His death comes as a great shock." His dark eyes are steady. "And for his sake, I'll help you. But first I've an errand to run. By any chance, are you hungry?"

7

THE BEST MEAT PIES IN ANDWARF

I guide Minx into a crowded square, staying close to Thomas, who's on foot. Above the heads of the vendors and patrons, a bizarre scene unfolds. It takes me a moment to figure out that two ragged men are clinging to the statue of a nobleman on a charger. At first I assume the wretches are up to some mischief, then realize they're trying to scrub away the red paint splattering the statue and pedestal. A guardsman oversees their labours.

Thomas drops back to walk beside my left knee. "The Duke of Anglia commissioned that statue after his troops wrested Andwarf from the Emperor," he says. "As you can tell from the paint, some folks still resent the Duke's authority."

His explanation reminds me of the rebel we encountered yesterday afternoon. Did the lad in the grey cowl light the fire that burned down the Governor's workhouse? Or splatter paint on the Duke's statue?

Beyond the statue, I notice wide gates, bolted to stone walls and wrapped in chains. Through the bars, I can see that weeds have overtaken the flagstone walkways while creeping vines entangle an elegant building.

"Is that the university?" I ask.

"It was before Visser closed it," Thomas replies. "Best not speak of it here, milady."

A pretty blonde maid balances a basket on her hip as she saunters over to us. "Back so soon, Mister Smithson? Will you have another pie then?"

My belly rumbles at the scent of fresh pastry. I missed breakfast this morning, and it's already well past noon.

"Not for me, but for the lady." Thomas places a hand on Minx's neck and gazes up at me. "Beef or pork, milady? You can't go wrong with either. They're the best meat pies in Andwarf."

"Beef, please."

He pays the maid, and she gives him a cheeky smile as she tucks the coins in her apron. From the basket, she extracts a parchment package and offers it to me.

"Eat hearty, milady," she says.

She slips her hand around Thomas' elbow, and they stroll a short distance away. She laughs when he leans over to whisper in her ear. Is he fond of her pies—or her pouting lips and generous curves?

I greedily unwrap the pie. The pastry and tender beef are delicious. Minx stands calmly and switches her tail while I eat. A man in a shiny yellow coat pushes between Thomas and the maid. I can tell his intrusion annoys Thomas, but he steps aside while the man haggles with the maid over the price.

Someone tugs on my skirt, and I look down into a freckled face. The boy, who could be ten years of age, holds up the stump of his right arm, and my heart goes out to him immediately. Then the poor child opens his mouth and gargles. He doesn't have a *tongue* either?

"Here." I wrap my pie in the parchment and offer it to him. "You need this more than I do."

Grinning his thanks, the boy takes the pie and sits on the broad steps to my right. He eats with great care—chewing slowly before he swallows. I watch him carefully, fearing he'll choke. Is he an orphan? The poverty of the children in this city is appalling.

"You shouldn't have done that. You're just encouraging the rascal to pick your pocket," a voice beside me says.

The man in the yellow coat takes a bite of his own pie and pats his mouth with a white silk handkerchief.

"What makes you think he's a pickpocket?" I counter.

The man chews and swallows before answering. "The authorities cut off the hands of thieves. And if the thief won't give up his accomplice's name, they cut out his tongue. You might disapprove, but strict punishments alone deter law-breakers," he declares.

"The funds from the sale of your handkerchief would feed a dozen children," I argue. "Are you as generous with alms as you are with opinions?"

"Don't lecture me, you ill-mannered chit!" The man snaps his handkerchief at me and storms away.

"Good day to you too, sir!" I call after him.

Thomas shoots me a concerned look. I smile reassuringly before turning my attention back to the steps—only to discover that the freckle-faced boy is gone.

Tiny yellow petals float on the breeze as it cools my neck. The broad steps ascend to four massive white pillars. The figure carved into the one on the far left is Zephrum, god of the North Wind. He clutches his cloak and bares his teeth. To his right is Inesol, the unsmiling East Wind, who folds his arms and glares in disapproval. Bactia, goddess of the South Wind, is next. She gazes seductively over her naked shoulder, but her smile promises warmth and fertility. Finally, Munificus, generous god of the West Wind, opens his palms in welcome.

Since she worships only the Goddess, Maman would dismiss these pagan deities. Still, I wonder if one of them would intervene if I offered a prayer for—

Wait a minute.

I raise my eyes to the promenade above the pillars. A statue of a woman rests her right hand on the head of a small girl. The foot of the statue is heaped with goldenrod.

By the Goddess' eyes.

I can't see the glass dome from down here, but I know exactly where Thomas has brought me.

"You lied about the errand!" I shout at him.

The pretty maid's peal of laughter infuriates me even more.

"You planned all along to bring me to the Temple!" To my dismay, my voice breaks on the last word.

Thomas sighs as he returns to me. "I did, and I'm sorry for the deception. I'll hold your mare while you go inside. Ask for Mother Celine."

Tears of frustration threaten to spill down my cheeks, but I won't let him see me cry. I tighten the reins, and Minx backs up.

Thomas grips my rein hand and moves with Minx. "If you love and honour your father, you must respect his wishes, Lady Gabrielle."

His plan all along was to dump me off like a sack of laundry. Well, it isn't mine.

I smooth the folds of my frock over my thigh in an attempt to compose myself. "You're right, Thomas." I butter my tone with reason as I meet his dark gaze. "I don't know what I was thinking."

He releases my hand, but his face is doubtful.

"*You* must speak to the Guardian," I suggest. "Explain

what's happened to my father. I can't bear the telling of it again." I squeeze out a tear and let it dribble down my cheek. "Please, Thomas. I'll wait here till you return."

I can read his thoughts as readily as the source of lameness in a horse's foreleg. Though he hates to do so, Thomas must take me at my word, for he was born a blacksmith's son while I am the lord's daughter.

"All right then. I won't be gone long." Thomas casts one last look at the square then hurries up the steps. When he pauses at the top, I raise a hand to him, and he disappears inside the Temple.

I *do* honour and love Papa—so much so that I will overturn every stone in Andwarf to find his son.

8

THE GREAT GONZALO

I BECKON TO THE MEAT PIE MAID, AND SHE SAUNTERS over. Her cheeks are aglow with anticipation.

"Can you point me in the direction of the Governor's residence?" I ask her.

She cocks her blonde head and considers my question. I'm about to repeat it when she says, "It's across from the courthouse and prison, milady. It won't take you long to get there, but I expect Thomas won't be pleased to find you gone when he returns. How do you know him—if you don't mind me asking?"

Even though she's given me what I wanted, I don't like her saucy looks or remarks. "I *do* mind," I tell her.

She screws up her pretty mouth.

Someone tugs my skirt, and I look down at the freckle-faced boy.

"Sam can show you exactly where the Governor lives," the maid adds. "You've already paid him with food, so don't let him pester you for anything else."

I feel guilty for my uncharitable thoughts about her. "Thank you for your help."

"Fare thee well, milady," she replies, "and good luck with the Governor. You'll likely need it."

Sam darts between the vendors and patrons in the square, heading north. I kick Minx, and she gambols after the boy. We nimbly dodge a man with two buckets dangling from a pole across his shoulders. I receive many a scowl for our hasty progress through the square. Ahead, Sam casts a look over his shoulder before slipping into the shadow of a narrow street.

I hope he won't lead me into a den of thieves. The weight of Papa's knife in my boot brings little reassurance since I've no notion how to defend myself with it.

Sam jogs past more shops and into another busy square where a man in a tall black hat clings to a lamp post and beckons his onlookers to come closer.

I realize I've lost sight of my freckle-faced guide.

"Ram's bollocks," I mutter, reining Minx to a stop.

Sam darts out of the crowd, latches onto my mare's bridle, and steers us towards the black-hatted man.

"This isn't where I want to go!" I protest.

The man steps down from the lamp post, and his audience parts like a flock of sheep. His long grey hair floats above the shoulders of his green coat as he strides towards us.

He halts and strikes a reflective pose, his fingers pinching his neat grey goatee. "What have we here, Sam?" The man waves an elegant hand. "Never mind. I'll conduct my own reconnaissance."

Like a cat, the freckle-faced boy slides into the crowd while the man crooks a finger at me. Though I've no intention of going closer, Minx has other ideas. Before I can stop her, she ambles over to him and thrusts her head against his chest.

The stranger rubs her ears. "She's a fine animal. Where did you acquire her?"

"That's none of your concern." I try to turn Minx's head but discover the man clutches both reins beneath her chin. "Let go of my horse."

To my consternation, Minx lifts her nose and whuffles in his face.

"Of course I do, my lovely girl," the man croons in reply. "Who could resist those brown eyes?" The crinkles deepen around his own bright eyes as he addresses me. "How much do you want for her?"

I tug on the reins, but it's pointless. "She's not for sale. And just who do you think you are!"

With his free hand, the strange man sweeps off his hat and extends it towards the crowd. "Gadzooks! Is there anyone here who *doesn't* know the Great Gonzalo?"

The crowd responds with laughter and catcalls.

Is this annoying man some sort of street entertainer?

"Excuse me, miss. Do you have a handkerchief I could borrow?" Gonzalo asks.

If only he knew how many times I've longed for my handkerchief today.

"Sir, I don't have time for this." I glance over my shoulder, hoping Thomas isn't already on his way to retrieve me. "And I don't have a handkerchief."

Gonzalo pops his hat back on his head and gestures dramatically. "By the frosty cheeks of Zephrum, can you imagine such a *travesty?*"

Ignoring my protests, he leads Minx—and me—to the middle of the square. Vendors and artisans form a circle. Children wriggle to the front and sit cross-legged on the cobblestones. From the edge of the crowd, a guardsman observes while stroking his prominent chin.

Arm raised, Gonzalo promenades us in front of his audience. "People of Andwarf, I know where a handkerchief might be found! Watch closely!"

I check the street again. No sign of Thomas. When I turn back, I realize that Gonzalo has unbuckled Minx's bridle.

"Stop! What are you doing?"

Gonzalo slips the strap over Minx's ears, freeing her head. "Such a clever animal needs no rein or bit!"

Minx prances in a circle, neck bowed, while I grasp her mane, and the children squeal in delight. Gonzalo hands my bridle to the big-chinned guardsman then whistles loudly. My mare rears and flails her forelegs, and I squeeze her ribs to stay aloft. I'm stunned by her bizarre behaviour.

"Let's see if we can hunt down this poor maid's handkerchief!" Gonzalo announces.

Snorting, Minx drops to all fours, and Gonzalo holds his palm beneath her nose. I can scarcely believe it when she plucks a red corner from his sleeve. Tossing her head, she jerks free a crimson scarf.

"Is that it?" Gonzalo demands.

Minx waggles her head.

"Are you certain?" Gonzalo asks.

She bobs her head, and the children giggle.

From his sleeve, Gonzalo extracts more colourful scarves—blue, yellow, green, and violet. He offers each one to Minx, but she refuses them with loud neighs and stomps. As Gonzalo flings each rejection over his shoulder, the scarves flutter like leaves to the cobblestones.

Gonzalo shakes an orange scarf at Minx. "Surely it's this one!"

Minx rolls back her lips and shakes herself from nose to tail, nearly unseating me.

The children's laughter bounces off the buildings beyond the square.

Gonzalo turns his back on Minx and extends his palms. "Help me, little ones! Help me find this poor maid's handkerchief!"

The guardsman, still holding Minx's bridle, watches Gonzalo while freckle-faced Sam sneaks along the edge of the crowd. Is he a pickpocket after all?

Minx plucks a white scarf from Gonzalo's pocket. She turns her head and offers me the scarf, rolling an expectant eye.

A small girl jumps to her feet and points. "There it is!"

Hoping to keep the guardsman's gaze from wandering towards Sam, I wave the scarf above my head. "She's right! Here it is at last!"

"Hooray!" Gonzalo cries.

"Hooray!" the children chorus.

The audience applauds warmly.

I vault from the saddle and stand with my back to Minx. "Little ones, do you think my horse is very clever—or very naughty?"

As the children clamour to answer me, Minx shoves me hard with her nose, and they clamour louder. I pretend to be outraged, then drop into a deep curtsey. Minx tucks a foreleg and bows.

Who taught her to do *that*?

Gonzalo holds out his hat. "Perhaps you generous citizens might reward this charming maid and her four-legged friend with a ferring or two."

Many folk deposit coins in his hat, but just as many shrug and walk away.

The big-chinned guardsman approaches and hands me my bridle. "Well done, miss. Your horse is gifted."

Minx lowers her head to accept the bit, and I slide the straps in place. "Thank you."

"But are you aware this sort of entertainment affords excellent opportunities for pickpockets?" Big Chin asks.

By the Goddess' eyes, he's about to arrest me.

"Zounds!" Gonzalo presses a thin hand to his chest. "I didn't see any!"

"I'm not a street performer." My fingers tremble as I buckle the last strap. "I just happened to be here."

Big Chin places his hands on his hips. "Is that so? Then you hoodwinked everyone—including me. You must be careful in choosing your associates, miss."

Am I about to lose my right hand?

As if unaware of my turmoil, Gonzalo swivels his head. "Sam, where are you?"

The freckle-faced boy peeks from behind Minx.

"Ah. There you are." Gonzalo slides an arm around the boy's shoulders. "Where are the fruits of our enterprise?"

Sam reaches into his shirt and withdraws a small pouch. He jingles it before placing it in Gonzalo's palm. The showman cocks a grey eyebrow. Sam sighs and withdraws a second pouch.

"Excellent work, my light-fingered friend," Gonzalo says.

How can they do this in front of the guardsman?

I gather Minx's reins and vault onto her back, preparing to flee.

To my surprise, Gonzalo tosses the larger pouch to the guardsman, who pockets it and strides away, twirling his baton.

I turn on Gonzalo. "That was a bribe!"

"I beg to differ." Gonzalo's long fingers reach behind Sam's ear and withdraw a ferring, which he places in the boy's grimy palm. "*That* was the price of doing business."

"You could have had me arrested!" I protest.

Sam gargles and shakes his head.

"Sam's right. You were never in danger, my lady of the horse," Gonzalo assures me.

I lean down. "The Great Gonzalo indeed. More like—the Great Exploiter of Children."

The showman stumbles back as if wounded. "I have spent my entire life bringing joy to audiences everywhere. Is it *my* fault the authorities take a dim view of my vocation?" He taps Sam's freckled nose. "I'll see *you* later."

Sam darts in the direction of the Temple.

Ram's bollocks. Gonzalo's performance has made me forget *everything*.

I spur Minx past him and gallop across the square. I'll find the Governor's residence on my own.

"Wait!" Gonzalo shouts behind me. "We still need to discuss your horse!"

9

THE GOVERNOR OF ANDWARF

As I trot Minx across the canal bridge, a sentry steps out of the guardhouse.

"What do *you* want?" he barks.

I lift my chin and look down my nose at him. Papa's name is all I have. "I must speak with the Governor. My father is Lord Simon March. He was here last night."

The sentry measures me, his gaze lingering on my bodice. Does he notice the bloodstains?

"You're wasting my time," I add, mimicking Papa's inflection. "Time I should be spending with the Governor."

Grumbling, the guardsman unlocks the gate to let me through, then passes me off to a pimple-faced servant. The lad speaks to yet another retainer who in turn sends for the chamberlain. While I wait, I dismount and let Minx drink from the courtyard fountain as the water gushes over the naked shoulders of stone mermaids. At this rate, my red hair will turn grey before I gain an audience with the Governor.

Beyond the fountain, a staircase leads to the villa's wide

terrace, which is flanked by pillars and more statues. I have never seen such opulence.

Does Governor Visser notice or care about the hardships of children like Sam?

The chamberlain arrives at last and curls his thin lips in disdain before agreeing to escort me to the Governor. I tie Minx to a post and follow the chamberlain inside the villa.

Directly across from me, two vases of red roses are displayed on pedestals in front of a small antechamber. To my left, an arch leads to a marble corridor. To my right, a dark wooden balustrade, spindles plated with gold, stretches to the upper floor. My boots echo on sea green marble as the afternoon sun beams through stained glass windows.

The door at the top of the stairs opens, and a young woman in a high-waisted white gown emerges. Her dark brown hair is piled on top of her head and raked back from her temples by jewelled combs. As she descends the staircase, she daubs her eyes with a lace handkerchief.

"Are you Katarina?" I ask when she reaches the bottom.

She clasps her handkerchief to her bosom.

I extend my right hand. "I'm Gabrielle—Lord Damon's sister. I look forward to the time when you shall be *my* sister as well."

Katarina blinks.

Behind me, the chamberlain clears his throat.

I lower my hand—since Katarina doesn't seem inclined to touch it. "Perhaps you haven't heard, but my father was murdered last night."

Katarina gawks.

"I must speak to Damon." I glance up the stairs. "Is he here by chance?"

Instead of replying, Katarina swishes past me and hurries down the corridor.

"Katarina?" I call to her, but she sobs and walks faster.

"This way please." The chamberlain gestures up the stairs.

I precede him, confused by the behaviour of my brother's betrothed. A crest which consists of two hands floating above a lighthouse and rocky headland is carved on the wooden doors at the top of the staircase.

What kind of man is the Governor?

I step aside so the chamberlain can knock. "Governor, please excuse the interruption, but there's a young woman here who claims to be the daughter of Lord March."

"Send her in, Peter!"

I sweep past the chamberlain into a spacious study adorned with gold velvet draperies and a marble fireplace. Conrad Visser's bald head is bowed over a ledger on his desk. The life-sized portrait of a skeletal man in rich blue attire hangs above him. I imagine the painting is a likeness of Duke Edmond of Anglia, but it's not flattering.

The Governor lifts his head. Though his face is fleshy, his gaze is sharp as a hawk's. "*You* are Simon's daughter?"

I nod. Should I curtsey? No.

Visser rises. "Leave us, Peter."

The door closes behind me.

Visser's white silk shirt and crimson brocade vest swell over his barrel chest as he rises and moves from behind his desk. The seams of his spotless breeches and hose strain against his broad thighs and muscular calves. From the tips of his polished black shoes to the top of his shiny head, Conrad Visser is not a man to take lightly.

Still, his gaze softens as he strides towards me. "My poor child. What terrible news you have received this morning." He takes my hand and brushes it with his lips. "I saw your father last night—though he left before supper, claiming that he felt unwell. I understand he was robbed and murdered on his way back to the inn. Most distressing."

Felt unwell? Papa seemed fine when he left me last night. I'll set aside that detail and press on.

"I came here as soon as I finished filing a report with the local constabulary." I concentrate on Visser's dark grey eyes. "And I should mention that—apart from one member of the City Guard—I was treated rudely and left with the impression that no one cares about finding my father's murderer."

"How unfortunate." Visser looks away and coughs. "Your father was the Duke's faithful vassal and my business associate." He leads me to a chaise in front of the fireplace. "Please rest. You must be quite overcome by this tragedy."

I sit, expecting him to do the same, but he leans his elbow on the mantel and stares at the door to his study.

I take a deep breath and launch once more into the tale of the discovery of Papa's body. The entire time, Visser drums his fingers on the mantel and darts glances at the door.

Is my visit burdensome? Does he expect Katarina to return? Why has he not asked about the health of my mother?

"I must also tell you about a rebel we encountered when we arrived in Andwarf," I say in an effort to gain the Governor's complete attention.

Visser's hawklike eyes return to my face and remain there while I outline what transpired with the rebel, the guardsman, and Rolf.

"Your father should not have interfered with the City Guard," Visser says when I'm finished. "I expend considerable funds to ensure our streets are free of ruffians and troublemakers."

"Are you acquainted with Mister Von Haugen, Governor?" I ask.

His response is a solicitous smile. "I am not."

Rolf said he worked for Visser, and Thomas confirmed it. Why is the Governor lying?

"Speaking of ruffians, is there someone to protect *you?*" Visser continues. "I can offer you a safe escort to the Temple."

Not a chance.

I quickly assure the Governor that I have Jack the sheep farmer's protection—a small but very necessary lie. "What I truly need is to find my brother. Can you help me?"

Visser's kind smile melts into one of regret. "I apologize, my dear, for the dire news I am about to impart. Circumstances have changed—irrevocably. Your father and I had once hoped to unite our separate enterprises through the marriage of our children, but last night we decided to dissolve the contract. Damon and Katarina are no longer betrothed."

I'm grateful to be seated. Is *this* why Katarina was upset?

"But do you know where Damon is?" I ask.

"I do not." Visser steps away from the mantel and offers me his hand. When I take it, he pulls me to my feet. "However, if you should happen to discover your brother's whereabouts, I would be delighted if you would share them with me. He and I parted on unpleasant terms, and I should like to make amends." The Governor's eyes dart towards the door again.

"What about my father? Did you part on unpleasant terms with him too?" I persist.

Visser's grey eyes are startled. "Of course not. Your father is —was—a gentleman. Now if you'll excuse me, I have affairs that require my immediate attention." He returns to his desk and sits. "Perhaps you've heard I had a fire at one of my workhouses this morning. The effect on production will be devastating. I bid you farewell." He dips his quill in the inkwell and scratches a figure in his ledger.

His sudden dismissal is infuriating, especially since Papa

mentioned that Visser owed him money. Does the Governor intend to ignore that debt now that Papa is dead?

I stand my ground. "Pardon me, Governor, but there's another matter I would like to discuss—the considerable sums my father left in your keeping."

The quill stops scratching. "Is that what Lord Simon told you, milady?" Visser's tone is condescending. "Because the reverse is true. Your family owes me over three hundred thousand talens."

He lies again.

"Only yesterday my father dropped off a cartload of wool at one of your workhouses. Wool of the finest quality." I lean across Visser's desk. "Furthermore, I have proof of your debt, which I will take to the Council."

Papa's own ledgers—which would support my assertions—are at the manor, but I hope Visser doesn't know that. Also, I have no notion whom to approach on the Council of Merchants, or if any of them would back my claim.

Visser sets down his quill. All semblance of courtesy vanishes as he clasps his powerful hands. "Miss March, you had best hie yourself to the Temple before I throw you in debtors' prison."

This bully will not frighten me with his threats.

"You will address me as *Lady* Gabrielle, and furthermore—"

"This audience is concluded," Visser snaps. "Show yourself out, *milady*. Peter! Come in here!"

Fuming, I turn on my heel and charge out of the study, narrowly avoiding a collision with Peter. If Visser won't give me what I want, I'll seek the assistance of the Council of Merchants.

At the bottom of the stairs, Katarina paces and twists her lace handkerchief. When she sees me, she beckons before disappearing into the small antechamber. I hurry down the stairs and join her behind the archway.

"I'm sorry, Gabrielle. May I call you that?" Before I can answer, she continues in a rush. "Your sudden appearance startled me. And Father had just informed me of your father's death. So shocking. Although I didn't know Lord Simon well, he was kind to me. And you say he was murdered?"

"Yes, but I don't have time to discuss the details," I say impatiently. "Please. Have you spoken to my brother recently?"

Her ringlets bounce when she shakes her head. "No, but you can look for him at the Black Bull."

At last!

"Is that an inn?"

"A tavern," Katarina corrects. "After his latest quarrel with my father, I had a servant follow Damon there. I sent several messages, but your brother didn't respond. I'm worried about him, and now that your father's dead, I fear the worst." She bites her lower lip as she tugs a gold ring from her finger. "When you see Damon, give him this. It might help if he finds himself in trouble."

I slip her ring onto my finger. "Why would my brother find himself in trouble?"

Katarina shakes her head again. "I cannot say. It's too dangerous."

She appears very concerned about Damon. Was he at least fond of her? What would it have been like for him to be betrothed to her if he wasn't?

Katarina retreats to the archway. "I must go. I can't be seen talking to you. Please tell Damon I shall always love him."

"First—tell me what happened last night when my father was here," I beg.

Katarina freezes as the door opens, and a yellow-haired man enters. A crossbow dangles from his shoulder.

Rolf!

I flatten myself against the wall. Visser denied knowing Rolf Von Haugen, and yet here he is. Blood roars in my ears as I consider the likelihood that Rolf and Visser are equally responsible for Papa's death.

"Good day, Miss Katarina."

Rolf's voice is ingratiating. Does he make Katarina's skin crawl too?

Katarina murmurs a reply and rustles down the marble corridor.

"The Governor's been expecting you, Mister Von Haugen," Peter says.

"Von Haugen's *here?*" Visser's voice sounds close, as if he's left his study.

Peter hurries past the antechamber and exits the villa.

When I hear the tread of boots on stairs, I peek around the archway. Rolf climbs while Visser watches his ascent.

"Where have you *been*?" Visser demands. "You were to report to me immediately!"

"I overslept," Rolf says. "I had a busy night, thanks to you. And also—too much ale." He belches. "I heard you had a fire."

I check the hallway then peer around the arch again. Rolf and Visser now stand on the landing at the top of the stairs.

"No doubt the work of rebels," Visser fumes. "When you sober up, you can root them out."

"I'm not too drunk to collect my fee," Rolf says. "Do you have it?"

Visser makes a disgusted sound before tossing Rolf a pouch.

I'm certain that pouch is payment for Papa's assassination. Oh that a bolt of lightning would strike these two murderers where they stand.

Rolf opens the pouch. He staggers a little as he shakes some of its contents onto his palm.

"Have you found the younger March?" Visser asks.

"It's only a matter of time." Rolf hiccups. "You'll need to pay me more when I do. You keep me far too busy these days."

By the Goddess' eyes. They mean to kill Damon.

"The daughter was just here," Visser says. "I sent her away."

"How long ago?" Rolf returns the items to the pouch and tucks it under his belt. He swaggers to the window overlooking the courtyard. "That's her horse."

They'll soon figure out I'm still inside the villa. I need to get to Minx, but how?

"Did you *see* her leave?" Rolf asks.

Men shout outside.

"Blast!" Visser pushes Rolf aside and, raising the casement, leans out the window. "What's going on, Peter?"

"A man scaled the wall!"

"Then arrest him!"

"We're trying, Governor!"

"Do I have to do everything myself?" Visser marches down the steps. At the bottom, he gestures at Rolf impatiently. "What are you waiting for? Load that weapon and make yourself useful!"

Visser sweeps out the door, which he leaves open. His broad back blocks my view of the courtyard. Upstairs, Rolf sways as readies his crossbow and inserts a bolt.

"Show me Lord Simon's daughter!" a man shouts.

Thomas!

Rolf raises the crossbow and aims through the window.

10

CHAOS IN THE COURTYARD

I topple a pedestal, and the vase of roses smashes on the marble.

Rolf swings his crossbow in my direction. I leap back as a bolt zips past my nose.

"My apologies, Lady Gabrielle. You startled me," Rolf slurs.

"Gabrielle!" Thomas calls outside. "Where are you?"

As Rolf reaches for another bolt, I lunge into the foyer. Rolf's footfall on the stairs spurs me through the open door.

Near the fountain, Visser rails at his servants while Thomas edges along the top of the stone wall. Two guardsmen track his movements like dogs hunting a squirrel. Minx, still tied to the post, tugs at her reins.

"I know Lady Gabrielle's here!" Thomas points at Minx. "That's her horse!"

I hurry down the steps, waving my arms. "Thomas!"

"Gabrielle!" Thomas waves back. "Mount up!"

"The *girl*, Rolf!" Visser thunders.

The mercenary is right behind me. At the bottom of the

steps, he grabs my wrist and spins me around. He stinks of sour ale and rotten teeth.

"Not so quick, milady," Rolf says.

"You're a murderer!"

The accusation startles him, and his crossbow clatters on the flagstones. I step closer and drive my knee into his crotch. He releases me and clutches his groin, gasping.

Visser curses his annoyance while Rolf coughs and hunches on his hands and knees. A pouch plops on the ground, and I reach between his arms to scoop it up. I jam the pouch in the top of my left boot. Papa's knife is in my right, and I'm tempted to draw it.

"I could end you here and now," I tell Rolf.

Oblivious to anything but his discomfort, the mercenary rolls onto his side and throws up.

This ale-soaked sack of bones killed Papa?

"Milady, what are you *doing?*" Thomas shouts. "Run, will you?"

I gather my skirt and sprint across the courtyard. Visser tries to cut me off, but I keep the fountain between us.

The Governor's grey eyes are fiery as he circles to the left. "You'll answer to charges of treason!"

I circle to the right. "You're the traitor!"

Out of the corner of my eye, I see Thomas lose his balance and crash into the shrubs at the base of the wall.

"Secure that man, and take him to the prison!" Visser commands.

Servants converge on the blacksmith.

I feint left then whirl and run for Minx. Visser pants and curses behind me. I tear Minx's reins from the post and spring onto her back. Before I can thrust my feet in the stirrups, Minx rears, and I grip her mane to stay aboard. Visser retreats, shielding his face from her hooves.

The servants propel Thomas towards the gates while he curses and struggles against the arms pinioning him.

Minx rears again, but I cling to her back, yelling at Visser, "Tell them to let him go! He only came here to find me!"

"You'll both hang!" Visser threatens.

I find my stirrups at last and thump Minx's ribs. Visser steps in our path, then leaps out of the way as we sweep past. Thomas' captors drag him through the gates, and the sentry begins to close them.

"Runaway horse!" I scream as Minx bears down on him.

I catch a glimpse of the sentry's shocked face as we thunder through the gap and barrel towards Thomas and his captors.

"Stop the girl!" Visser yells behind me.

Instead, the servants release Thomas and peel in either direction. I reach a hand to Thomas, but he waves me on.

"Go!" he calls. "I'll be all right!"

Maybe it's a good idea to split up to confuse our pursuers.

Thomas races for the canal and dives into the murky water. Meanwhile, Minx and I thunder across the square and over the bridge, heading south. The glass dome of the Temple looms in the distance, but I have no intention of going there.

Thanks to Katarina, I know where to look for my brother.

11

THE BLACK BULL

When I'm certain no one can catch us, I slow Minx to a trot and venture into the maze of Andwarf's narrow streets. There's no sign of the City Guard.

A garishly painted woman leans from an upper casement and hurls abuse at the two drunks lurching out of the tavern below her.

"Excuse me, miss, but could you tell me where to find the Black Bull?" I call up to the woman.

She laughs and points down the street. "It's close to the harbour. But that district's no place for a lady."

One of the drunks points at me. "You think *she's* a lady?"

His companion roars.

I leave the laughter and insults behind, glad at least to know where to go.

Squalor and poverty abound in the crumbling plaster walls and thatched roofs of every house. Thin-cheeked children stare at me from windows and doorways. A woman sweeping her stoop harangues a crone in a tattered blanket. The crone's ancient eyes reproach me as I ride past. I can't wait to find my brother and put leagues between us and this horrible place.

The tang of saltwater fills my nostrils as at last I approach a row of fishermen's stalls. I must be getting close to the harbour. A young woman crouches on a stool as she guts a fish, tossing the scraps to a trio of mewling cats.

"Is the Black Bull nearby?" I ask hopefully.

The maid points her knife. "End of the street."

I nod my thanks and ride towards the setting sun, which silhouettes the masts of fishing boats against the blush of clouds. Further out, tall ships at anchor ride peacefully on the swell. The beauty of the sky and sea lightens my heart.

However, the rough fellows who loiter outside the Blue Harp, White Lion, and Dancing Pig reawaken my fears. I keep to the middle of the street to avoid them.

What will I tell Damon when I find him?

If he learns Visser and Rolf are responsible for Papa's death, my brother might try to go to the authorities—which would be pointless, even dangerous. I must get him back to Lille before Papa's powerful and ruthless enemies find him. This city isn't safe for either of us.

My mare quickens her step as we approach the final tavern, which has two storeys and a slouched roof. Laughter pours from the open windows, and a black bull exhales smoke and flames on the sign above the door.

"We found it." I give Minx a pat. "Good girl."

The door of the tavern flies opens, and a body hurtles at Minx's feet. She jumps sideways, nearly unseating me. While I tighten the reins and try to calm her, a heavily-built woman strolls out of the tavern, carrying a club. The projectile—a wiry fellow in loose-fitting clothes—scrambles to his feet and draws a knife. Men spill out of the tavern in twos and threes. More faces gather at the open windows.

"Don't even think about it, Tim," the woman warns. Her skin and hair are white, though she doesn't speak or act like someone old. "You've been at sea too long, and you've forgotten the house rules."

"You tell him, Molly the White!" someone urges.

Tim the sailor shifts his knife from hand to hand. Though small, he's muscular and tough—a dangerous opponent.

Unperturbed, Molly flips her thin, white braid over her shoulder and smacks the club across her palm. "Rule number one: if you cheat at cards, be prepared for a thrashing."

What a woman.

12

ALE AND A TALE

Tim lunges at Molly.

Nimble despite her bulk, she dodges him and smacks the knife from his hand. Howling, Tim drops to his knees and cradles his hand against his chest while the other men cheer.

Molly bends over and scoops up the knife. "Don't return to the Black Bull for a year and a day."

Still howling, the sailor lurches past me and up the street.

"What's your business, girlie?"

I realize that Molly now addresses *me*.

"I'm looking for Damon March. Is he inside?" I ask.

"Oh, he's inside all right," Molly replies.

Praise the Goddess!

Molly surveys my mare from ears to hooves. "Where'd you find her?" She takes a step towards me, and I back Minx up. "Don't play games with me, girlie. It's been a rough day."

"I'll bet mine's been rougher."

"She's a feisty one, Molly!" a hoarse voice yells.

"If you want to see March, come with me." Molly disappears into the shadows between the Black Bull and the Dancing Pig.

Reluctantly, I follow. In the yard behind the tavern, a lean-to is divided into three stalls. Ale kegs are stacked in the stall on the left. A colossal black bull dozes on the right.

I slide off Minx. "So there *is* a black bull."

Molly chortles as she leans her club against a keg. "His name is Magnus. Zoh rides him in festival parades. He's tame as a kitten."

The bull snorts awake, raises his tail, and breaks wind.

Molly rubs her nose. "But his farts will be the death of us."

A rancid odour fills my nostrils, but I'm well-acquainted with all manner of bovine smells.

Molly coaxes Minx into the middle stall and unbuckles her bridle.

"I'm not leaving her here," I say quickly.

The woman turns her head towards me. Her eyelashes are snowy, and her eyes are pale blue. "You can't bring her inside my tavern, girlie."

Molly's appearance reminds me of a white-coated, blue-eyed calf born at our fief. The local wise woman pronounced it a bad omen, but Papa claimed such occurrences were natural, though rare.

As Molly slips a halter over Minx's ears, I notice a slender building beside the stable. "Might I use your privy?"

"Suit yourself," Molly says with a wave of her white hand.

I enter the privy, hike my frock, and drop my breeches. What if Molly has some mischief—or worse—planned? I open the door a crack and watch her ease the saddle from Minx's back.

Why is this woman so interested in my horse?

When I come out, Minx's nose is buried in the manger, her

teeth grinding oats. Molly rubs her neck with a handful of straw, and Minx heaves a contented sigh.

"You act like you know my horse. You're actually the second person today who—"

"We'll speak of that another time. Come with me." Molly gives Minx a final pat and retrieves her club.

She elbows past me and opens the back door of the tavern. Male voices and ale-soaked air rush out. I tuck myself inside Molly's wake as she navigates the restless sea of patrons. Most look like sailors. I don't see Damon anywhere.

A clammy hand grasps my arm.

"Here's a red-headed wench. Tall and skinny but ripe as a plum." A black-toothed man breathes in my face. "Buy you a drink?"

Molly turns and grabs Black Teeth by the throat. "Let her go, or you'll eat this club."

Black Teeth backs away, gasping and sputtering.

Molly steers her bulk behind the bar and faces me. "What's your poison, girlie?"

I push my way between two sweaty sailors and lean on the counter. "Stop calling me that."

"What's your name then?" Molly demands.

What use is there in taking on airs in such a place? Besides that, I have a fearsome thirst.

"You can call me Gabby," I tell her. "And I'll have a pint of ale. Please."

The husky fellow next to me laughs.

Molly fills a tankard to overflowing and slams it on the counter. "Then drink up, Gabby. It's on the house."

Faces leer on either side of me. I've never tasted ale since Papa wouldn't allow it. I raise the mug, gulp the contents, and pause to belch.

"Well done!" The husky fellow laughs and jabs a finger in my ribs.

A raven-haired maid with silver hoops dangling from her ears jostles the sailor on my right and sets empty tankards on the bar. Scarlet sleeves sag below her bare shoulders. She could be Thomas' age.

Molly folds her white arms and leans them on the counter. "Gabby, what's your connection with March?"

I set down my tankard and wipe the foam from my lips as I consider my answer.

The barmaid turns curious violet eyes on me. "You know zee Leetle Prince?"

"Are you jealous, Zoh?" Molly asks.

Zoh shrugs her left shoulder, and her sleeve dips lower. "She don't look hees type, eh?"

"No, she doesn't," Molly concurs. "She doesn't look worldly enough to be anyone's type."

"Please tell me where Damon March is," I beg.

"Tell us first what you want with him," Molly insists.

I've no intention of pouring out my sad tale for a taproom stuffed with strangers, but I need time to think of a different version. I push my tankard towards Molly. "I'll have another please."

Molly purses her pale lips, but she refills it. Zoh saunters to the end of the counter, and the sway of her hips reminds me of Fanny Miller.

Fanny. Yes.

While Molly's patrons wait with expectant smiles, I sip my ale and fetch details of Damon's infatuation with the miller's pretty daughter.

"Let's have the story," Molly presses.

I sense her impatience, and truth be told, I enjoy it. A delicious confidence flows through my veins. I take another sip, set down the tankard, and turn to the husky fellow beside me. "Help me onto the bar."

He grasps my waist and lifts me easily. I sit, surveying the crowd of shiny faces, and begin to weave my story.

"I'm a miller's daughter, and I know how it is with the son of a noble. If his eye should fall on me, my virtue is in peril." I glance over my shoulder at Molly the White, whose pale blue eyes seem to doubt the truth of my words. I return to my audience. "But he duped me. He carved my name in a tree and bought me a cheap bauble at the town fair, and so I let him make love to me behind my father's mill."

Husky Fellow places a hand on my knee, and I smack it away. The others yowl, and I have to raise my voice, so I can be heard over them.

"Yes, I gave myself to him, never guessing what lay in store!" My cheeks burn at my sordid lies.

Molly taps my finger. "Is this the bauble he gave you?"

I drag my hand beneath my skirt, concealing Katarina's ring. "It is—since you mention it. And then he left me, never to return. He never told me he was betrothed to a rich man's daughter."

Zoh curses in an exotic language I do not recognize.

"Quite a story," Molly observes.

Her tone sounds suspicious, but I forge ahead. "Should I let the rake go unpunished? Me with no brothers to defend my honour or my good name?"

"No!" Husky Fellow shouts.

I brandish my fist. "I stole a horse, and I came here to find him!"

"Stole the horse from *where*?" Molly asks.

Why is she so obsessed with Minx?

I jump off the counter and confront Molly. "Never you

mind where! I demand you take me to that villain Damon March!"

My audience roars in agreement.

Molly cocks a white eyebrow. "Show her, Zoh."

The barmaid jerks her dark head, and I follow her across the taproom, a boisterous entourage at my heels.

As we mount the staircase to the upper level, Molly booms, "It's nearly curfew! Time for you drunken wastrels to go home!"

The sailors grumble and protest.

Molly waves a powerful arm. "Off with you now! And Gabby, I'm tossing your pretty boy in the street tomorrow. His money's run out."

I have no doubt Molly can make good on her threat.

When Zoh and I reach the passage at the top of the stairs, I try not to imagine what lies behind each closed door. Zoh opens the third one and ushers me inside the small room.

I look around hopefully for my brother, but see only a naked bed, a chair, and a washstand.

Why would Damon choose to stay here instead of the Garland?

A snore rattles from behind the bed. I look down and find my brother at last.

13

THE LEETLE PRINCE

Bare to the waist and tangled in a sheet, Damon is crammed between the bed and the wall, his bearded face pressed to the plaster.

"Is he hurt?" I ask Zoh.

"No. Drunk." Her forearm rests on the door frame.

After all I've been through today, *this* is my reward for finding him?

I open the window, welcoming the draught of cool, salty air and the view of the stable and docks. It will be fully dark soon.

"He hasn't left zee Black Bull seence he fought weeth hees friends." Zoh's full mouth twists in disdain. "Stupeed boys."

Why doesn't she leave? What is she waiting for?

"Could you please bring me some fresh water and towels?" I ask her.

She lowers sooty lashes. "Are you hees lover—or hees nurse?" She sounds suspicious.

Does she doubt my story too?

I turn my back to her and light the candle on the washstand, flooding the room with shadows. With a sound of disgust, Zoh turns on her heel and tromps down the hall. Relieved, I close the door, shift the bed to the side, and stand over my brother.

A dark bruise mars his cheek. Did he get that falling out of bed—or in the fight with his friends? It's hard to imagine Damon fighting at all.

"Wake up." I shake his shoulder with my boot. "Damon, it's me."

He tucks his hand beneath his cheek and heaves a sour sigh.

"Have it your way." I retrieve the basin from the washstand and slop him with the contents.

Damon shoots up, sputtering and gasping. He doesn't seem drunk.

"Why did you do that?" He wipes the sopping hair from his eyes and blinks at me. "Beetle?"

It's hard not to smile. No one has called me that for four years.

"It *is* you!" Damon leaps to his feet and clasps me to him, transferring the damp from his body to mine.

His embrace is paradise—so familiar and so dear, like sun-warmed earth or fresh-baked bread. I didn't realize till now how much I've missed him.

And yet. Something feels peculiar.

When he steps back to look at me, I realize what it is.

I've nearly caught him in height.

"You're—you're grown," he observes. "Those coltish limbs aren't so . . . coltish."

"I suppose they aren't," I admit.

"And I shouldn't be calling you Beetle anymore," he reproves himself. "From now on, it's Gabrielle. I promise."

"I'll settle for Gabby," I reply.

Damon has the face of a poet. Like Maman, he's light-boned, and he shares her blue eyes and brown hair. The town maids and the crofters' daughters blushed and giggled whenever he rode past. And even in this haggard state, he's still handsome.

"Why are you here?" His gaze flies to the door. "Where's Papa?"

My joy in seeing him is quashed. "I needed to find you. To tell you what's happened."

His brows curl in confusion. "Tell me what?"

I start at the beginning, but the retelling of Papa's death, while shock and horror flicker across Damon's face, fans the embers of my own grief.

Damon sinks onto the bed. "I can scarcely believe it. How can he be gone?" His slender hands hang between his knees. "I feel terrible that our last words were spoken in anger."

"Was that last night?" I ask.

He gives me a strange look. "No. Several months ago—when Papa came here after the university closed and sent me to work for Conrad."

I would give anything to know where Papa went after he left the Garland—and whom he met. I can't believe Visser's version.

"Well, the Governor saw Papa last night," I inform my brother. "And whatever they discussed concluded with the breaking of your engagement to Katarina."

"I ended it myself a fortnight ago." Damon slips a hand beneath his damp brown hair and massages his nape. "Wait a minute. You *talked* to Conrad? Did he tell you where to find me?"

I reconstruct the details of my visit to the Red Nag and to the Governor's villa—excluding my argument with Thomas, foray into role of street performer, and confrontations with Visser and Rolf. The curtailed account doesn't take long.

"I'm glad Conrad treated you courteously," Damon says when I'm finished, "but don't be deceived. He's ambitious and corrupt, and his days as Governor are numbered."

His ominous tone frightens me. "What do you mean?"

Damon sighs. "You're too young to understand."

I've had quite enough of being forced to stand on the boundaries of my own life.

"Try me."

He shrugs. "I have companions who won't rest until that evil man is toppled from power."

Companions. In other words—rebels.

"Are these companions the same ones you quarrelled with?" When he gives me a sharp look, I add, "The barmaid told me."

Damon sighs again. "When they found out about my engagement to Katarina, some thought I was a traitor to our cause."

Our cause? He counts himself as a rebel?

"But I'm no traitor," Damon continues. "I must prove to them that I'll stand shoulder to shoulder with them when a new age dawns, and a man is free to love whomever he chooses."

The miller's daughter again.

Damon fingers the bruise on his cheek. "I never wanted to marry Katarina. Still, I'm thankful she knew where you could look for me, or I wouldn't know what happened to Papa. I still can't comprehend it. It's unthinkable."

I go to the window and lean on the sill. Minx dozes in her stall. With any luck, she'll carry Damon and me home, so my brother can take over Papa's role. How strange it will be for Damon to preside at the Lord's Court and settle the disputes of our folk. Somehow I cannot imagine it.

How much easier life would be if I looked like him, and he looked like me. What strange quirk of fate decided that the warrior's daughter would love the land while his son would dream of books?

"We must return to Lille, Damon. The fief belongs to you now," I tell him.

"I won't go," Damon says quietly.

Does he mean—not yet?

"There's nothing for me there." His voice is devoid of emotion. "I will never be Lord of Lille."

I focus on the wooden floor beneath my feet, fearing it will open up and swallow me. It's impossible for Damon *not* to be Lord of Lille. It would be easier for him to say, "I shall tell the wind to stop blowing and the river to cease rushing."

I meet his gaze and speak slowly—as if to a child. "You don't mean that. You can't. Lille is your birthright."

Damon puffs his cheeks and expels his breath. "If you could decide, what fate would you choose, Gabby?"

"What a ridiculous question, Damon. We don't choose!"

"But what if we could?" His poet's face is eager. "Do you know what I'd do? I'd travel to Marianas and study at the university. Maybe I could teach there one day."

What folly!

"There's no money for you to live in Marianas, much less here," I inform him. "And speaking of *here*, you're supposed to clear out tomorrow. You've left unpaid bills all over the city. Which raises the question—why does Thomas Smithson have your horse?"

My brother looks sheepish as he smooths his beard. "I sold it to him a week ago."

"Let me guess. You needed funds to pay your room and board, but you *drank* it."

"It's Visser's fault," Damon says defensively. "He wasn't inclined to hand over a talen of what he owes Papa. And he owes him a fortune. I know full well Visser used it to build his merchant fleet, and he lost three ships last year to pirates and storms."

"Why would Papa give it to Visser in the first place?" I ask.

Damon rolls his eyes. "Papa banked the funds with Visser in order to collect interest. It's the way business is conducted. But he never authorized Visser to squander it on his own enterprises. I would guess Papa tried to call in his credit last night after Visser told him about the broken engagement." Damon stiffens. "Rather a strong coincidence that Papa ended up dead."

His thoughts have taken the exact direction I feared. I turn away to hide my alarm. "The guardsmen assured me it was thieves." I shut my eyes to banish the image of Papa's mutilated hand.

"If you think Visser isn't capable of having Papa murdered, you're mistaken. And with him dead, this city isn't safe for either of us."

Damon already suspects what I know to be true. What will he do with the knowledge? He's no fighter. He'll end up dead if he seeks revenge.

"We'll talk more tomorrow," I tell him. "You should get some rest."

"You're right." Damon stifles a yawn. "I'm glad you're here, little sister." He looks around the room. "I suppose this isn't the sort of place you'd have expected to find me, but I'm done with living a life of ease while others starve." He stretches out on the bed and closes his eyes.

Despite statements like that, he seems rational. Perhaps in the morning I can convince him it's his duty to claim his title. I could even help him settle into his new role as I have a good grasp of all there is for him to know.

"Blow out the candle, will you?"

His drowsy voice disturbs the tangle of my thoughts. Still, I manage to unsnarl one more question. "Damon, did Papa know you've been consorting with rebels?"

A soft snore answers me.

How did he fall asleep so quickly? I nudge his shoulder, but he doesn't move.

Exhaustion tugs my eyelids. I prop the chair under the door handle to secure it. When I lean over to blow out the candle, the gold ring on my finger glints. In the flickering flame, I study the embossed lighthouse, rocks, and hands of the Visser crest. Tomorrow, I'll give Damon the ring—if he'll take it.

I snuff the candle and curl up in the corner where I found Damon, not bothering to remove my boots. Folding the sheets under my head as a pillow, I try not to think about the hard floor and the chamber pot behind my hip.

Instead, I let my thoughts wander to Thomas. Did he return to the Red Nag after we were separated? Guilt twinges when I consider how close he came to being imprisoned. Why did he insist on following me to the Governor's? Then again, what would have happened if he hadn't?

My morning began with news of Papa's disappearance. So much has happened since then. I can scarcely believe one day contains it.

I close my eyes and listen to the clang of a ship's bell and the wash of waves, wishing I could answer the call of the sea.

"DAMON MARCH!" A fist pounds the door. "Open in the name of the Governor!"

I lie in a pool of darkness. My bones ache. Am I dreaming?

"Get under the bed, Gabby," Damon whispers.

I know where I am—the upstairs room at the Black Bull. I slink on all fours to peer around the end of the bed. My brother perches on the edge. Shadows and light steal through the crack beneath the door.

A fist hammers again. "Open I say!"

"Gabby, for the last time. Get under the bed." Damon seems remarkably calm.

I wriggle underneath. The space between the mattress slats and the floor is tight. I straighten my right leg, and the chamber pot sloshes my thigh.

Damon snatches the sheet I used for a pillow and tiptoes to the window. What's he doing? Wood splinters as a body hurtles against the door. When the assault is repeated, the door bangs open, and light floods the room.

"You're under arrest!"

I'm sure it's Rolf.

"What's the charge?" Damon replies calmly.

"Never mind the charges! Where's your sister?" Rolf hisses.

"I'm alone," Damon maintains.

I'm grateful he wants to protect me, but it's my fault the mercenary is here.

"Check the yard. Hurry!" Rolf orders.

Boots race down the hall.

"I'm the one you want, Von Haugen," Damon insists. "But first admit you murdered my father."

A fist smacks flesh, and moaning, Damon drops to his knees.

My poor brother.

"That's enough out of you," Rolf says.

Heels drag across the wooden floor. Boots thunder in the hall and down the stairs.

Where are they taking him?

Molly cries, "You can't arrest him before he's paid his rent!"

Silence.

I hear the rise and fall of breath. Rolf is still in this room, waiting for me to give myself away. I fear I'm lost.

Outside, Minx neighs, and a monster bellows. Men cry out in alarm. Rolf curses softly and exits.

I wait until the sounds and voices outside have faded before I crawl out from under the bed. The chair is broken to bits, and the door hangs by a hinge. A sheet, knotted to one of the bedposts, dangles out the window. Had Damon planned to escape, or had he intended for it to appear that I had? He is no longer here to ask.

I should venture into the night. Find out where Rolf is taking him. The very thought of doing so—alone—turns my knees to butter.

I sit on the bed and push the heels of my hands into my eyes to banish the image of Damon's head on display at the bridge.

14

DISCOVERY

Minx whinnies outside. At least Rolf's thugs didn't take her.

I hear a light footfall and the swish of clothing. Zoh leans through the doorway, holding a lantern. She wears a violet satin dressing gown, and her black hair tumbles to her waist. "Zey are gone. Zee leetle prince too. Zee red hair breeng zee bad luck, eh?"

"I don't think my hair or bad luck had anything to do with it," I reply.

But inwardly, I am wailing: Oh Maman, what a mess I've made.

Raising her lantern, Zoh enters. "Who weel clean thees?" Her slipper kicks aside a piece of the broken chair. "Not Zoh."

The trickle of water outside rouses my curiosity, and I go to the window. In the stable yard, my mare fusses in her stall while Magnus' long tongue slurps the ale draining from a split keg.

"I thought I heard a monster earlier, but it was only your bull," I remark.

"*My* bull." Molly, wrapped in a white sheet, fills the doorway. She looks like a ghost. "Magnus serves better than a watch dog. You can thank Zoh for setting him loose, so they didn't take your horse—or my ale. The City Guard has a bad habit of confiscating it when I fail to render a suitable bribe."

"Thank you, Zoh," I say, sitting on the bed.

The barmaid smirks and sets the lantern on the table.

When Molly enters, the room seems even smaller. "I don't much like the authorities breaking down my doors in the middle of the night. This is a respectable establishment."

"Eet ees?" Zoh says as she tugs on the borders of her dressing gown.

Molly ignores her. "Gabby, you haven't done me the courtesy of telling the truth."

What's the point of hiding it *now*?

"Lord Damon's my brother," I admit.

"The leetle prince's *seester*?" Zoh breathes.

Molly folds her arms across her chest. "I knew the jilted lover story was false. What's your real name, milady?"

"Gabrielle March."

I hope the interrogation won't last long. I want them to leave, so I can start thinking about how to rescue my brother.

The bed creaks and sags as Molly sits beside me. Since I'm not sure the frame will support both of us, I stand.

"Let's have the whole story," Molly says, leaning her meaty fists on her knees.

"First, promise you won't turn me over to the authorities."

"I'd have done that already if I wanted to," she replies.

"She ees right," Zoh says, sinking down next to the tavern owner.

By the time I finish relating a condensed version of yesterday's events, Zoh—chin cupped in her palms—is stretched across the bed beside Molly. Of Rolf, I say nothing, focusing on the Governor.

"A gritty tale, no?" the barmaid concludes.

"Indeed. I'm right sorry for you, Lady Gabrielle," Molly says. "Losing your father like that."

"Thees Thomas who help you. Ees Thomas Smeethson?" Zoh shifts so her weight rests on her elbows.

"Yes. Do you know him?"

Her violet eyes are mysterious. "We are acquainted, eh?"

I wonder how.

"Visser has made himself popular by doing away with many of the city's riff raff." Molly tucks a fold of her sheet against her substantial bosom. "Next, he targeted the rebels, blaming them for everything. That Von Haugen fellow is one of his toadies. His executions aren't civilized, and his curfew is an abomination. How am I supposed to make a living?"

The word 'rebels' sparks my interest. Might they be the key to rescuing Damon?

"What rebels are you talking about?" I ask.

Zoh flutters her thick black lashes. "Eediots! Zey want to change everytheeng. Your brother theenk the same. Look what eet did for heem."

"Before the Governor shut down the university, they used to come here to drink," Molly says. "You should have heard their wild notions. Bactia's buttocks, what a world we'd have with those school boys running it." The tavern owner shakes her white head. "You'd best steer clear of them, milady, if you don't want to end up in chains." She spreads her hands on her knees and rises. "I know someone else who might help you, but we'll save that discussion for tomorrow."

A cock crows.

"Eet *ees* tomorrow," Zoh observes with a yawn.

"All the more reason to get some sleep." A corner of the

sheet trails as Molly drifts like a white barge towards the door. "I'll make sure you get a change of clothes, Lady Gabrielle. That frock and hair of yours can't be seen again in *my* neighbourhood."

After Molly and Zoh leave, I reposition and close the damaged door. I may be exhausted and beaten down by a succession of disasters, but I still have to muster the strength to strip off this stained and smelly frock. What I'll wear to the prison, I've no notion, but whatever it is, I *will* find out what the Governor intends to do to my brother.

As I unlace my bodice, something bounces on the floor and rolls beneath the washstand. Confused, I reach behind it and discover the talen George gave me this morning.

How long ago *that* seems.

I place the talen on the table and slip out of my frock, letting it pool around my ankles. I already feel cooler and lighter in my chemise and breeches. Looking down, I realize I still have Papa's knife and sheath in my right boot—and something else jammed in my left. I reach down the side of it and retrieve the pouch I took from Rolf—payment for Papa's murder.

I'm wide awake now.

I turn up Zoh's lantern and empty the pouch's contents on the table.

Seven diamonds—all large and finely cut—sparkle.

No wonder Rolf is hunting me.

15

BREAKFAST AT THE BLACK BULL

I awake to the scrape of furniture downstairs. I have no idea what time it is, but the sun is up and the room is already warm. I sit on the edge of Damon's bed and stare groggily at my surroundings. The sight of the broken chair rips away the wool swaddling my brain. I shove aside memories of Rolf's midnight intrusion, for today I must rescue my brother.

The water in the pitcher is scummy and tinted with rust, but I use every drop to splash away yesterday's grime. As I dry myself with the sheet, I ponder what to do about the tangled debacle of my hair.

A light knock startles me. I grip the sheet against my chest and ease the door open, lest it fall in on me. In the hall, Gonzalo's little pickpocket presents a bundle of clothing.

"Sam, what are you doing here?"

He grins, passes me the bundle, and dashes down the hall. Instead of a clean frock, I find a white linen shirt, a brown wool vest, and a cap.

Is this Molly's idea of a joke?

Still, Rolf won't be looking for someone dressed as a lad.

I quickly put on the clothes, which fit well enough. I slip the pouch of diamonds and George's talen into the vest's inside pocket and scoop up the cap, which at least will hide my hair.

Hearing voices in the yard, I go to the window. Magnus dozes in his stall while Molly the White—fully clothed, thank the Goddess—paces behind him. I can't hear what Molly's saying, but the perpetual motion of her white hands suggests she's agitated.

A grey-haired man in a green coat and black hat exits Minx's stall. I should have guessed Gonzalo would be here since I've already encountered his freckle-faced accomplice.

Molly ceases pacing and pokes Gonzalo's chest with her forefinger. Gonzalo makes a submissive gesture, reaches into his coat for a pouch, and bowing, offers it to her.

Did that old crook just buy Minx?

I jerk the door open, and it crashes to the floor. Zoh curses from somewhere up the hall. I race downstairs to the taproom, where a drunk sprawls across a table while Sam mops the floor.

Molly lumbers through the tavern's rear entrance. She smiles broadly when she sees me. "Good morning, Lady Gabrielle. I see that you—"

"Did you just sell Gonzalo my horse?" I interrupt.

Molly sets her hands on her broad hips. "What a silly notion." She nods at Sam. "Bring her some breakfast, boy."

Sam shoves the mop in the pail and disappears behind the stairs.

"I'm not hungry." I peer around Molly, looking for Gonzalo. "Why did he pay you then?"

"With all due respect, that's none of your concern, milady, but since it might put your mind at ease, the money was for his room and board."

"Oh." As I sink onto a bench, my stomach gurgles. "In that case, maybe I *am* hungry."

The drunken man behind me snores.

"Are you still here, Olaf?" Molly strides past me, hoists the man by the collar and coattails, and drags him across the taproom. "On your way then."

The back door squeaks as Gonzalo enters. Seeing me, he winks and places a skinny finger against his lips then ducks behind the counter. He sneaks a small wooden chest from underneath, plucks a key from his pocket, and wiggles the lock. When a man's muffled cry announces Olaf's exit, Gonzalo sweeps the chest behind his back. His bright eyes will me to remain silent.

"What are you doing back there, you thief!" Molly accuses.

Gonzalo retreats a step. "I was about to pour you a libation, my darling."

Darling?

"Give me the chest," Molly commands.

"What chest?" Gonzalo asks.

Molly closes in on him. She's a full head taller and several stone heavier. An entertaining game of cat and mouse ensues with Molly lunging and Gonzalo dodging.

"Gonzalo, this is far better than your street act," I observe.

Molly wrestles the chest away from him at last and thrusts the key between her breasts. "You'd best think more carefully about whose pockets you pick," she says as she dumps the contents of the chest on the counter.

Gonzalo drops out of sight—I assume—to seize the coins that have rolled to the floor.

Molly stacks the rest into piles. I wonder where she squirrels away the tavern's profits. Surely not in one of Visser's banks?

"Not a bad night—if I discount the loss of an entire keg." Molly shakes her head and smiles. "At least that glutton Magnus got to enjoy some of it."

A clatter from the kitchen reminds me that breakfast is on its way. My stomach gurgles again.

"Does Sam work here?" I inquire.

"The poor little fellow earns his keep." Molly moves a coin from one stack to the next and measures them with her pale blue gaze. "Sam's mother worked here before she died of consumption. Shame about his hand and tongue. The Governor's a brute."

I couldn't agree more.

Gonzalo surfaces and leans close to Molly. "Have I mentioned you look radiant this morning, my beautiful buttercup?"

Molly smacks the spindly fingers reaching for a stack of coins. "You're a scoundrel and a liar. I don't believe your story of being on the Redemption last night."

Gonzalo caresses her arm. "Are you jealous, my pet?"

"Don't be daft," Molly says. "No other woman would have you."

These two are lovers?

"Here's proof of my affection." Gonzalo removes a necklace from his pocket and dangles it.

Molly clasps the necklace. "Those sapphires look real. Where did you steal it?"

"Does it matter?" Gonzalo fastens the chain around her white neck. "There. A perfect complement to your beauty."

Molly grasps him by the lapels. "Come here, you handsome scallywag."

As their lips meet, I decide that Gonzalo has met his match.

Sam enters and sets a platter in front of me.

"Thanks for breakfast, Sam." Starving, I reach for a slice of bread and a wedge of cheese.

Molly releases Gonzalo and drags a forearm across her lips. "Sam, go get Zoh. Make sure she brings her shears."

Sam darts up the stairs.

Gonzalo straightens his rumpled coat before sauntering to the table and sitting across from me. He surveys the contents of the platter.

Molly swipes the coins into a sack and disappears behind the counter. The creak of a board suggests that she hides the tavern's profits below the floor.

I wait until a wedge of cheese is halfway to Gonzalo's lips before asking, "Why did my horse know how to do those tricks yesterday?"

"*Tricks?* I, who have performed for royalty, do *tricks?*" Gonzalo points the cheese at me. "Still, I'm pleased you've raised the subject of Perdita."

"Perdita?" I ask, confused.

Gonzalo chews and swallows a bite of cheese before continuing. "Four years ago, I fell on hard times and was forced to sell her."

Molly sits next to Gonzalo. "In fact, he has sold her more than once."

Ah. This is beginning to make sense.

"You trained her to run away," I accuse Gonzalo. "No wonder we had so much trouble keeping her at first! She jumped out of every pen!"

Gonzalo draws a crimson handkerchief from his sleeve and dabs the corners of his mouth. "The little minx must have decided she preferred her new home. You named her well." He leans on his elbows. "I'll give you fifty marks for her. It's an exorbitant sum, but you saw how the crowd responded yesterday."

"Minx is *not* for sale," I assert.

Gonzalo waggles a finger at me. "You're a bold one, my lady of the horse." He straightens and smiles. "As a compromise, shall we try our luck this afternoon at the square in front of the Temple?"

"That's a terrible idea," Molly says. "After what happened to her father and brother, the last thing she needs is to draw attention to herself."

My brother. Molly and Gonzalo have been a huge distraction from the daunting prospect of arranging Damon's rescue.

"Indeed, I'm sorry to hear of your misfortunes, milady," Gonzalo says. "I offer my sympathies for the untimely death of your father."

He seems sincere.

"What you need Zoh for, eh?" The barmaid, still wearing her violet dressing gown, descends the stairs.

"We're going to give Lady Gabrielle a disguise." Molly flicks a white hand at Sam, who has resumed mopping the floor. "Boy, go muck out the stalls. Take Gonzalo with you."

Gonzalo, grumbling, follows Sam outside.

"Can I trust those two with my horse?" I ask nervously. "I need her to go to the prison. To see what's happened to my brother."

Molly sighs. "Didn't you hear what I just said about drawing attention? A guardsmen might recognize her from your adventures in the Governor's courtyard. It'll be safer if you hire a canal boat. Zoh can help."

"I suppose that'll be all right," I reply.

Zoh sits next to Molly and cocks her dark head. "Zoh theenk she make a good boy, eh? She got no chest or heeps."

I wish I could think of a retort.

"Leave her be, Zoh. When we're done, she'll go anywhere without being noticed," Molly says.

"What do you mean—*done?*" I ask.

"You could use a trim," Molly suggests.

Though I've never been fond of my braid, I'm not about to allow Zoh or Molly near it.

The barmaid places a pair of shears on the table and gives me a wicked grin. "Zoh look forward to thees."

16

DISGUISE

The blades of Zoh's shears scrape and squeak as red strands sift to the tavern floor, joining the coil of my thick auburn braid. My head feels lighter without it, but I'm not sure I enjoy the sensation. I've had hair to my waist my entire life, and Maman will be shocked to see me without it.

Whenever that is.

"Give me the shears, Zoh." Molly holds out a white hand. "Do you have dye on hand?"

"Zoh always have eet." The barmaid rolls her violet eyes. "Men like zee black, eh?" She disappears into the kitchen.

"Black?" I wonder.

Molly combs my hair over my face, then hunches in front of me and makes a pass across my brows with the shears. I brush away the strands that tickle my nose. I've never had bangs before.

Molly's face hovers before me. "Lady Gabrielle, your mother's not here to give you advice, so will you take some from me?"

I open my mouth to inform her she is nothing like Maman,

then think better of it. Molly has been courteous to me, and I'm curious to hear what she has to say.

I nod. "All right then."

"Don't throw your life away over your brother's foolhardiness," Molly warns.

Here we go.

"If you're going to tell me to go home, it's too late for that," I argue.

Molly sets down the shears and cradles my face in her palms. "My father was killed in a quarrel over cards. I know how it feels to lose someone you love and to long to bathe your hands in his killer's blood. But such urges will only bring pain and regret. Promise me you won't walk that path."

Molly means the path of revenge. She has no idea how close I've already come—with Rolf gasping at my feet while I considered drawing Papa's knife.

"I don't want to *kill* anyone," I say slowly. "I just want to save my brother."

"And how far will you go to do that?" she asks.

"As far as I have to," I affirm.

She releases my face and steps back. "The Goddess protect you then."

I'm surprised Molly has religious convictions.

Zoh returns with a bowl containing a dark concoction. She uses a wooden spoon to spread it on my scalp and then combs it through my shortened hair.

"Zee black will fade, eh? But for now, eet stay." The barmaid positions my cap on my head and tucks my hair behind my ears. "Not bad."

"Not bad at all," Molly agrees.

The tavern owner gives me a hand mirror, and I gaze at my reflection. A stranger stares back. Surely even Maman wouldn't recognize me. I turn my head from side to side.

Molly frowns. "Zoh will go with you to the prison. But after you've seen that nothing can be done for your brother, you'd best go to the Temple and speak to the Guardian."

Everyone seems to think that's the best place for me. They want me locked up and out of the way.

"I'm certain Mother Celine can help you," Molly adds.

"Help *hide* me, you mean," I reply sarcastically.

"She can do much more than that." Molly leans over my shoulder, so I can see her pale reflection in the mirror. "She's Duke Edmond's sister."

17

THE PRISON GATES

A crow lights on the crossbeam of the gallows. The sea breeze teases the two corpses swaying beneath and carries the creak of ropes and stench of rot to where I stand. These poor souls are the victims of the Governor's last set of executions. On Saturday, Damon could be next.

Will Visser bother with a trial?

I don't want to consider the possibility that Rolf's thugs cut my brother's throat and threw him in a canal instead of locking him up.

I rub the gooseflesh on my arms as I meet the stern gaze of the grey-mustached sentry on the left side of the gates. I turn away, intending to rejoin Zoh at the courthouse steps.

The square, bordered by the Governor's residence, the courthouse, and the prison, is nearly deserted. Not far from the pillory, a kerchiefed woman squats on a stool in the shade of her hand cart. She wasn't there when Zoh and I stepped off the canal boat.

"Care to buy a tomato or a pepper?" the woman calls to me.

"Better do it now! This place will be crawling with folk by three o'clock!"

I check the clock above the courthouse portico. It's half past two.

The woman's wares are bruised, and many have black spots and grey fuzz. These vegetables aren't for eating.

"Will there be a trial today?" I ask her.

"That's what I hear." The vendor smiles, obviously pleased by the notion.

"Do you know whose?" I persist.

"Does it matter?" The woman unties her kerchief and mops her damp face with it.

A mule and cart rumble out of a side street. The woman driving wears a white bonnet. A man with thin shoulders is perched on the back of the cart, which rattles up to the prison gates. The woman speaks to the sentry on the left and gives him something.

What does she want? Did she just offer him a bribe?

The sentry on the right opens the gates, which squeal in protest, then closes them once the cart passes through.

"Zee Levers," Zoh remarks.

I hadn't heard the barmaid approach, and it takes a moment for me to connect her remark to the couple I confronted at the constabulary.

"Those people tried to buy my father's body yesterday." The admission makes me queasy. "Why would they do that?"

Zoh sighs. "Zey render zee fat into soap."

Soap made from dead bodies? How revolting.

"One time Zoh work for zem, but zey not pay enough for zat."

I can't see what the soap makers are doing inside the gates, but I picture guardsmen cutting down the corpses and transferring them to the Levers' cart.

Zoh jingles her tambourine and calls, "You pay and Zoh dance for you, eh?"

I look over at the three young sailors she's addressing. Their skin is tanned mahogany, and their hair is sun-bleached.

"See?" The vegetable vendor points at the sailors. "The crowd's arriving already."

Laughing and elbowing each another, the sailors sidle up to Zoh.

"Like flies to honey," the vendor observes.

Zoh begins her dance with shoulder twitches and suggestive eye rolls. She transitions to stomping her sandalled feet, smacking her tambourine on her hip, and weaving between the members of her audience. When one of them grabs at her, she slithers out of reach. Shoulders swimming, she bends her knees and arches her spine until her long black hair brushes the cobblestones. The sailors leer and make crude gestures.

A loud screech announces that the prison gates have opened. A tarp conceals the back of the Levers' cart as it jiggles over the cobblestones. I shove aside the vision of Damon's body exiting the prison in the same way. I can't let that happen.

I study the sentries at the gate. I saw Gonzalo bribe a guardsman yesterday, and I'm fairly certain the Levers bribed the sentry with the grey mustache.

I fish the talen out of my vest. It seems fitting to use the money to procure Damon's release since I earned it through the sale of Papa's sword.

Maybe *that* is the answer to my prayers.

First, I ensure that Zoh is still busy with the sailors. Then, eyeing the older sentry, I walk quickly back to the gates.

"What do you want *now?*" the sentry asks, pawing his grey mustache.

"I'm curious about the hangings. I've never seen one before," I reply.

"Then be here early on Saturday, so you can get a spot near the front." Grey Mustache gestures at the empty gallows. "And see that?" He points to a roofed, curtained platform—higher than the gallows—in the middle of the prison yard. "That's the Governor's Perch. Visser has the best view of all. I hear the sight of young rebels swinging gives him an appetite."

I set aside my revulsion and fear. Now is the time to offer the bribe. The talen should be enough. If it isn't, I still have the diamonds.

"Excuse me, sir, but—"

"Another rebel's to be tried today," Grey Mustache interjects, lowering his voice. "Not much of a trial though. The merchants on the Council are Visser's puppets. The Rechter too. And the sentence is always the same." He sticks out his tongue and pretends to choke, then guffaws and slaps his thigh. When I don't respond in kind, he glares at me suspiciously. "You look just like one of those blasted rebels."

My pulse leaps.

"Move along—before I arrest you as a spy," he threatens.

I retreat across the square. I'm a coward and a failure. All I can do now is wait to see if Damon will be the one taken to the courthouse and pelted with tomatoes.

Two of Zoh's admirers sit on the courthouse steps while the third attempts to juggle some peppers.

When I reach Zoh, she jerks her dark head at the sentries. "Eediot! Why you talk to heem? You want to join zee leetle prince? You would not like eet. Ees very wet and smelly. Zoh been een a time or two. Don't ask for what."

More citizens drift into the square. The vegetable vendor implores them to purchase her rotten goods. Bit by bit, the crowd grows.

The clock above the courthouse portico chimes once. Twice. Three times. The prison gates creak open again, and two pikemen march a man out of the yard. Shackled at the wrists and ankles, the prisoner moves in a peculiar shuffling gait.

Is it Damon?

The prisoner's shirt and breeches are torn, and his shoulders droop with exhaustion. As he hobbles closer, I recognize my brother. Though I'm relieved he's alive, I feel little joy. I must let him know that I'll do everything in my power to save him.

"*Now* don't you wish you had bought my wares?" the vegetable vendor asks.

"I hear he burnt down the Governor's workhouse," another woman says.

All eyes are riveted on Damon and his escort as they move towards the courthouse. I start to follow, but Zoh seizes my arm.

"You must not speak to heem," she whispers. Her musky perfume washes over me. "Ees too dangerous. Zee wheels of justeece weel turn." She gives me a tug. "We go to zee Black Bull now."

"You go," I urge. "I'll come after the trial. I promise I won't do anything rash." I avoid her violet eyes.

She slips into the crowd while my brother and the guardsmen disappear behind the courthouse.

One way or another, I must get inside.

18

THE WHEELS OF JUSTICE

"Look at that. Visser's daughter is here." The baker's wife ceases peddling her gossip and day-old loaves to point in the direction of the Governor's residence.

The woman has plagued me ever since Zoh left. I look beyond the crowd to the curtained litter bobbing towards us. Four men in Visser's livery carry the litter on their shoulders.

Hope flutters. Perhaps Katarina can prevail upon her father to take mercy on Damon.

"I hear she was betrothed to the rebel they're trying today." The baker's wife rubs her flour-streaked nose. "Do you think she's come to plead? Or gloat?" She sniggers and wails in a high voice, "Oh Father, please save him!"

I must speak to Katarina before she disappears inside the courthouse. I make my way closer to the steps. Guardsmen armed with batons and chest plates deter the crowd from venturing up to the terrace. By the time I arrive at the bottom of the steps, Katarina, her head concealed beneath a lilac veil, is already at the top.

"Miss Visser!" I call. "Katarina Visser!"

She turns, but I can't see her face because of her veil. I take the steps two at a time.

The guardsman closest to Katarina points his baton at me. "Go back down!"

"Katarina!" I wave the hand bearing her ring. "You gave this to me!"

"What?" She peers at me through her veil. "Oh!" She seems to recognize me. "Let him by," she says to the guardsman.

He lowers the baton. Katarina reaches around him and grasps my fingers, pulling me close.

"What are you doing?" she asks. "Why are you dressed like this?"

"Help me get inside," I beg.

She looks towards the courthouse. I wish I knew what she was thinking.

She straightens and throws back her shoulders. "This lad is coming with me," she announces.

I stay close as she swishes across the terrace towards the portico. The beefy guardsman protecting the entrance looks hesitant when Katarina tries to enter.

"My father is expecting me," she insists. "The trial won't begin until I take my place."

I'm certain she's lying, but the guardsman opens the door and steps aside for her.

When I move to follow, he grabs my shoulder. "Where do you think *you're* going?"

I press the talen into his palm.

The guardsman stares open-mouthed at the gold coin, and I slip past him.

Ahead of me, Katarina sweeps across a foyer populated with statues. I duck behind one while the Governor's daughter argues with yet another guardsman. I notice an open door to my right and move quickly towards it, anticipating but never receiving a shout to stop. The opening leads to a narrow staircase.

I ascend to a deserted gallery. The heat up here is oppressive. I crawl on hands and knees to the brass rail and look down into a rectangular chamber.

Dressed in a crimson coat, Conrad Visser struts up and down the chamber, his shoes reverberating on the marble floor. His bald head and chain of gold medallions reflect the sunlight streaming through the upper windows.

A clerk scribbles at a desk on the dais at the north end of the chamber. Twelve men in silk, brocade, and velvet watch the Governor from their chairs on the west wall. I gather these wealthy men belong to the Council of Merchants.

A door creaks, and slippers patter. The merchants murmur and shift in their chairs.

Visser turns slowly. "Go home, Katarina." His voice is devoid of sympathy. "Women are not permitted to witness our deliberations."

Katarina rustles into view. "But someone must speak for Damon. He couldn't have done those horrible things."

"He did do them, Katarina, and for that, he will pay." Visser's tone is sharp.

The heads of the Council swivel between father and daughter, but not one merchant speaks in her defence—or my brother's.

Katarina wrestles the veil from her face and drops on her knees. "He's not like the others! Father, please!"

The scene is playing out exactly the way the baker's wife predicted. Yet I admire Katarina. At least she has spoken, while I do nothing.

"Katarina, cease this silly display." Visser beckons to someone I cannot see. "Remove her."

What kind of man treats his daughter this way?

A yellow-haired man strolls into view and stands over her. Rolf—of course. She turns a terrified face towards him. Is he giving her his broken-toothed smile?

Katarina cranes her head back to her father. "I can't bear it if he dies. Please spare him!"

She's not afraid of the mercenary but of the fate awaiting my brother. As I am.

Visser waves an impatient hand.

Rolf stoops, slips an arm around Katarina's waist, and whispers in her ear. She rises, then collapses, sobbing, in his arms. Rolf half carries, half drags the poor girl out of my range of vision.

"All rise for the Rechter!" Visser commands.

Chairs scrape as the Council of Merchants obeys.

A portly man in red robes and cap enters through the curtained archway behind the dais. He sinks into a high-backed chair and swabs his round, flushed face with his sleeve.

This man is the head of the Council of Merchants, but I sense that if I had sought his help yesterday, he would have thrown me in prison—or worse.

"Bring in the prisoner," the Rechter orders.

Chains clink and drag on marble as Damon shuffles into view. He holds his head high as he climbs the steps to the prisoner's box and faces the Council. Somewhere along the way, he has discarded exhaustion and fear. His proud shoulders and straight spine remind me of Papa. A small part of me wishes my father could be here to witness the bravery of the son who disappointed him so many times.

The Rechter glowers at my brother. "You are Lord Damon March of Lille?"

"I am."

The Rechter clasps his podgy hands. "Read the charges against the prisoner."

"Charge Number One—consorting with a treasonous faction," the clerk intones. "Charge Number Two—plotting to assassinate the Duke's lawfully appointed governor. Charge Number Three—arson."

My spirits sink with each accusation.

"Damon March, how do you respond to these charges?" the Rechter asks.

Damon's chains rattle as he raises his hands to grip the rail. "What is it I am supposed to have burned?"

"My workhouse!" Visser barks.

"The fire was the result of the abominable conditions in that deathtrap," Damon announces. "The innocent workers who lost their lives rest on *your* conscience, Conrad. As to the other charges, I won't deny my friends or our efforts to free this city from tyranny."

I've never been prouder of Damon—or more afraid for him.

The Rechter rises. "Are you aware of the penalty for treason?"

"I never swore an oath of fealty towards the Duke of Anglia," Damon declares. "Even so, I have committed no crime against him. However, perhaps the Governor will enlighten the Council about his treasonous communications with Emperor Maximillian of Berengaria."

Is this what Damon and Visser quarrelled about two weeks ago?

"You're lying!" Visser's face is as crimson as his coat.

"Conrad, isn't it true that you wrote to the Emperor, promising to open the gates of Andwarf to his army in return for a gift of territory that includes my father's estate?" Damon demands.

No wonder Visser wanted Papa out of the way.

"That's enough of these wild and unfounded accusations!"

Visser yells. "Gag the prisoner before he utters another poisonous lie!"

Damon stands calmly while a guardsman secures his mouth, and the Rechter orders a vote. The clerk invites each merchant, including Visser, to place a pebble—white for innocence and black for guilt—on a silver tray. The clerk returns to the Rechter and shows him the tray.

Every pebble is black.

I shouldn't be surprised. The sentry with the grey mustache told me how the trial would proceed:

"The merchants on the Council are Visser's puppets. The Rechter too. And the sentence is always the same."

"It is decided," the Rechter says ominously. "Damon March, this assembly finds you guilty of all charges. You will be held in the dungeon until Saturday—when you shall be taken to the prison yard and your head shall be struck from your shoulders."

Oh Damon.

My brother's chin drops to his chest, exposing his white nape, where the executioner's axe will strike.

"Wait one moment." Arms folded, the Governor commands the attention of every person in the chamber.

My chest swells in optimism. Is he about to pardon my brother?

The merchants' bland expressions give no clue, nor does Damon raise his head.

Visser approaches the Rechter, then asks in a muted tone, "Since when do we execute rebels in this fashion?"

Dread's icy fingers freeze my hopes.

The Rechter blusters and squirms. "I assumed—er—Damon March is the son of a landowner, Governor. And in light of what just happened to his father . . . . we cannot hang him like a common criminal."

"We can't?" Visser gestures to the merchants, as if seeking confirmation. "Why would we afford March the slightest dignity? He has betrayed this city and his family name. I say we *hang* him."

The merchants murmur and tap the arms of their chairs in agreement.

"Is anyone opposed to the Governor's suggestion?" the Rechter asks.

I want to scream at this assembly of cowards.

The Rechter continues, "Very well. Damon March, on Saturday next, you shall be hung from the neck until you are dead. May Inesol show you mercy."

My clever, gentle, handsome brother has been consigned to the gallows like a common thief or murderer.

"I will inform the people of the prisoner's crimes. Bring him this way." Visser strides from view.

While two guardsmen haul Damon out of the prisoner's box and drag him from the chamber, I run onto the balcony overlooking the square.

Visser's bald head gleams as, arms raised, he addresses the crowd from the terrace. "Citizens of Andwarf! Another rat has been brought to justice! A rat responsible for setting fire to my workhouse and murdering innocent men and women!"

The crowd boos.

I recall the poverty of the tent village beyond the city walls. Do these citizens actually care about the workers who died?

"Bring forth the rat!" Visser shouts.

Two guardsmen propel Damon to the edge of the terrace. He stands, head bowed, a few paces from the Governor. My poor brother is alone and undefended.

"Damon March was a guest in my home—betrothed to my daughter. And how did he respond to my hospitality? He plotted to take my life! Thanks to rats like him, I have been forced to impose curfews and hire mercenaries to preserve *your* safety!"

"The rat must die!" a voice rasps.

Rolf Von Haugen, the Governor's toady, stands on the right side of the terrace.

"What say you, good citizens?" Visser demands. "Shall we tolerate such *vermin* in our midst?"

"No!" a woman shouts.

Why can't these people see that Visser—not my brother—is the dangerous one?

Visser gestures at the guardsmen, and they shove my brother down the steps. Damon stumbles, and his chains drag him to his knees. He crouches, arms shielding his head, while the crowd pummels him with rotten vegetables.

A lilac blur emerges from the crowd. The Governor's daughter lifts her skirts as she mounts the steps, but the crowd is undeterred. By the time Katarina reaches Damon, her gown is splattered with green, red, and yellow pulp. She huddles protectively over my brother.

As I should be doing.

"Katarina, I told you to go home! Get her away from here!" Visser orders.

When a guardsmen attempts to wrest Katarina away, he too is showered with vegetables. The crowd surges up the steps and overwhelms the line of guardsmen, who flail their batons to safeguard the Governor's retreat.

In this confusion, I see the opportunity to rescue my brother.

I bolt for the staircase and join the other guardsmen streaming through the foyer. Under the portico, I encounter a furious Visser, who curses as he brushes pulp and seeds from his coat. Behind him, Katarina sags against the grip of the guardsmen who hustle her along. No one pays me the slightest attention.

The terrace is an ocean of heads, bodies, and arms. I duck and dodge them to avoid being knocked over or trampled or have my head cracked open by a baton.

I hunt for my brother and find him, still cowering on the steps.

"Damon! Come with me!"

He shakes his head and contracts even further into himself. Why won't he run?

I lift a heavy length of his chain and realize that getting him away from here is impossible. I wrap my arms around him instead—as Katarina did only moments ago. Someone steps on my thigh.

"Don't give up," I tell Damon. "I'm here. I won't leave you."

He shudders and sobs against the gag still tied to his mouth. Here is something I can do for him. I can give him back his voice. I fumble with the knot and tear off the rag.

"Get away from the prisoner!" a voice shouts.

I raise my head.

Rolf stares down at me from the terrace.

Does he know me?

"Go, Gabby," Damon begs. "Don't let them take you!"

Rolf shifts the crossbow from his back. "It's another rat! Seize him!"

I jump to my feet. "If I'm a rat, you're a snake, Von Haugen!"

"Go!" Damon insists.

Though I hate to leave him, I have no choice. As Rolf loads his crossbow and the guardsman close in, I turn tail and desert my brother, fleeing across the square with the rest of the cowards.

. . .

I'm a toy boat, abandoned in a pond and certain to sink. All is lost. All is hopeless. Damon will die on Saturday, and I've squandered the chance to save him.

I run aimlessly up a street. An intersection looms ahead. Do I turn left or right or keep going straight? As I reach the crossroads, I realize someone light of foot pants behind me.

"Weel you stop?" a familiar voice scolds.

Gasping for breath, I turn to face Zoh. I have no idea why her stormy face fills me with such joy.

"Why you draw attention, eh?" Hands on her hips, she paces, her chest heaving. Still, she finds enough wind to berate me. "Zoh geeve you deesguise, and look what you do!" She shoves me hard as she strides past. When I move to follow her, she whirls and points a threatening finger. "You cannot come to zee Black Bull *now!*" she states, as if that should be perfectly obvious. "You must go to zee Temple!"

Muttering to herself, she stalks down the street to my right, which leads to a canal.

I choose the street to my left, but it leads to a dead end. I maneuver into the space behind the wooden casks stacked against the high stone wall. While I ponder what to do next, I become aware that someone approaches on confident feet.

Is it Rolf?

A young man thrusts himself into my hiding spot and squishes me against the wall.

"Hey!" I exclaim.

"Were you trying to save Swordthrust?" he asks.

"Swordthrust?" I repeat, confused.

"You wouldn't have gotten far." The stranger sidles closer. "How do you know him?"

Does he mean my brother?

Hearing more running feet and shouting, I peer between

the casks. Rolf and two guardsmen stare at the stone wall for few fearful heartbeats, then head back the way they came.

"Thanks be to the Goddess," I murmur. "They must have thought we went over the wall."

"The Goddess helps those who help themselves," my fellow fugitive declares. "Now tell me how you know Swordthrust."

"I'm from his fief." It isn't exactly a lie. "Who are you?"

He shifts his body and leans against the cask, his hands cupping his knees. "They call me Firebrand."

By now, my eyes have adjusted to the shadows. Dark curls poke from beneath Firebrand's grey cowl, tweaking my memory.

Could he be the rebel Papa and I encountered when we arrived in Andwarf?

"Who calls you that?" I ask.

"My companions in the fight for freedom," he replies. "We'll do whatever it takes to end corruption and poverty. Not just in this city, but in the world."

It's him, I'm certain of it. Did *he* light the fire my brother is accused of setting?

"Does that include burning workhouses and killing innocent people?" I accuse.

Firebrand frowns. "Perhaps you'd like to learn more about our cause before you judge us." He extracts a handbill from his coat. "We didn't set fire to the governor's workhouse—though Visser leaped at the opportunity to blame Swordthrust. Poor fellow."

Zoh said Damon quarrelled with the rebels, but Firebrand seems sympathetic.

"Will you help Swordthrust escape?" I ask.

Firebrand raises an eyebrow. "We'll discuss it at our meeting on Thursday night. Perhaps you'd like to come. We'll have to blindfold you on the way there of course. Where are you staying?" He folds the handbill and stuffs it in my vest.

"What are you two doing down there?"

An old woman in a night cap leans out a window above us. She brandishes a chamber pot.

Firebrand springs to his feet. "It's best we part for now!"

He yanks me up as the contents of the chamber pot splatter the cobblestones behind us.

"You're a brave lad," he says, releasing me. His eyes are as blue as the summer sky. "I liked the way you stood up to Von Haugen. I shall call you . . . Spark."

With that, he leaps onto a cask, thrusts his toe in a notch on the wall, and scrambles to the top.

"But where are you meeting on Thursday?" I call up to him.

"Don't worry. I'll find you." He disappears on the other side of the wall.

By the time I scale it, the maze of streets have swallowed Firebrand. Sitting on top of the wall, I heave a sigh of frustration.

How will he find me on Thursday if he doesn't know where I'm staying? *I don't even know where I'm staying.*

The Temple rises above the rooftops, its magnificent dome glistening in the sun. Molly and Zoh have urged me to go to the Temple, and I seem to have no other choice—though I'll stick to shadows and side streets until dark.

As the Duke's sister, Mother Celine might have some influence over Visser and the Council. I push away the thought that if I'd gone to the Temple in the first place, Damon might not have been arrested.

Five days remain until his execution. Is that enough time to save him from the gallows?

19

THE TEMPLE OF THE GODDESS

Dusk casts long shadows as pigeons flutter and settle on the Temple roof. Ahead of me, a small figure scurries up the steps and vanishes behind Bactia's pillar. I follow at a slower place. Before the open doors, a stooped old woman holds up a lantern while a little boy clings to her.

Is she Mother Celine?

"Why are you so late, Jacob? A few minutes more, and the doors would have been locked for the night." When he starts to babble an explanation, the old woman shushes him. "Never mind that now. Go inside."

"I want to go inside with you, Sister Agnes." His voice is muffled since his face is pressed against the folds of her grey robe.

She's not the Guardian after all.

"As you wish." She peers up at me. "I haven't seen you before. What's your name?"

It's a question I anticipated. "Will," I reply.

William is my father's middle name.

"Welcome, Will. I'm Sister Agnes," the old woman says. "What brings *you* to the Temple?"

"I wish to ask a boon of the Guardian."

Sister Agnes holds her lantern high and bathes me in golden light. Her rheumy eyes explore my face. "And what is it you wish?"

"My words are for her alone," I answer firmly.

Sister Agnes' lips quirk in curiosity, but she turns and precedes me into the Temple, still holding Jacob's hand. Two young women in kirtles bang the doors shut behind us and slide a metal bar through brackets to secure them.

Is this a Temple—or a fortress?

My boots echo as I follow Sister Agnes across a dark sanctuary. Her swinging lantern provides the only light. Each swing reveals more of the colourful murals painted on the walls. Children cavort in a forest of beech and oak with all manner of wild animals—rabbits, squirrels, foxes, martens, and hedgehogs. The divine scent of fresh bread grows stronger with each step, and I realize I'm ravenous.

We approach a towering marble statue of the Goddess. This statue clasps a quill in one hand and presses a thick tome to her breast with the other. I nearly flood my breeches when a creature leaps out from behind the pedestal and emits a bloodcurdling scream that reverberates off the vaulted ceiling.

"That will do, Con," Sister Agnes says. "Let's go have our supper, shall we?"

The creature is a skinny girl with blonde braids. She stomps, fists clenched, ahead of us.

"Con is bad," Jacob observes.

"No. Con is lonely," Sister Agnes replies.

The sanctuary leads to a spacious room with a hearth, long trestle table, and benches. Three children sit at the table while a young woman my own age saws thick slices from a round loaf.

She wears a milk white kirtle, and her brown hair is twisted on top of her head. She must be a vestal.

Sister Agnes directs us towards a side table which holds a pitcher, basin, and bar of soap. I wash my hands and dry them on the towel provided.

"Will you help me?" Jacob asks.

He's too short to reach the basin. I lift him while he attends to his own hands. His body feels so light.

"Thank you," he says when I lower him to the floor.

I do the same for Con, although she offers no words of gratitude.

"Will, this is Anne." Sister Agnes gestures to the young woman. "If the rest of you are finished eating, let's go find Sophie." The old woman and the three children disappear through an archway at the opposite end of the room.

I sit at the table. Jacob plops next to me while Con scrambles onto the bench directly across from us. Anne fills three wooden bowls from the black pot hanging over the embers and places the bowls before us.

"Let us offer thanks to the Goddess, who knows the good within us and assures our sustenance and protection." Anne bows her head. Her long neck is slender and graceful.

Jacob rests his elbows on the table, clasps his hands, and ducks his head. I imitate his pose.

"Sela," Jacob and I murmur.

"What's sustenance?" Con asks.

"Food," Anne replies.

"I don't believe in the Goddess," Con asserts, "but I do like food."

"Then you're fortunate the Goddess believes in you, Con," Anne admonishes her. "Now remain silent until the prayer is finished."

Con squirms, but she offers no more comments or complaints as our thanksgiving concludes.

The bowl's carved handle makes it easy to raise the creamy soup, which smells of garlic, basil, and thyme. When I take a sip, I discover pieces of flaky fish and hints of butter. The bread is also delicious.

"I like soup," Jacob says.

"Is Will a boy or a girl?" Con asks.

Coughing, I try to distract the little scamp. "How long have you been living here, Con?"

She holds up two fingers. "Two nights. My mam is gone away. I have my very own room."

The trade seems to suit her well.

"Her mam died in the fire," Jacob informs me.

"She did not!" Con shouts.

"There now, Jacob." Anne places her hands on Con's trembling shoulders. "If Con says she didn't, we must believe her. For Con knows we love her and want what's best for her. Isn't that right, Con?"

Con nods as tears drip down her cheeks.

Could she be the skinny girl I saw in the tent city outside the walls?

While we share the rest of our meal, Anne tells Con and Jacob about the antics of one of the Temple's goats. If the vestal is suspicious that I am someone other than a mysterious lad named Will, she gives no sign.

How different the Temple is from the rest of Andwarf. If Papa had brought me here yesterday, as planned, what would I have thought of this place? Would I be helping Anne feed the city's orphans?

I'm scarcely finished eating when Sister Agnes reappears and calls to me. I hope she means to take me to the Guardian. Lantern swinging, the old woman totters down a long corridor.

Through open doors, I catch glimpses of children of various sizes and ages preparing for bed. In one room, a young woman with blonde hair cradles two tiny waifs in her lap while she sings a lullaby.

How many children does the Temple shelter?

At the end of the corridor, Sister Agnes climbs a stone staircase which curves round and round and opens onto another long passage. At last, she stops in front of a door and opens it.

"You are to stay here tonight." Sister Agnes waves me into the room. "Mother Celine will see you in the morning. In the meantime, someone else wishes to speak to you."

The old woman closes the door.

Lit by a single candle, the room is unremarkable. Its only furnishings are a narrow bed, a small table, and a stool. As I toss my cap on the bed, a figure steps from the shadows, startling me.

"Good evening, lass."

20

NIGHT VISITOR

"Thomas!" I throw my arms around him. "Where have you been? So much has happened! I don't even know where to begin!"

The young blacksmith stiffens.

"Damon's been arrested. He's sentenced to hang." The velvet beneath my cheek smells of sandalwood.

Thomas places his hands on my shoulders and sets me at arm's length. "I know about Damon." His dark eyes are serious. "Why are you dressed as a lad? And what've you done to your hair?"

I smooth my bangs. It still feels strange to be free of my braid. "Molly and Zoh thought I needed a disguise. Molly owns the Black Bull Tavern, and as for Zoh—" I recall that Zoh said she was acquainted with Thomas. "You know them, don't you?"

"I do."

"Did Molly tell you I might be here?"

"She did."

Thomas looks more like a nobleman than a blacksmith. He

is now clean-shaven, and his dark hair is drawn back and tied at his nape. Besides the black velvet coat fastened with gold buttons, he wears a fine white shirt, spotless tan breeches, and knee-high brown boots.

"Where did you get these clothes?" I finger the lace at his throat. "And what happened after you jumped in the river?"

He grasps my hand and tugs it down but doesn't release it. "Never mind where I went. Why did you go to the Governor's residence instead of remaining outside the Temple, as you promised?"

Irritated, I wriggle my hand free. "I wouldn't have run away if you'd told me the Guardian is the Duke's *sister*. Can she influence the Governor? Because if she can't, we need to make a plan to rescue Damon."

"Don't get ahead of yourself. You're safe here, and that's enough for now." Thomas turns his back and leans on the window sill. "Tell me what you've been up to since you left the Governor's."

"Didn't Molly tell you?"

"I'd like to hear your version." He throws the remark over his left shoulder.

It seems that I irk him. Well, his attitude irks me.

Nevertheless, I settle into an explanation of my activities. When I come to the point of outlining the accusations Damon made against the Governor, Thomas straightens and faces me.

"You should never have gone in the courthouse," he says when I'm finished. "You put yourself in grave danger."

"But I learned more about Governor Visser from Damon's testimony than I would have if I'd remained outside. Do you think Emperor Maximillian has designs on Andwarf? And if so —why?"

"It would be the perfect place to launch an assault on Marianas," Thomas says, more to himself than to me.

"But that would mean another war between the Duke and the Emperor," I point out.

Thomas rests against the window sill, arms folded across his chest. "It does indeed."

His words hang in the air between us.

I've never known war. I cannot imagine Imperial troops marching through Lille. It's been twenty years since Papa wrested those lands from the Emperor, thereby giving the Duke of Anglia a foothold on the continent. But none of this matters right now. What matters is my brother.

"You *knew* Damon was at the Black Bull." I don't bother to mask my resentment. "If you had told me that in the first place, you would have saved us both a great deal of trouble."

"You'd find trouble no matter where it hid," he mutters.

Heat pricks my throat. "If not for me and Minx, you'd be awaiting your turn on the gallows next Saturday!"

One corner of Thomas' mouth twitches. "You have me there, and I'm very grateful for your assistance. But I never would have been arrested if you hadn't gone to see Visser in the first place." He takes a step towards the door.

Oh no. He can't leave just yet.

"I have the means to bribe the sentries at the prison," I say in a rush.

He cocks an eyebrow. "You do?"

I reach inside my vest and touch a piece of paper. Confused, I withdraw the handbill Firebrand gave me. I'd forgotten I had it. I place it on the table and reach into my vest again.

Thomas picks up the handbill. "Is this what you'll use?"

"No." My fingertips poke about for the pouch of diamonds. "I took something from—" Should I tell Thomas that Rolf is looking for me? No. Thomas would only stop me from helping Damon. A lie is wiser. "I *stole* something from the Governor's residence." Exasperated, I unbutton my vest and shrug it off, still searching.

"Indeed you did. From Rolf Von Haugen. I could scarcely believe it when you kneed him in the—" Thomas clears his throat. "What did you take from him, lass?"

I throw down my vest, frustrated by this sudden and unwelcome plummet in my fortunes. "Diamonds."

"Diamonds?"

"Yes, and now someone has stolen them!" I try to recall who might have been close enough to pick my pocket.

Firebrand—of course. That wall-climbing thief has rendered me penniless once more.

"Bribing a sentry is a daft notion," Thomas says as he unfolds the handbill. "Promise me you'll stay here. Sister Agnes and the others will take good care of you."

"But I don't want to be taken care of!"

As Thomas peruses the handbill, he sinks onto the stool. "Where did you say you got this?"

I wave a hand. "From one of Damon's friends. He calls himself Firebrand." I don't mention Firebrand's invitation to the rebel meeting. I don't know where it's to be held, and Thomas would only try to stop me from going if I did. "Do you know him, Thomas?"

Thomas doesn't answer. Instead he extends the handbill. "You keep dangerous company, lass. Look at this."

I take the paper. The large print grabs and holds my attention.

A TREATISE ON FREEDOM
Addressed to the
CITIZENS
OF
ANDWARF

On these SUBJECTS:
I. The Unequal Burden of Taxation
II. The Corrupt State of Governor Visser's Affairs
III. The Dubious Sovereignty of the Duke of Anglia

"This is sedition against the Duke," Thomas says. "In Marianas, just for having this in your possession, you would be drawn and quartered."

Though the room is warm, I shiver. My father's loyalty to the Duke has never been questioned. What would Papa think of this?

Thomas takes back the handbill and thrusts a corner in the candle flame. He watches the parchment blacken and curl as blue fire laps the edge.

"Thomas, are you involved with the rebels?" When he doesn't answer, I study the angle of his handsome, stubborn jaw. "Please, Thomas. Look at me."

He raises his dark eyes. I resist the urge to drown in them.

"I won't stand by and watch Damon die. Please help me save him."

Why is he staring at my mouth? His gaze drifts lower, and I realize my collar has slipped, and the pale flesh of my shoulder is exposed.

Recalling the maid with the meat pies, I decide there might be another way to bend Thomas to my will. I step between his knees, put my hands on his cheeks, and press my mouth against his. His lips are soft and warm, but my first ever kiss is fleeting.

He shoves me away and rises, knocking over the stool. "What do you think you're doing?" He shakes his fingers, then slaps the fiery embers on the table.

"I'm sorry." But I'm not sorry at all. Blood pounds in my ears. "I thought you wanted me to."

"Promise not to do that again. Ever."

"To you? Or to anyone?" My face burns, but not from shame.

Thomas opens the door.

"Wait! Will I see you tomorrow?" I ask.

He slams the door in my face.

What an infuriating man!

I scoop up my vest and hurl it against the door. I listen to the tread of Thomas' boots in the hall, anger and frustration—and something entirely new—bubbling in my veins.

I touch a fingertip to my lower lip, remembering Thomas' warm mouth. I know it's a mistake to step over the hard boundary separating a landowner's daughter and a blacksmith's son. One thing's certain—I only did it because of Damon, and I won't do it again.

21

MISSIONS

Bells chime.

How long did I sleep?

Last night, thoughts of Papa, Damon, and Thomas kept me awake for hours.

Still drowsy, I climb out of bed and go to the window. I'm high enough to see the rooftops of the city and the sea beyond. Below me, the Temple's high stone wall encloses a thatch-roofed barn, several smaller buildings, a large garden, and a vineyard.

A skinny, braided girl who could be Con squats between the leafy rows of the garden. Sister Agnes totters towards her, scolding and waving her arms. The old woman wears an apron, gloves, and a wide-brimmed hat with netting. She shoos Con back inside the Temple then makes her way towards a line of white boxes. Sister Agnes must keep bees.

Turning from the window, I notice a pitcher, towel, and basin on the table. Whoever brought them did so while I slept. I wash and dress, wishing I had a mirror to check my appearance. As I pull on my boots, I notice the ashes on the floor, a reminder of my argument with Thomas. I was a fool to think kissing him would make a difference.

Someone raps on my door. Before I can open it, a slender vestal with a thick brown braid enters. I don't recall seeing her last night.

"Good morning, Will." She sets down a plate of grapes and sliced bread. "I'm Margaret. Did you sleep well?"

"I slept very well. Thank you." I hasten to put on my cap. "Sister Agnes said I could see the Guardian this morning."

Margaret frowns at the ashes on the floor. "And I am to take you to her—after you eat."

I barely mask my impatience as I pluck a grape and crush it between my teeth. My mouth is flooded with sweetness. I chew and swallow before remarking, "This is good."

The vestal rolls her brown eyes. "Of course it's good. We make excellent wine here. Also, Anne baked the bread this morning, and the honey is from Sister Agnes' bees."

I bite a bread slice drizzled with honey. It's delicious.

"Mother Celine often uses honey to dress wounds," Margaret continues. "Did you know that it fights corruption and speeds healing?"

Since my mouth is full of bread, I shake my head.

"I thought you might not," she replies.

What does she mean by *that*?

The vestal speaks at length about Sister Agnes' beekeeping operation while I consume my breakfast. When Margaret begins to ramble about the Temple milk cow and cow pox, I decide it's time to extract the information *I* need.

"Excuse me, but have you seen Thomas Smithson this morning?" I ask.

"Thomas?" Margaret arches a slim eyebrow. "How do you know *him?*"

"That's none of your business."

"I'll tell you what *is* my business." She folds her arms. "You don't speak or act or eat like a lad, though you dress like one. Are you an imposter?"

I am beginning to hate this girl.

I push the plate away. "I'm done eating. Please take me to Mother Celine."

Chin raised, the rude young woman sweeps past, leading me up the passage and down the stone staircase. At last she opens the door to an airy room lined from floor to roof with bookshelves. A wooden ladder is suspended from the highest shelf. In front of the glass garden door, a marble Goddess holds a large ball between her palms.

I walk over to the statue and spin the ball, which turns on a rod, and stare at the peculiar blue and green shapes. "What is this?"

"It's the earth." Margaret's tone suggests I'm a simpleton. "Haven't you seen a globe before?"

Stupid girl.

"Everyone knows the earth is flat," I declare.

"You're wrong," she contends. "Astronomers know it is round, and cartographers and seafarers have confirmed it."

I've seen maps of Papa's lands, but I've never seen anything that shows more of the world. Should I believe her?

"Here's Andwarf." Margaret points to an inlet on a green coastline. "Across the Great Sea is Anglia—and Marianas, the Duke's capital." Her finger moves to a large island, then drifts east of Andwarf. "And this is Colognia, the capital of the Berengarian Empire."

I wonder where Lille is, but asking might further stir her suspicions.

The door to the garden opens, and a woman the height of a child enters. Her blonde hair streams over her shoulders and hangs past her waist. Her light blue robe matches her eyes.

"Good morning, Margaret," she says. "Thank you for showing our guest to my study."

Margaret bows her head. "Good morning, Mother Celine."

This tiny woman is the Temple Guardian?

I whip the cap from my head. Recalling the Duke's portrait from the Governor's residence, I search Mother Celine's placid face for a family resemblance, but I see none.

"Margaret, you may return to your mission. I prefer privacy for my conversation with Will," Mother Celine says.

Margaret nods politely. "As you wish."

I throw Margaret a triumphant look. She narrows her eyes at me before exiting into the garden.

I make a little bow. "I'm pleased to make your acquaintance, Mother Celine."

"And I am pleased to make yours, Lady Gabrielle," she replies. "I've been expecting you for several days."

She already knows who I am? Did Thomas tell her?

Mother Celine gestures to two chairs in front of the hearth. One chair has much shorter legs than the other. "Please sit." The Guardian sinks onto the smaller chair and rests her slippers on a footstool. "Thomas told me what happened to your father. What a harrowing time you have had. I offer you my deepest sympathy."

A lump fills my throat.

Mother Celine clasps her hands on her lap. "May I ask why you didn't come here after you'd dealt with the authorities?"

I move to the cold hearth and face her. "That's of little importance now. My brother has been arrested and sentenced to death—mainly because he knows things the Governor does not wish to be brought to light. The Governor has also seized my family's fortune and—" I pause when I notice Mother Celine's serene expression hasn't changed. "Would you consider intervening with the Governor on Damon's behalf?"

"I have not left the Temple in years," she states. "However, I can send word to the Governor—though it's unlikely I will make any impression on him. Conrad Visser and my brother—the Duke—are at odds. Still, Visser might at least consider delaying the execution."

"Thank you." I'm relieved.

"Lady Violet will be most distressed to learn of your father's death," Mother Celine observes.

"She'll be devastated." I wonder how Mother Celine knows my mother. "I hope you understand that I cannot consider becoming a vestal after all that's happened."

Mother Celine nods. "As you wish. And while you're here, I ask that you maintain the identity you have recently adopted." With a simple gesture, she acknowledges my boyish appearance. "That will be safest."

For me or for you, I wonder.

I clear my throat. "Mother Celine, have you seen Thomas Smithson this morning?"

"Briefly." She rises and opens the glass door to the garden. "Life at the Temple is not what you have imagined. Let me show you some of our missions."

I don't have time for a tour. I need to find Thomas and concoct a plan for Damon's rescue—in case Mother Celine is unable to make headway with the Governor. Then again, perhaps Thomas is somewhere on the Temple grounds.

I give her another little bow. "I would be delighted."

Once we are outside, Mother Celine names some of the herbs flourishing in neatly tended plots. Maman has many of these plants in her own garden. Mother Celine continues along a flagstone path that meanders towards the east wing of the Temple.

Inside a solarium, Sister Agnes is perched on a high stool,

and at her feet, a dozen children hold small glass jars containing bees.

"It's Mother Celine!" Con cries. "And Will!" She lifts her jar. "We're learning about bees!"

I smile and wave at her.

A small boy runs to Mother Celine and hugs her. She bends over to kiss him—though she doesn't have to bend far—then urges him to return to his place.

"Some children belong to street gangs and cannot remain here during the day," Mother Celine says. "Life can be cruel, but we do our best to help children discover their own worth."

Shame flushes my cheeks as I recall the unfair judgments I made about the Temple.

Mother Celine clasps her hands behind her. "Perhaps you would like to sit in on the class."

"My mother also keeps bees," I inform her.

"Excellent. While you are here, we shall try to discover the gaps in your education. Your father's letters indicated there are several." Mother Celine opens another door.

Ignoring the reference to my failings, I hurry after her. "Mother Celine, I must speak to Thomas."

But Mother Celine has already walked into an adjoining room in which children are seated at long tables. Several young women lead lessons in mathematics and geography. Mother Celine wanders about the room, pausing to ask each child a question.

Near a window, more children surround Anne. A child turns his freckled face towards me and grins.

What's Sam doing here?

"Come here, Will," the vestal says, beckoning.

Curious, I move closer. Anne holds a wooden paddle with several knobs and a lengthy screw.

"What is it?" I ask.

The children giggle.

Anne smiles. "Place your eye against the lens."

I peer through it while she adjusts the height of the screw. "All I see is a wavy blur," I say after a while. "What am I supposed to see?"

A gap-toothed girl guffaws out loud. Anne hushes her, and the child covers her mouth with her hand.

"Keep looking," Anne instructs.

I start when strange shapes wiggle into view. How peculiar!

"What *are* they? They look like they're *swimming*," I remark.

The children laugh. Sam pokes me with his stump.

The vestal sighs. "Tell her, Philip."

"Of course they're swimming," the little blonde boy says with elaborate patience. "They're in a drop of rainwater. They're called animalcules."

"There are animalcules in *everything*," the gap-toothed girl states.

The sight of the wriggling creatures makes me queasy. "Where did you get this device?"

"Anne made it," Philip informs me. "She calls it a microscope."

"My father's a wool merchant," Anne explains. "He needed a way to examine fabric threads so he could judge their quality."

"Tell her what he said when you showed him the microscope," the gap-toothed girl urges.

Anne tightens her hair twist and re-pins it before answering. "He was certain it was witchcraft. When I argued that it was science, he sent me here. Little did he know—my experiments were just beginning."

My skills and knowledge are paltry compared to Anne's—and the children's. I could study every minute of every day for a year and still fall short. No wonder Papa said I have 'gaps.'

"Will, would you like to see a rose petal up close instead?" Anne asks.

"Or maybe some sheep shite?" a small boy wonders.

"Anne's very skilled at developing poultices and other remedies," Mother Celine says behind me.

I didn't realize that she has been listening.

"Lately she's had some marvellous results with bread molds, isn't that right, children?" Mother Celine asks.

Anne blushes.

The children nod. While their adoring gazes shift between the vestal and Mother Celine, I discover that I'm envious.

"Come, Will. Let's leave the children to their lessons," Mother Celine says.

I return the microscope to Anne and smile my thanks, then wave goodbye to Sam. With a shy grin, he waves back.

Next, Mother Celine takes me on a tour of the vineyard, where two youths aged twelve or thirteen are harvesting grapes. They remove their straw hats as we approach. She speaks with the youths briefly before entering a long storehouse.

"Can boys be vestals?" I ask.

"We call them altons. They stay only until they're old enough to go to university. Now that Andwarf's is closed, I've made arrangements for them to go to the one in Marianas," Mother Celine explains.

Is it possible Damon knows some graduates of the Temple school?

As I enter the storehouse, I assume I'm about to receive a lesson in vinting. However, Mother Celine walks past the vats and wine press into a connecting room, where two vestals—one of whom is Margaret—operate the handles of a tall wooden framework. A powerful smell assaults my nostrils, but it isn't wine. Sheets of parchment are stretched on racks and stacked on shelves. Printed pages flutter on a clothesline when Mother Celine opens the window.

"Will, this is Sophie," Mother Celine says, indicating the short, plump vestal with large brown eyes and wavy blonde hair. "You've already met Margaret."

Sophie returns my smile, but Margaret ignores me.

"Sophie, please explain your mission," Mother Celine says.

"We print books," Sophie says as she adjusts the shoulder strap of her ink-stained apron. "Margaret started it all by adapting a wine press." She points to the parts of the framework as she explains. "See this handle? It turns this screw and puts pressure on the paper, which is laid over the type." She pushes on the handle, raising the plate so I can see it.

"You mean you don't copy books by hand?" I ask.

"Of course not." Margaret gestures to the wooden tray on the table. "That's the type for the next page."

I study one of the pages pinned to the clothesline. "What do you use for ink?"

"We used wine at first, but it wouldn't adhere to the paper without blurring." Sophie fans beneath each of her arms. "Now we mix soot, turpentine, and walnut oil."

"This looks like a page from a science book," I observe.

Margaret sighs, as if the question is beneath her. "We print books on every subject."

Sophie's face shines. "Mother Celine says books will change the world."

"As long as we can produce enough paper." Margaret wipes her cheek, smearing it with ink. "We print on one side, so the paper must be glued together."

"Why couldn't you print on both sides?" I suggest.

Margaret places her hands on her hips, spreading the ink to her kirtle. "The paper isn't thick enough."

"Will's right," Sophie agrees, turning her quizzical brown gaze on Margaret. "Haven't I said we should make it thicker?"

Margaret shoots me a look of consternation.

So there.

While Mother Celine and the vestals discuss the possibility of two-sided paper, I glance at a smaller printing tray on a nearby shelf. The letters are backwards, but if they were reversed, I'm certain they would read:

A TREATISE ON FREEDOM.

22

THE QUEST FOR KNOWLEDGE

Are Margaret and Sophie writing and printing handbills for Firebrand and the other rebels? And if they are, does Mother Celine know?

Margaret scowls at me, confirming my suspicions.

I'll keep their secret for now, but do they realize how dangerous this is? Thomas said that—

Thomas! I've been so distracted by the missions, I forgot about looking for him. Before I can ask Mother Celine, she crooks a finger at me and exits the print house.

"Sophie was a baby when her mother brought her to the Temple," Mother Celine explains when we are both outside. "Sophie had seven siblings, and both her parents needed to work. They had no means to feed them all."

"Mother Celine, I—"

"And Margaret is the daughter of a tailor." Mother Celine walks towards a low stone structure surrounded by pink rose bushes. Steam billows from the open windows. "She came to us four years ago. She has a brilliant mind."

Also, a rebellious one.

"*My* mission is to make sure all young persons within these walls discover their potential," Mother Celine continues. "This is often accomplished through cooperative learning. One idea builds on another."

The bright morning sun shines on the Guardian's blonde hair, highlighting streaks of silver. How old is she?

"Mother Celine, when did *you* come to the Temple? Is this the way you wanted to spend your life?"

She turns her head, and her voice floats over her shoulder. "Because of my size, my father decided he would never find a husband for me. I was nearly thirty when he sent me here. Once I became Guardian, I decided to put love into action."

We now stand just outside the low building, and the steam moistens my cheeks. It's peculiar that Mother Celine has not mentioned the Goddess at all. Even Molly the White appears to have stronger convictions.

"So you don't believe in the Goddess," I remark.

Mother Celine's face shines with purpose as she looks up at me. "Of course I believe in Her. But I don't believe She resembles the statues erected in her honour, and I don't believe She is wholly female. Instead, I worship the beauty and the logic of Her creation."

What would Papa have said about such unorthodox views?

"Not everyone values our quest for knowledge." Mother Celine leans over to study a fuzzy black caterpillar inching along the window sill. "I dismissed the Temple Guard. Most of the older priestesses left—since the penalty for heresy is burning at the stake."

I shiver.

She lets the caterpillar crawl onto her tiny forefinger before transferring the creature to a rose leaf. "I tell you this, Lady Gabrielle, because your parents are people of character. I assume you can keep a confidence."

I consider the poverty, oppression, and violence I have seen in Andwarf. How can Mother Celine pursue knowledge so tenaciously without fear of betrayal?

"You assume correctly." I wipe a drop of sweat from my brow. "Now, will you please tell me where Thomas is?"

"Mister Smithson is no longer here." Mother Celine smiles. "But I'm certain he'll return. In the meantime, it's best you make yourself useful." She gestures to the door. "Welcome to the laundry."

23

A BARGAIN

Perching on the edge of the vat, I stir the contents with a wooden paddle. Robes, kirtles, and children's clothing float, dive, and resurface. Because of the heat, I've shed my vest.

I fish out a sopping kirtle and feed it through the wringer. The resulting flattened fabric reminds me of the stacks of paper I saw earlier today. Would the addition of a crank handle improve the efficiency of the Temple printing press? I'll suggest it to Sophie the next time I visit the print house. I'll especially enjoy watching Margaret's reaction.

Later, while I pin garments to the line outside, the breeze cools and dries my skin.

I consider all that I have seen since I arrived at the Temple. I've never had the opportunity to associate with young women my own age. How diverting each day would be with clever companions like Anne and Sophie.

Impossible. Not with Damon awaiting execution. How will Governor Visser respond to Mother Celine's request to delay it? And when will Thomas return?

I notice Margaret making her way towards me from the

print house. She carries something under her arm, and her stride is purposeful.

She's thoroughly unlikeable, but I'm determined not to give her the satisfaction of knowing just how much she annoys me. Therefore, when she stands, sighing, right behind me, I take great pleasure in ignoring her.

"There's no use in pretending you don't know I'm here," she says at last.

"Oh, it's you, Margaret. Did you need something?"

She marches to the other side of the clothesline and presents me with an ink-stained kirtle. She looks like she's outgrown the one she's wearing.

"You should consider putting on an apron at the print house." I hold up and examine the kirtle. "Furthermore, I have no idea how to get rid of these stains."

"I knew you wouldn't. That's why I brought this." Margaret produces a small bottle and pulls the stopper.

I wrinkle my nose at the smell.

She pours some pale liquid onto the stain. "We call it ammonia. It's made from fermented urine. Too harsh for silk or wool, but it won't damage this fabric. Let it soak before you launder it." She stares at me, one slim eyebrow raised. "And if you want everyone to think you're a boy, you shouldn't take off your vest."

I blush and clutch the kirtle against my chest.

"I thought at first you were a rich girl who'd run away to be with her lover. With Thomas," she adds. "But he couldn't possibly be interested in *you*—whether you're rich or not."

My palm itches to smack the smug smile from her face.

"I know about the handbills," I counter. "Firebrand—or whatever his real name is—gave me one yesterday. You print more than books. I might be hiding, but *you* are aiding seditionists."

Margaret blanches. "Please don't tell Mother Celine."

It's gratifying to know I've bested her—if only this once.

"I won't tell her, I promise." I hold out my hand. "As long as you don't tell anyone I'm a girl."

"Agreed." Margaret clasps my hand.

It occurs to me that the promise I've just made could be dangerous for Sophie and Margaret. Then again, they're both safe inside the Temple walls and under the protection of the Duke's sister. What could harm them here?

I drop Margaret's kirtle on the grass and return to the task at hand. To my surprise, Margaret scoops up a garment from the basket and pins it to the line. We work together in a silence that is almost companionable.

"When did you meet Firebrand?" Margaret asks after a moment.

I attach a small frock to the line before replying, "After the riot at the courthouse yesterday."

"What riot?" Margaret pulls the garment aside and gapes at me.

The shock on her face is rewarding.

Though I can't tell her that Damon is my brother or reveal what I saw during the trial, I quickly summarize how the crowd reacted to Katarina's presence on the courthouse steps.

"Whom did you say was on trial?" Margaret probes.

"I don't know," I lie. "I was only there because I want to join the rebels. Firebrand invited me to the next meeting."

I'm hoping she'll let slip where and when the meeting will take place. I can't wait to confront Firebrand since I'm quite certain he's the one who stole my diamonds.

Margaret's brown eyes narrow. "He invited *you*?"

I fasten a boy's shirt to the line. "Yes, and he'd only just met me. He should be more careful. The Governor deals harshly with rebels."

"I know." Margaret untangles a pair of breeches from the basket. "Some have already paid with their lives."

Her words are a grim reminder of my brother's predicament.

"Why are you involved—when you know how dangerous this is?" I ask.

Margaret stares at me for a moment, then hands me the breeches. "I must go back to the print house, but we should talk later. Meet me in the sanctuary after supper."

As Margaret walks briskly in the direction of the vineyard, I stifle my impatience. If she knows Firebrand and the young men who were executed, she probably knows Damon too, but I'll have to wait until tonight to find out for certain. I'm determined to attend the rebels' next meeting—if only I can trick Margaret into telling me where it will be.

24

THE TEMPLE ROOF

THAT EVENING, I HELP ANNE SERVE BREAD AND CHICKEN soup to the children. I hope for a glimpse of Thomas or Mother Celine but see neither. Although Margaret told me she would meet me at the sanctuary—where children's voices echo off the walls and roof as they play a lively game of tag— there's been no sign of her either.

"What happened to your hands, Will?" Anne asks when we're finished eating our own supper.

I look ruefully at my chapped, red palms. "The water in the laundry is very hot."

"Am I done yet?" Con remains at the table, brooding over her meal. "I want to go play."

"You may go." Anne holds Con's arm as the little girl jumps up. "But please show Will to Sister Agnes' room first."

Con runs the entire way, raps once on the door, and deserts me.

Sister Agnes ushers me into a bedchamber that appears to double as a storeroom. Jars of all shapes and sizes line the shelves, as well as racks of drying herbs. The smell reminds me pleasantly of Maman's pantry.

Sister Agnes takes a jar from the shelf and rubs a fragrant salve on my skin.

"Is this made from rose hips and peppermint?" I ask.

The old woman clasps my hands between her gnarled ones. "You truly are Violet's daughter." When I draw back, startled, she quickly adds, "Mother Celine told me what happened to your father, Lady Gabrielle. I'm so sorry, and you can be certain I'll keep your secret."

The papery network of wrinkles around her rheumy eyes are mesmerizing. "Sister Agnes, just how do you know my mother?"

The old woman leans closer. "You can be quite certain I'll keep that secret as well. Now. You've seen many of our missions. I have a very special one of my own. May I show you?"

I nod.

When I leave Sister Agnes' room, Margaret paces in the hall, a lantern swinging from her fist.

"Why didn't you meet me in the sanctuary?" she demands.

"Why didn't you come for supper?" I counter.

"Never mind!"

She leads me down the hall and, producing a ring of keys, unlocks a door.

"Why do *you* have keys?" I ask.

"I have privileges because I'm the oldest vestal," Margaret says with a hint of pride. "This is one of the few doors Mother Celine insists on locking. You'll soon see why."

On the other side, a metal staircase spirals upwards. After

she relocks the door, Margaret begins to climb, the glow of her lantern providing the only light.

I try not to look down as I ascend. "Mother Celine told me you're a tailor's daughter. Why did your father send you here instead of arranging a suitable marriage?"

"I'm the second youngest of five sisters." Above me, Margaret's voice echoes on metal and stone. "My father didn't wish to pay my dowry."

Perhaps Margaret and I have something in common after all.

"Did you *want* to marry?" I ask.

"My three older sisters are married to men twice their age while the youngest cares for my grandmother, who is an invalid. Am I not the lucky one?"

I ponder her question until we reach the top of the staircase, where Margaret pushes open a trap door.

"Is this the roof?" I ask.

"In a manner of speaking." She levers herself through the opening and reaches a hand down to me. "Welcome to the observatory."

Darkness enfolds the glass dome. Beneath it, a long cylinder is suspended from a massive wooden framework.

"What *is* this?" I gasp.

"A telescope," Margaret says. "For gazing at the stars. I suppose I shouldn't be surprised you didn't recognize it. You don't know much about anything, do you?"

Maybe I've grown accustomed to her insults. They don't sting as much as they did this morning.

I walk around the telescope. "How does it work?"

"The cylinder's hollow," Margaret explains. "Through trial

and error, Mother Celine determined that the eye lens should be concave while the other should be convex."

"I don't know what you mean."

Margaret rolls her eyes as she draws in the air with her forefinger. "Concave. Convex. Do you see now?"

I nod, though I'm not sure I understand.

"Mother Celine experimented with the sizes and distances between lenses until she arrived at this model." Margaret crosses her arms and tilts her head back to gaze at the top of the telescope, which is nearly as high as the dome. "It is by far the most powerful and accurate."

Incredible. I wonder if Mother Celine has ever glimpsed the Goddess from down here.

Margaret uses a hooked stick to release the catch holding a pane of glass. It swings open on a hinge, and a breeze freshens the dome. Next, she repositions the telescope, which moves clumsily on wheels. When she beckons at me impatiently, I help her align the telescope according to the diagrams etched on the flagstones.

"Star gazing is one of my favourite missions." Margaret points to the small chair behind the cylinder. "Climb up there, and see for yourself."

I mount the telescope and slide into the seat while Margaret gives me directions on how to focus the eyepiece.

I gasp when a grey wasteland of ridges and gullies appears. "What in the world is *that?*"

"The moon," Margaret says.

"But it can't be! The moon is the wheel of the Goddess' chariot." The words are out of my mouth before I can pull them back.

Margaret laughs. "Who told you *that?*"

Why do I always feel so backwards around her?

"My brother," I explain.

Damon told me many stories about the Goddess, but from the look on Margaret's face, I now know they came from his fertile imagination.

"Not everything your brother told you is true," Margaret says in a gentler tone. "What a strange childhood you must have had."

I'd like to assure her it was a *useful* childhood, learning about livestock ailments and crop failures, but I doubt this would impress Margaret.

I adjust the lens again. "It's very desolate up there. It makes me feel lonely."

"Science sometimes does that," Margaret says. "But wouldn't you prefer the truth over fantastical stories of chariots?"

"I suppose." The curve of the moon reminds me of the globe in Mother Celine's study. "You could also be right about the earth being round."

"Of course I'm right." Margaret sets her lantern on a podium next to a thick ledger. "Lately we've been recording the ocean tides along with the phases of the moon. Mother Celine believes there's a connection."

While Margaret flips the pages of the ledger, I rub the telescope's eyepiece with the hem of my shirt. "So, how did you meet Firebrand?"

Margaret turns another page. "He was a Temple orphan. I've known him most of my life." Her voice sounds dreamy. "Mother Celine arranged for him to attend university. She said a mind as clever as his shouldn't be wasted."

"And when the university closed, he and the other students continued to trumpet their ideas," I conclude. "Did Firebrand convince you to join the rebels?"

Margaret shuts the ledger. "No. He wanted me to stay here

—where I'd be safe. But I don't want to be safe. Besides that, I have skills he can use."

She blushes and looks away, but she can't deceive me. She's in love with Firebrand.

"I'll not be won over by a handsome face," she asserts—to my surprise. "And when I take a lover, I won't ever have children. I've had my fill of the brats at the Temple school."

Take a lover? Never have children?

Shocked by these notions, I start to climb down from my perch.

"I thought I might find you two up here," a familiar voice says.

Startled, I tighten my grip.

"Hound's spit!" Margaret exclaims.

How did Mother Celine enter through the trap door without us hearing her?

Moonlight transforms Mother Celine's blonde hair into silver ripples. "Did you enjoy using the telescope, Will?"

If she overheard any of our conversation, she gives no indication.

"It's a marvel. Just like everything else at the Temple," I confirm.

The Guardian looks tiny next to the bulk of the telescope. "Then come out to the roof. You'll enjoy the view."

Mother Celine opens a glass door in the side of the dome.

As I step outside, a wind gust nearly tears off my cap. The stars peek between cloud-drifts in an inky sky while the moon rides on the shoulder of distant hills. White caps ripple towards the bright flame flickering within the great lighthouse, and a boom announces their arrival on the rocky shore. Yellow rectangles glow in the darkness as the residents of Andwarf prepare to end another day. It feels like a lifetime since Sister Agnes ushered me inside the Temple.

I lean against the parapet. "The city looks peaceful."

"Only because of the Governor's curfew," Margaret says dryly.

The Governor. And my brother. My thoughts of peace are shattered.

"That's Mother Celine's dovecote," Margaret continues, touching my arm and pointing.

Mother Celine disappears inside a small building tucked in the corner of the roof.

"She's probably sending a message to one of the Temple's patrons. There are many of them," Margaret explains.

The moon shines on the Duke's lead statue in the square below. Is Mother Celine sending her powerful brother a message about Damon? I hope so. In any case, she'll be back any minute, and Margaret has information I need.

"Will you attend the rebel meeting on Thursday?" I ask.

Margaret frowns.

"I've already promised not to tell Mother Celine about the handbills. If you're going, I would like to come," I beg.

"I don't think the Heron would approve," Margaret replies.

Her face is averted as she gazes north. Patches of light bob in the darkness.

"Are those torches?" I ask.

"Probably. Can't be the Night Watch," Margaret states. "They use lanterns. I wonder where the City Guard is headed at this hour."

Mother Celine emerges from the dovecote cradling a bird. She holds the pale plumage against her cheek, then extends her arms and parts her hands. The dove spreads its wings and flutters into the night.

The patches of light, now arranged in two rows of six, bob closer. Mother Celine joins us at the parapet.

"Are they coming *here?*" I ask fearfully.

"I believe they are," Mother Celine says. "Margaret, summon Sister Agnes and the others. Tell them to bring the thunder balls."

The vestal turns and runs towards the dome.

The clink of metal and the tramp of boots echo in the night. When the cohort draws closer, torchlight reveals the livery of the City Guard. I tremble as the two lines of guardsmen turn at the bottom of the Temple steps and begin to climb.

"Halt!" a voice rasps.

The City Guard freezes, their torches illuminating the yellow-haired man mounting the steps between them. I have no doubt he conceals a crossbow beneath his cloak.

Horrified, I back away from the parapet. Has Rolf come for *me?*

25

CONFRONTATION

"Guardian of the Temple!" Rolf shouts. "Open in the name of the Governor!"

I freeze. Did he see me?

Mother Celine leans over the parapet, and the wind fluffs her hair in a silver cloud. "We close our doors at sunset and open them for no one—not even the Governor!"

What a warrior!

"Mother Celine, I am Rolf Von Haugen." The mercenary sounds unimpressed. "Governor Visser wishes to make certain you are not harbouring rebels. No harm shall befall you and your charges if you permit me to search the Temple and its grounds."

"Mister Von Haugen, why can't you carry out this investigation in daylight?" Mother Celine counters.

"You take in street urchins at *night,*" Rolf replies. "The rebels executed last week had connections to your Temple. One sentenced to hang on Saturday has a sister who may have come to you seeking sanctuary."

Rolf wants his diamonds back, and he's had no difficulty determining where I am because of what Papa told him:

"*My daughter is to become a vestal. I'm taking her to the Temple.*"

Still, convincing the Governor to allow him to search the Temple might have taken a day or two.

Mother Celine draws herself to her full height. "The Governor has a vivid imagination regarding the activities within these walls. I will not permit him—or you—to violate our sacred laws."

Silence falls. What will Rolf do now?

"Then I will batter down your doors," Rolf threatens. "And the children you claim to protect will suffer the consequences of your disobedience. The safety of the city's highest official takes precedence over your laws. This building is a haven for rebels and witches."

Gooseflesh ripples over my arms.

Altons and vestals—Margaret, Sophie, and Anne amongst them—pour out of the dome and arrange themselves along the parapet. Each holds a basket. Sister Agnes totters behind them, bearing a torch.

Mother Celine turns her back to the parapet. "Sister Agnes, give me your torch before you burn yourself. Anne, bring a thunder ball."

From her basket, Anne removes a pod the size of her fist. When Mother Celine holds the torch to the wick dangling from the pod, a spark sizzles.

"Begone while you have a chance!" Sister Agnes rails, shaking her fist. "Or you shall know the Goddess' wrath!"

Anne leans over the parapet and drops the pod. I peer over the edge and shield my head as the pod explodes to the left of the assembled guardsmen, leaving a crater in the step. The concussion knocks Rolf off his feet and scatters the guardsmen into the square.

Inside the Temple, children scream.

"Ram's bollocks!" I blurt. "What's in those things?"

"Black powder." Margaret removes a pod from her basket. "Want to light one?"

"No!"

I've heard Thomas' father Andrew speak of black powder, which he used to fire the Duke's cannons. Where on the Temple grounds has Mother Celine hidden the manufacturing of explosives?

"Another!" Mother Celine commands.

Sophie's pod explodes to Rolf's right. He retreats down the steps,

Serves him right.

"Not so bold now, are you?" Sister Agnes calls gleefully.

"You may have won the battle, Mother Celine, but you won't win the war!" Rolf rages. "No one will enter or leave this building! If you don't open these doors, your children will starve!"

I'm doubtful this will happen soon. The Temple garden and livestock can provide sustenance for many weeks. Still, Mother Celine looks concerned as she hands the torch to Anne.

"A siege will deter others from seeking shelter," Mother Celine says. "I cannot tolerate this interference."

"Does that mean you'll send out the person he's searching for?" I ask.

"Absolutely not," Mother Celine says. "The Governor has no authority here."

Praise the Goddess.

"Conrad Visser is a braying donkey," Sister Agnes asserts.

"That will do, Sister Agnes," Mother Celine reproves. "Go

downstairs and console the children. They must be terrified. Anne, Sophie, Margaret—stay up here and keep watch. If the City Guard approaches, do not hesitate to use more thunder balls."

While Rolf instructs the City Guard to surround the Temple, I linger at the parapet and turn my gaze to the prison.

Leaving has just become impossible. I can't rescue Damon or attend a rebel meeting now.

26

UNDER SIEGE

The following day after I finish my chores in the laundry, I join Anne's lesson on magnets. However, I'm unable to concentrate, knowing that Rolf and the City Guard prowl outside the Temple walls.

When her lesson is concluded and the children are dismissed, Anne calls me over. "Will, I'd like you to read this." She gives me a copy of *Everyman's Journey*. "It's an allegory about the quest for scientific methodology."

"My father had a copy," I tell her. "I'm not sure where it is now."

"So, you've already read it?" When Anne cocks her head, her brown twist of hair lurches to the side.

"No, I haven't." I don't have the heart to tell her I don't feel much like reading.

Tucking the book under my arm, I retreat to a bench shaded by a walnut tree. I open *Everyman's Journey* and attempt to give the first page my full attention.

An Apology

When at first, I took my quill in hand,
To write this book, little did I understand
The power of words to instruct
Or impair the souls of man.
But bear in mind, O reader wise
That my purpose is but to surmise
The truth in all its radiant glory
Through Everyman's humble allegory.

"Truth," I say out loud. "I wish I knew the truth about even one thing."

I've seen and experienced so much since I arrived in Andwarf, I hardly know what to think. I lie on the bench and read a few chapters, but the book makes no more sense than it did the first time I opened it. I'm too thick to learn anything new.

Between the walnut's sturdy branches, a white wisp of a moon floats in the blue sky. On the other side of the wall, a guardsman shouts a crude jest to his companion, reminding me of my helplessness.

What good is viewing the moon through a telescope when I only want to know if my brother is all right?

The seed of an idea takes root.

I jump off the bench and hurry to the print house in search of Margaret.

"Why do you want to look into the prison?" Margaret asks as she helps me climb through the trap door into the observatory.

I promised Mother Celine I'd keep my identity a secret. But hasn't Margaret already guessed much of the truth?

"You were right when you wondered if I was born to a family with means," I explain as I strip off my vest. The heat trapped beneath the glass dome is overpowering. "My father was a vassal of the Duke."

"Was? What happened to him?" Margaret asks, moving to the north region of the dome.

I take a breath to fortify myself. "He was murdered a few days ago. And my brother Damon March has been imprisoned. I believe the rebels call him Swordthrust."

"Hound's spit! Swordthrust is your *brother*?" Reaching for a lever, Margaret gapes at me over her shoulder.

"You know him?"

"Of course! Because of his betrothal to Katarina Visser, some of the rebels accused him of being an informant for the Governor!"

"My brother broke that engagement," I point out.

Margaret engages the lever, and a pane of glass above us pops open. "So he said, but the Heron didn't believe him. Firebrand alone spoke in your brother's defence."

I grunt and strain against the framework of the telescope. It won't budge, and I'm already sweating like an ox. "Tell me about the Heron."

"He's one of our newer members. No one knows his real name, but he went to university in Berengaria." Margaret brushes aside the brown strands that have blown across her face. "There's something different about him. I'm just not certain what it is."

There's something she's not certain about? What a refreshing change.

I put my back against the frame and push harder. At last, the telescope moves. "What would your father say if he knew you consorted with rebels?"

"My father abandoned me to what he thought would be a life of servitude," Margaret says as she helps me swivel the telescope so that the cylinder faces the prison. "Meanwhile,

Mother Celine helps create a world in which we are free to choose our destinies. She hopes that one day the Temple will become a university for young women." She climbs up to the chair, kneels on it, and peers through the lens.

"Is that what *you* want?"

"Why not?" Her brown eyes are defiant as she gazes down at me. "I'm as smart as Firebrand and the others. In many cases —smarter. Tell me. What path would *you* choose if you could change the future your father arranged for you?"

When my brother asked me a similar question at the Black Bull, I had no answer. But now I shake my head to dispel the vision of a young blacksmith with dark hair and eyes. "I should like to raise superior sheep and cattle," I tell her instead.

Margaret makes a disgusted sound as she uses a winch to lower the chair. "Don't you want to travel? Learn new things?"

Indeed, is life on a fief truly what I want? Or have I never allowed myself to imagine anything else?

"How did you come to be in Andwarf in the first place?" Margaret asks as she climbs down from the telescope. She frowns and stares, arms folded, while I explain my parents' decision to send me to the Temple.

"Didn't you even consider running away?" she asks when I'm finished.

"Run where?" I argue. "And if you're so adventurous, why didn't *you* run away when your father sent you here?"

She shoots me an exasperated look before turning her back and repositioning the telescope's framework once more. "Give it a try," she says at last.

I climb into the chair and press my eye against the lens. At first, I'm not sure what I'm seeing, so I expand the focus. I finally recognize the Governor's Perch, the empty gallows, and the tower. I refocus to take in the entire yard and the sentries on the walls. I could watch the activity within the prison and record it, like Mother Celine does with the tides. Such information could prove useful later.

"*If* I ever get out of here," I murmur.

"What's that you're saying?"

"Nothing." I narrow the focus so I can see through the largest window of a low building.

"I'm getting bored watching you. What are you looking at now?" Margaret asks.

"I'm not sure. Stop talking," I say impatiently.

The room is richly furnished, and a wide desk is positioned so that anyone sitting behind it would have an unimpeded view of the prison yard. Have I happened upon the warden's office?

A fat man in a red coat walks into view and sits behind the desk. His mouth and hands are moving. Who is he talking to?

"Well?" Margaret prods.

Another man steps in front of the window and blocks my view.

"There are two men in a room," I inform her. "One might be the warden, but I can't see him anymore. I wish the second man would move or turn around."

"We're like *spies*," Margaret says excitedly. "I wonder what Hen—what Firebrand would think of that."

When the second man faces the window, a black mask conceals his eyes and nose. In fact, he's entirely dressed in black.

"What's wrong?" Margaret asks. "You look like you've seen a ghost."

"Not a ghost." My hopes plummet. "My brother's executioner."

27

THE WALNUT TREE

Footsteps approach.

I peer over the window sill and watch the slender figure in coat, cap, and breeches race towards the print house. The moon shines through the glass dome, peopling the Temple grounds with bizarre shapes, but it also reveals the thick braid bouncing against the runner's back. Margaret opens the door and disappears inside.

I haven't seen Mother Celine or heard from her since Rolf's siege of the Temple began. She has obviously made no headway with the Governor, which means I have one hope remaining for Damon's rescue.

Margaret exits the print house, a satchel dangling from her shoulder. She sprints towards the walnut tree, jumps onto the bench, and scales the tree. From within the branches, a dove calls, and a dove on the Temple roof answers.

Another dove—or Sophie?

Loud pops echo in the Temple square. Running feet and shouts fade on the other side of the wall. Sophie must have provided a diversion for the guardsmen.

Margaret sidles along a thick branch, climbs onto the wall, and straddles it. She takes off the satchel and drops it on the other side, then eases her body over. I hear a soft thud and a curse.

I must move fast if I want to keep up. Tonight, the rebels will meet, and hopefully, Margaret will lead me to them.

Excitement flutters as I exit the laundry. The evening air is cool, and I'm grateful for the boy's coat I borrowed. I run for the walnut tree, keeping low. The wind tickles the leaves as I scramble up, then venture onto the wall on my hands and knees. Shadows conceal what's on the other side. I hang by my fingertips for a nervous breath or two, then let go.

I FOLLOW the echo of Margaret's footfall down eerie streets. What if she disappears into a dark passage or building before I catch her?

Someone steps in my path, and we collide.

"Hound's spit! Stop making so much noise!" Margaret's pale face is annoyed. "You'll alert the Night Watch!"

She doesn't seem surprised to see me. Was she expecting me to tag along?

"Are you going to the meeting?" I gasp.

Margaret adjusts her cap. "What else would I be doing? Now stay close!"

Confused, I run after her. She shadows buildings and checks each thoroughfare before setting foot in the next street. She ducks into a passage that twists and turns, then pushes open a gate and enters a small yard. A youth slumps on a bench, his back braced against the brick wall of the building. Above him, orange light escapes a shuttered window.

"Wake up!" Margaret hisses.

The youth leaps to his feet, knocking over the bench. He

wrestles a knife from its sheath and holds the blade at arm's length, his hands shaking.

"Hammer of Justice, do you even have a clue how to use that?" Margaret demands.

Her satchel bumps him as she stomps past, and he nearly drops the knife.

"Sorry, Maggie." He straightens when he sees me. "Who're you?"

"Never mind. Firebrand invited me." I try to sound confident. "Who came up with these ridiculous names?" I ask Margaret as she opens the door.

She doesn't answer.

Inside, a huge man pumps a set of bellows, feeding the fire in the forge. When he turns his head towards us, I see his eyepatch. Margaret has brought me to the Red Nag.

28

MEETING OF MINDS

THE FOUR YOUNG MEN SEATED ON STOOLS IN THE CORNER of George's shop don't seem aware of us. One bows his head, his features concealed by his grey cowl, but I'm certain he's Firebrand. A lad in a tricorn hat is addressing another wearing a red cap though I can't hear him over the wheezing of George's bellows and the roar of the fire. The fourth youth, gangly legs outstretched, observes the others through wire-rimmed spectacles.

Margaret approaches George. The blacksmith ceases pumping while she whispers urgently in his ear. She opens her satchel and shows him the contents. He places his huge hands on her slender shoulders and steers her away.

How does Margaret know George? Furthermore, will he recognize *me*?

His eye roves past me—thank the Goddess—to Hammer of Justice, who lurks in the doorway. George jerks his head, and his message is clear. The youth withdraws and closes the door.

George sets aside his bellows and uses tongs to insert a

small pot in the forge. I start to sidle closer to the rebels, but Margaret pulls me back and puts a finger to her lips.

"The time for action is *now!*" The speaker is the stocky lad in the red cap.

"Don't be a fool. We'd be cut down by the City Guard in an instant," says the youth in the tricorn hat.

"I'd rather be a fool than a coward," Red Cap blusters.

"Are you accusing *me* of cowardice?" Tricorn Hat retorts.

"We mustn't quarrel. A divided house will fall." Firebrand rises and props a foot on his stool. With a flourish, he tugs off his cowl, revealing the riot of brown curls. He flips a few pages of the slim volume he holds. His showmanship reminds me of Gonzalo in the square and Visser in the courthouse.

"Listen up, lads," Firebrand says.

Red Cap groans.

"'And Everyman said, 'This hill, though high, we must climb; the difficulty of the ascent makes it more sublime.''" Firebrand waves a forefinger as he reads.

I'm astonished that *Everyman's Journey* keeps cropping up.

"'For I discern the way to freedom lies above,'" the rebel continues. "'Pluck up your courage, my comrades; let it fly like a dove. Better should we die in the endeavour, than chart an easier course, and freedom find never.'" He snaps the book shut and holds it in the air. "One sentence at a time, Fierelli revolutionizes our world."

Tricorn Hat yawns. "I grow weary of your philosophy lessons, Firebrand."

"All we do is *talk!*" Red Cap jumps to his feet. His round face is flushed. "Scatter handbills! Run from the Night Watch! When do we *fight?*"

"Saturday!" Firebrand shakes the book. "*Saturday,* we bring freedom to the citizens of Andwarf!"

Yes! And freedom for Damon!

"At last!" Red Cap shouts, echoing my excitement.

"Is it freedom that motivates you, Firebrand—or a desire for fame?" Tricorn Hat sneers.

Firebrand spreads his arms. "Can't it be both?"

Red Cap laughs and smacks Tricorn Hat's shoulder, spilling the lad from his stool. The two wrestle on the floor while Firebrand doubles over in laughter.

The gangly fellow, unsmiling, watches them. He seems like an outsider. Is he the one Margaret referred to as the Heron?

Margaret steps into the circle of rebels. "I've brought the new handbills," she announces.

"Maggie!" Firebrand's smile is brilliant. "How did you get away from the Temple? We heard it's under siege."

Margaret gazes at him adoringly. "I went over the wall—as we used to do together."

Despite her bold words in the observatory, the poor girl's fallen hard for this pickpocket.

"Hello, Firebrand," I say.

Startled, he peers in my direction. His smile fades.

Yes. He remembers me, and he didn't expect me to appear at this meeting.

He looks away and tucks *Everyman's Journey* into his coat. "Ah. Spark, isn't it?"

"My name is Will," I say slowly.

Firebrand turns to his companions. "Lads, this fellow stood up to Von Haugen outside the courthouse a few days ago."

The gangly one rises and clasps my hand. "Welcome, Will. I'm called the Heron. I'm pleased you've decided to join us. Did you attend the university here?"

"He did not." Tricorn Hat scratches a sideburn. "He could be a spy."

"I'm not a spy," I assert. "And to my regret, I'm not a university student, but I *am* sympathetic to your cause."

"I'm certain we can trust Will," Margaret says quickly.

I give her a grateful smile.

Tricorn Hat's gaze remains suspicious. "Then why didn't you join earlier?"

"I arrived in Andwarf this week. From the country." I try to stick close to the truth. "And since then, I've seen the tyranny of Governor Visser. When I read Firebrand's handbill, I knew I had to join."

I give Firebrand a hard look, and he averts his eyes.

"Bravo!" Red Cap's grin dimples his ruddy cheeks.

Tricorn Hat folds his arms over his chest. "We don't accept country bumpkins."

"'Each man is a brother no matter his station, and each woman is a sister no matter the nation,'" I quote.

"You've read Fierelli?" Firebrand gasps, looking up.

I nod and hope he won't ask for a longer recital.

"Ah. You are *self*-taught. That's unusual but admirable." The Heron's eyes glow behind his spectacles. "I hail from the university at Colognia, which offers a superior education. There I was exposed to the greatest of teachers and ideas—"

Tricorn Hat sighs. "Not this again."

"—ideas which have opened my mind in ways these young men have yet to grasp," the Heron concludes.

"And what of young *women?*" Margaret asks.

Good question.

Tricorn Hat laughs. "I hear the Temple offers a superior education in *sewing*. Maggie must teach it—since her father's a tailor."

Margaret swings her satchel at his head, and he ducks.

"Easy, Maggie," Firebrand intervenes. "I'm sure he intended no offence. Now show us what you've brought."

Muttering, Margaret opens her satchel and passes some

pamphlets to Firebrand. Fingers pinching his beardless chin, Firebrand reads.

What manner of sedition does *this* pamphlet propose?

"Well?" Red Cap urges, echoing my thought.

"Pretty Maggie has done well," Firebrand approves. "Visser has turned us into monsters. This." He raises the pamphlet. "This reveals who the *true* monsters are."

Margaret beams. "At least *someone* appreciates me."

Firebrand gives the pamphlets to his companions. "Memorize the most inflammatory phrases. We'll distribute them tomorrow."

Has he forgotten how easy it is to be arrested?

When he offers a pamphlet to George, the blacksmith holds up his giant palms in refusal.

Tricorn Hat scans his copy. "Do you think the common folk will be able to read this—much less understand the arguments?"

"A revolution has to start somewhere," the Heron observes, one hand resting on his hip.

When Firebrand extends a pamphlet in my direction, I declare, "The last time you gave me one, you took something from me."

"I don't know what you're talking about," he replies, avoiding my gaze.

I take a step closer. "Give me back my diamonds."

"What diamonds?" Margaret sputters. "You never mentioned any diamonds before. How dare you make such an accusation against Firebrand!"

George clears his throat. His eye is fixed on my face.

Ram's bollocks. He's seen through my disguise.

"I too would like to know more about the diamonds," the Heron says. "As leader, it's my right to know every detail of this rebel chapter's activity."

"*Leader?*" Tricorn Hat shakes his head. "You arrived far too late for that. Tell me, is there any truth to the rumour that you were expelled from the university at Colognia?"

The Heron looks dismayed, and I suspect the rumour is true.

Firebrand waves the pamphlet under the Heron's thin nose. "Since when do we take direction from *you,* you pompous egghead? I don't have to justify the use of assets I acquire!"

Firebrand *does* have the diamonds. Excellent. I can use them to save Damon.

Firebrand and the Heron glare at one another. Animosity crackles. There's so much petty jealousy amongst these young rivals, I doubt they could mount a successful campaign against the Governor. They're a divided house indeed.

George steps between Firebrand and the Heron and clenches their collars in his powerful fists, lifting them like a pair of schoolboys. "Enough of your squabbling!"

Exactly.

Firebrand's boots barely touch the floor. He still clutches the pamphlet. "Thunderer, please."

Thunderer. What an appropriate name.

George gives them each a shake. "I take considerable risk letting you fools meet in my shop, and I only allow it because of Lord Damon. Furthermore, my name is George, not Thunderer."

Firebrand looks chastened while the Heron looks peeved. I gather the latter's not accustomed to being manhandled by giant blacksmiths.

"And just who is this Lord Damon?" I ask, seizing the opportunity.

Margaret and George both eye me doubtfully. They haven't given me away so far. Will they now?

"Damon March—formerly known as Swordthrust." Tricorn

Hat curls his lips in distaste. "The traitor. All those fine words when the whole time he was betrothed to Visser's *daughter*."

The blacksmith releases the two rebels.

"But since Damon's arrest, he's not turned even one of us over to the authorities." Firebrand smooths a wrinkled pamphlet against his chest. "He's no traitor. Our plans for Saturday must include a rescue attempt."

Yes!

"Too risky." The Heron tugs on his sleeves. "We'd never get him free."

"You're wrong about that." When Firebrand faces me, his gaze is apologetic. "Will, I admit that I took your diamonds, but I used them to finance the revolution. I intend to purchase the services of the Duke's privateer."

Firebrand can't be serious.

"The Duke is a worse tyrant than Visser!" The Heron's thin face twists. "We can't use *his* ship. It's a violation of my principals."

Tricorn Hat folds his arms. "As if we give a fiddler's fart for your principals."

Red Cap laughs.

George clears his throat in warning.

"How did you gain access to the Duke's privateer?" Margaret wonders.

Another good question.

"It was Ironfist's idea," Firebrand explains. "He's with the privateer right now. And when he returns, he'll show us new weapons. Weapons we'll use to overthrow Visser and free Swordthrust."

"Huzzah!" Red Cap shouts.

These revelations make my head spin.

"What weapons are you talking about, Firebrand?" the Heron persists.

"Maybe George would like to show them to us now," Firebrand suggests.

"Not until *Ironfist* arrives," the blacksmith replies.

"Who is Ironfist?" I ask.

Margaret frowns and shakes her head at me.

The Heron removes his spectacles and polishes them on his sleeve. "Firebrand, tell us more about your plans for Saturday."

Firebrand beams with excitement. "During the executions, the City Guard will congregate at the prison. We'll seize the opportunity to take control of the courthouse. Once we're inside, just let Visser try to force us out!"

Red Cap clenches his fists and cheers.

This is Firebrand's plan? How will storming the courthouse benefit my brother?

"What if the Guard brings cannons or a battering ram to bash open the courthouse doors?" I have to shout to be heard over Red Cap's cheering. "I've been inside that building! It isn't fortified!"

George narrows his eye at me, as if willing me to be silent. What does *he* know?

"The people of Andwarf will rally to us," Firebrand affirms. "They'll help us overpower the City Guard."

"No. The people of Andwarf will be inside the prison, watching the executions," I point out. "The prison is a better target."

"Will's right." The Heron perches his spectacles on his nose. "The prison *is* fortified, so it wouldn't be easy for the guardsmen to oust us once we've taken control."

Margaret wrinkles her brow. "But how would we get past the sentries?"

We? Is she part of this outlandish scheme?

"You'll be allowed to enter the prison yard to watch the hangings," I remind her. "The crowd can then be rallied to overpower the City Guard." I turn to Firebrand. "You saw what happened at the courthouse."

Firebrand scowls. "But the courthouse is the *symbol* of Visser's power."

"You're wrong," Red Cap's voice is hushed. "Our friends have given their lives on the gallows."

"Though not one of us has had the courage to watch them die," Margaret says.

The rebels exchange somber glances.

"We must take over the prison, not the courthouse," the Heron states.

"For once, I agree with you." Tricorn Hat grips the Heron's shoulder. "What say you, Firebrand?"

"I say . . . the majority rules," Firebrand replies quietly. "That's what we're fighting for, right?"

The four lads link hands and raise them. I can't believe I've convinced these rebels to change their plans. George and Margaret appear to be equally surprised.

Firebrand turns his gaze on me. "Will, since you seem well acquainted with the activity within the walls, how would you propose we attack the prison?"

"Attack?" the Heron repeats.

Before I can answer, the door to the shop opens, and a tall figure in a black cloak and hood enters.

"Ironfist! Your timing is perfect!" Firebrand cries.

The stranger pulls down his hood.

It's Thomas—of course.

29

IRONFIST

Firebrand grasps Thomas' hand and shakes it. "Did you meet with the privateer?"

"I did, and he's amenable to the plan." Thomas surveys the room and locks eyes with me. "Why are *you* here?"

My answer is a self-assured smile. Serves him right for trying to shut me out.

Thomas looks at George, and the huge blacksmith shrugs.

"You *know* Will?" the Heron asks.

"I have for many a year." Thomas unfastens his cloak and hangs it on a nail. "But the lad has a way of surprising me."

"We've been waiting for you, Ironfist. Please show everyone the weapons," Firebrand urges.

Thomas jerks his head at George. The blacksmith unlocks and opens a wooden chest. He removes an object with a smooth wooden handle and a metal barrel the length of my forearm.

Strange.

"What *is* that?" Red Cap asks as he leans over Thomas' shoulder.

"We call it a pistol," Thomas replies. "Very deadly."

Firebrand takes a second weapon from the chest and sights along the barrel. "Show them how it works, Ironfist."

Thomas pushes on Firebrand's arm, forcing him to lower the weapon. "Do you think firing one of these in the dead of night will fail to attract the Night Watch?"

"Firing?" the Heron asks, stepping forward. "Is it a cannon of some kind?"

"You might say that," Thomas says. "From fifty paces, it'll blow a hole the size of your fist in a man."

These weapons are like the Temple's thunder balls—only worse.

Red Cap whistles appreciatively. "Where did you get these?"

"I made them," Thomas says.

"Here?" the Heron asks.

Thomas rolls his dark eyes. "Never mind where."

Obviously these young men irritate him. It's hard to believe only a few years separate them.

"They're portable. Easy to conceal. Far more effective than a sword or a crossbow," Firebrand says to his companions.

Red Cap and Tricorn Hat appear awed. The Heron looks mortified.

"There's more black powder at the Temple if you need it," Margaret says.

Thomas gives her a worried glance. Has he just noticed her?

Margaret smiles and folds her arms across her chest. "We had occasion to use some a few nights ago."

"I can attest to that," I say.

Thomas shoots me a hard look.

Red Cap runs a fingertip along a pistol barrel. His round face is curious, admiring. "Do we have ammunition?"

"Working on it," George says. "Bring the lead molds, Thomas."

While Thomas unhooks two trays from the wall and sets one on the anvil, the one-eyed blacksmith uses tongs to remove the pot from the fiery forge. After George pours the silvery contents of the pot into the depressions in the tray, Thomas places its mate on top and clamps it in place.

"I've made a few rounds already," George says, dipping the molds in a bucket of water. "But I can't melt all my horseshoes for lead balls. I still have to earn a living."

"Outstanding." Tricorn Hat shakes his head in disgust.

Firebrand and Margaret exchange secretive smiles. He whispers in her ear, and she nods.

What are they scheming?

Red Cap hefts a pistol. "Ironfist, show us how to load and fire. We'll practice until we can do so without thinking."

The rebels—except for the Heron—gather around Thomas.

Is the Heron reluctant to use the weapons because he fears the consequences, or is he merely upset this is Firebrand's notion, instead of his?

"This contains enough powder for one shot." Thomas holds up a small bottle, uncorks it with his teeth, and spits the wax seal on the floor. "Pour a little into the priming pan and close the lid. The rest goes into the muzzle." He demonstrates, then reaches for one of the lead balls. "Insert the ball." He mimes doing so then raises the weapon to eye level, left arm straight. "Pull back the hammer."

"Boom," Red Cap murmurs.

"Show us again. Slower," Tricorn Hat says eagerly.

I watch with growing trepidation as Thomas answers the rebels' questions while he reviews the loading, firing, and care of the pistols. He is placing deadly weapons in the hands of young folk who are as distant from trained mercenaries as doves from hawks.

"You don't approve of these weapons, do you?" I whisper to the Heron.

"I don't believe in using violence to achieve our goals," he whispers back. "I'm curious about how you acquired those diamonds."

"I stole them," I say simply.

He nods. "I shouldn't be surprised. You're clearly a resourceful lad."

"Was it your idea to defame the Duke in these pamphlets?" I ask him. "I thought Visser was the enemy of the people."

"Heron, take the watch if you're not going to learn how to use a pistol." Firebrand looks irritated.

The Heron shrugs at me and ducks out the door.

A moment later, Hammer of Justice stumbles into the shop. When he's given a weapon, his fingers tremble so badly he can't load or aim it. Finally, Margaret takes it from him. Holding the pistol steady with two hands, she turns her pale face towards me.

"Your turn, Will." Her tone is a challenge.

I start to refuse, then notice that Thomas bristles with disapproval. I take the pistol from Margaret and repeat the steps, then aim at the wall and conjure the executioner's mask.

Would I shoot him to prevent him from killing my brother?

Vaguely, I hear Firebrand say, "I thank you all for your attendance tonight and look forward to standing shoulder to shoulder with you lads on Saturday."

Thomas wrenches the weapon from my hand. *"This* lad will not be standing next to anyone's shoulder. He'll come along when I take Margaret back to the Temple."

"I won't go," I say.

"The City Guard watches the Temple too closely. There's no way back in," Margaret argues.

Before Thomas can answer, Firebrand turns to George. "Thunderer, do you have a length of chain I could borrow?"

George looks at Thomas.

Thomas nods his head. He looks resigned—even defeated.

Firebrand embraces Margaret and swings her until her cap comes free and her braid whips behind her. She squeals in delight.

What are Firebrand and Margaret planning?

Red Cap raises a fist above his head. "On Saturday, we take Andwarf!"

"You'd best lie low until then." Thomas thrusts two pistols in his belt and fetches his cloak. "Step outside, Will."

"As you wish, *Ironfist.*" I raise my chin and breeze past him, shoving open the door to the yard. I've a few things of my own to say.

"You test my patience," he says once we're alone. "I'll not have you popping up like a weed all over town."

My own anger catches fire. "The other night, you suspected Firebrand had taken my diamonds. Then you talked him into giving them to you, so you could buy the services of the Duke's privateer!"

Thomas folds his arms. "And just when did you establish ownership of them—seeing as how you stole them in the first place."

Someone clears his throat.

The Heron stands, hands in pockets, near the gate. I'd forgotten he took the watch. He moves swiftly towards us.

"Ironfist. A moment." The rebel touches my arm. "I'd like to speak to Will alone."

Thomas snorts. "Be quick." He walks to the gate and peers out, checking the street.

The Heron draws me under the eave of the blacksmith shop. "I couldn't let you go without mentioning how much I value your insight. You have a broader vision than the others."

Across the yard, Thomas curses under his breath. I'm impatient too. We have much to discuss.

The rest of the rebels exit the shop. Firebrand and Red Cap carry a length of chain between them. Thomas grabs Margaret's arm and whispers to her urgently. She tears free and runs after the others, stuffing her braid under her cap. The rebels' mysterious enterprise worries me.

"Let's go, Heron!" Tricorn Hat shouts.

The Heron grasps my shoulder. "I'll go with the others—wherever they're headed, so I'll say goodbye. But be leery, Will. Be leery of old men who know too well the rules of the game." The Heron hurries to catch up to the rest.

Before I can ponder what these cryptic words mean, Thomas growls at me, "Let's go, milady." He opens the gate.

"Where are we going?"

"To the Redemption." He swirls his cloak around his shoulders. "If you want your diamonds back, you'd best speak to the Duke's privateer."

30

THE REDEMPTION

While I struggle to remember where I've heard the ship's name before, two rough-looking wretches step out of the shadows.

"Good eventide," one says. "What brings you out past curfew?"

Moonlight reveals the man's blunt features and greasy lips, but if he has weapons, his cloak conceals them.

Neither of Thomas' pistols is loaded. What now?

The other stranger has pock-marked cheeks. "Mayhap you're looking for a wench."

"No, we're headed for the harbour," Thomas says in a congenial tone. "We're part of the Redemption's crew."

The men look at each another. Greasy Lips touches the brim of his hat and bobs his head. "Safe travels to you both. There's ne'er-do-wells aplenty in these streets."

Yes, just like them.

"I'm grateful for the warning," Thomas says.

I let out my breath when we're safely past. "As soon as you mentioned the Redemption, those two scoundrels left us alone," I observe.

Thomas tugs my forearm. "Keep your voice down and walk faster."

He stays close to the shuttered shops. I lengthen my stride to keep pace. A window above us slams, and I squeak. A dog bays, and I squeak again.

"And quit starting at every sound," Thomas mutters.

"Sorry." I clutch the lapels of my coat to keep out the night chill. "How long have you been involved with the rebels?"

Thomas grunts. "I wouldn't say I'm involved. Your daft brother dragged me into their reckless schemes. George let them meet at the shop so I could talk sense into them, but there was no sense to be had."

My heart slams against my ribs as Thomas shoves me in a doorway, his chest pressed against mine.

"What—"

"Hush now. It's the Night Watch," he whispers.

Fear grips my throat, and his closeness is disconcerting. I place my cheek against his chest and feel the throb of his heart. Has the pace quickened only because of the Night Watch?

I shift my body, so I can peer under his arm. A circle of light approaches. Five men in dark surcoats and wide hats walk single file up the street. The first man carries a long pole from which a bright lantern is suspended. His four robust companions are armed with pikes and batons.

When the Watch moves on, Thomas relaxes and steps away from me. "I'll do everything in my power to protect your father's family," he says quietly.

His words disappoint me, though I don't know why.

A TALL SHIP, lit with lanterns, bobs at the harbour entrance.

The darkness and distance make it impossible to discern the ensign, but I assume this is the Redemption.

Thomas leads me to the dock adjoining the esplanade. After we climb in a longboat, he unfastens the rope and lays into the oars. His strokes are sure, and his gaze is fixed on the ship behind me. As our boat glides through the water, I look over my shoulder. The details of the vessel take shape: three masts, a female figurehead—

"Tell me about the Temple, lass," Thomas says.

It's the first time he's called me that since I kissed him. My cheeks burn at the memory. I shove aside my embarrassment as I describe the Temple missions.

"And have you seen Margaret making black powder?" Thomas asks when I'm finished.

"No. But I know Mother Celine used it to keep the City Guard away when they came in search of rebels."

What would Thomas do if he knew Rolf had been searching for *me*?

A star falls, disappearing beyond the city in a streak of gold.

"Oh!" I exclaim.

"What is it?" Thomas stops rowing and looks over his shoulder. "Is it trouble?"

"No. A shooting star," I say quickly. "It reminded me of one of Damon's tales."

"Tell it to me." Thomas pulls on the oars.

"Very well." I hope he won't think me a silly girl with silly stories. I shift and draw one knee against my chest. "According to Damon, the Goddess had two children—a boy and a girl. One night they begged to accompany her when she drove her silver chariot across the sky. She allowed them to come, but she warned them to sit quietly. When she wasn't looking, they teased and tormented one another. The boy fell from the chariot, and his body became a shooting star."

"A pleasant ending," Thomas observes with a hint of irony. "I hope you could sleep after Damon told you that one."

We've drawn close to the ship's hull, and I look up. The clouds part, and the moon shines on the ship's ensign fluttering in the breeze. Bordered in silver, a white dolphin leaps in the centre of the flag. Thomas draws in the oars as the boat's prow bumps the hull.

There's more to the tale, but I'm too nervous to finish. I'm about to meet the Duke's privateer.

"Who goes there?" a voice calls down.

"Smithson!" Thomas calls up.

A rope ladder drops from the deck.

"You don't answer to Ironfist here?" I tease.

Thomas grunts and ties the boat to the iron ring on the hull. He holds out a hand. "Up you go."

Conserving my breath, I scale the swaying, creaking ladder in the dark while Thomas puffs beneath me. The ascent is far more taxing than the tree in the Temple yard. Once on deck, I cling to the rail until my breath returns and my legs adjust to the rolling of the ship. I've never been aboard one before. The vast deck is deserted, apart from two barefoot men in rags. If the Redemption is the Duke's ship, his sailors look like pirates.

"Who's the lad, Smithson?" A sailor with a gold earring asks. "Shall I take him to the brig?"

"Not this one," Thomas replies. "He'll stay with me."

The sailor guides us to a cabin and opens the door, revealing Molly the White's broad back. She's seated between Gonzalo and another man, a map unrolled on the large oval table before them.

Why are Molly and Gonzalo here?

The stranger's wavy black hair reaches the shoulders of his dark blue velvet surcoat. He wears light blue silk breeches, and the handle of his dirk is a silver dolphin. If he is the Duke's privateer, his attire is at odds with his ragtag crew.

Gonzalo sees me first. "My lady of the horse!"

So much for my disguise.

"Thomas, where in the world did you find her?" Molly's grin is wide as she turns in her chair. "I'm glad to see you, Lady Gabrielle. I was worried when you never came back from the prison."

I'm glad to see her too, but I have business with the man in the blue coat.

I approach him, hand outstretched. "I'm pleased to meet you, Captain."

Thomas coughs. Did he think I'd remain silent and submissive?

The captain sweeps a courtly bow and brushes my hand with his lips. His mustache tickles. "And I am pleased to meet you, milady. I'm the Duke's esteemed privateer Captain Hernando Enzio Varga."

I withdraw my hand. "When Thomas mentioned the Redemption to some rough fellows, they acted as if it might be crewed by pirates."

I'm shocked when Hernando's smile reveals pearly teeth that are sharpened to points. "I used to be a pirate. Now I rob and sink the ships of the Duke's enemies—of whom there are many. The Seven Seas are ripe for picking." He tugs a lace handkerchief from his sleeve. "Lady Gabrielle, I wish to express my deepest sympathies. I never met your father, but I've heard of his exploits. The Duke will be greatly disturbed to learn of his untimely death."

"Not only untimely," I tell him. "My father was murdered."

Hernando dabs his nose with the handkerchief. "Unspeakable."

He seems sincere, but will he return my diamonds?

"Did you meet with the rebels, Thomas?" Molly shifts in her chair.

"I did," Thomas says.

"Hopefully the lads will stay out of our way while the Redemption's cannons blast the prison to bits." Hernando flashes his pointed teeth. "Those walls will crumble like biscuits."

Disconcerted, I glance at Thomas, who is now studying the map. Did Firebrand or one of his companions mention that they now intend to attack the prison?

Before I can point this out, Thomas says, "After we rescue Damon, we need to prevent the City Guard from closing the gates."

Rescue!

"I've got that covered," Molly says.

"And what of a diversion inside the prison walls?" Gonzalo asks.

"And a means to smuggle in weapons," Hernando states.

"There are *more* pistols?" I ask.

Thomas' sound of annoyance cannot extinguish my excitement. All the while that I've been worrying about how to free my brother, these people have been plotting to help him.

"Zoh could steal a set of keys and get swords to the prisoners," Gonzalo affirms. "I taught her everything she knows."

"What's keeping Zoh so long?" Hernando smacks his lips. "All this talk of revolution makes a man thirsty."

"Speaking of revolution, don't you have a great deal to lose by conspiring against the Governor that the Duke appointed?" I ask Hernando. "Isn't this the *Duke's* ship?"

Thomas curses under his breath.

"This is *my* ship," Hernando corrects. "And I'm not acting against the Duke. I'm acting against Conrad Visser. Duke

Edmond is most perturbed with him for imposing exorbitant tariffs on Anglian goods."

"I suppose that makes sense," I reply.

"It's never wise to bite the hand that feeds you." Gonzalo strokes Molly's white forearm.

"I'm accustomed to changing course with the wind," Hernando continues. "And the present wind blows towards the removal of Governor Visser. How providential to be so handsomely rewarded for helping to oust a tyrant whilst appearing to quell an uprising."

"Rewarded in *diamonds*?" I ask.

Hernando raises both eyebrows.

"Those diamonds are mine," I assert.

"In truth, they belonged to Visser," Thomas says.

"Even better." Hernando intertwines bejewelled fingers. "How appropriate that the Governor should finance his own removal."

I'm confused. I've seen the pamphlet Margaret and Sophie printed. It defamed both Visser *and* the Duke. What would Hernando think about that?

I open my mouth to ask, then close it when I notice Thomas' icy glare. If Hernando knew the rebels were set on deposing both Visser and the Duke, he might not be as sympathetic to their cause—or to rescuing Damon.

I turn to Gonzalo instead. "I don't understand why *you* are here."

"Hernando's my nephew," Gonzalo explains.

I should have noticed the resemblance.

Hernando inclines his dark head. "What a fine example Uncle Gonzalo set for me. From him, I learned every trick in the book."

"You mentioned a diversion earlier," I say to Gonzalo. "Has anyone in Andwarf actually seen the Duke?"

"He hasn't traveled beyond Anglia in years," Hernando says.

"Who's to say the Duke won't make an appearance at the prison on Saturday? He could have been aboard the Redemption all this time," I suggest.

Gonzalo extends an arm dramatically. "It shall be my greatest performance."

Thomas shakes his head as he sinks in a chair. "That plan would take too much time. We only have a few days."

"All Gonzalo needs is the right clothing." I turn to Hernando. "Yours would serve the purpose."

"I'll need a retinue." Gonzalo strokes his goatee. "Men-at-arms."

"And a page," I say. "A Duke should always have one, shouldn't he?"

Gonzalo winks. "Excellent. Did I mention this would be my greatest performance?"

"And if you think you'll be playing the role of page, milady, think again," Thomas growls.

The cabin door opens, and Zoh backs in, a tray of tankards balanced on her palm. Her curves press against the bright red silk of her dress.

"Finally," Hernando says, rubbing his hands. "I had begun to despair, my raven-haired beauty."

Zoh scoffs and sets the tray on the table. The tankards shift with the motion of the ship.

"Zoh," Molly says. "Gonzalo wants to talk to you about stealing a set of keys."

Zoh casts a heavy-lidded glance at Thomas before she hands Molly a tankard.

Zoh said she and Thomas are acquainted. Heat floods my cheeks. Are they *lovers?*

"And as for Thomas—" Molly begins.

"Smeethson can go to hell, eh?" Zoh says mildly.

"You've offended her, Thomas." Molly peers around Zoh. "And now you need her. 'Tis a pity."

Zoh extends a tankard to Gonzalo next. "Zoh doesn't theenk about heem anymore, eh? Now that Hernando promise Zoh fine house een Marianas."

Hernando blinks as he accepts his mug. "I did?"

Zoh slams one in front of Thomas. "Let's dreenk." She raises hers.

"Salut," Thomas says.

Thomas and Zoh take sips, eyeing one another over the rims of their tankards. Molly elbows Gonzalo.

What's happening?

Zoh tosses her dark head. "So, what breeng you back, Smeethson? You miss Zoh?"

"Very much," Thomas replies, knuckling away the foam on his upper lip.

"He's lying," Molly says. "He wants us to help break Damon March out of prison."

Zoh sighs. "Heem again?"

Thomas sips his tankard.

"The easiest way to get weapons into the prison is in the Levers' cart," I suggest. "Isn't that right, Zoh?"

Thomas coughs and wipes his mouth. "Who are the Levers?"

"You know. Zee soap makers," Zoh says. "Zoh not see how zey weel help."

Thomas stares at me in surprise. "How do *you* know them?"

"I don't know them. I just know what they *do*." I blush as I explain, "They buy the bodies of the dead and render their fat into soap."

"I can think of better ways to make a living," Gonzalo says.

"On Saturdays, zey come to zee prison early and leave right after zee hanging." Zoh pretends to tighten a noose around her own neck. "Sometime, Visser like to leave a body sweeng, so zey come later. But in zee end, zee Levers always get zere soap."

"And no one searches the cart when they enter?" Thomas asks.

Zoh shrugs. "No one bother, eh?"

"Then I'll pay the Levers a visit," Thomas decides.

"And why you not veesit Zoh anymore?" Zoh pouts as she plops on Thomas' lap and wraps her arms around his neck. "You break Zoh's heart."

Before Thomas can reply, Zoh presses her mouth to his.

What?

Molly roars and pounds a white hand on the table. Hernando clears his throat.

"You dead to Zoh," Zoh murmurs against Thomas' lips.

I watch in dismay as his hands creep around her waist.

Gonzalo sets down his tankard. "Maybe not so dead as one would hope."

31

THE GREEN-EYED MONSTER

My annoyance grows when Thomas makes no attempt to push Zoh away. Instead, his arms enfold her, fingers splayed on the red silk. Warmth pulses in my throat and floods my cheeks.

Zoh reaches beneath her skirt to draw a stiletto attached to her calf. I watch in horror as she presses the tip of the blade beneath Thomas' left ear. "Why you go away, eh?" she whispers.

Thomas cups Zoh's head and kisses her until she drops the knife with a twist of her wrist.

My fear vanishes. The nerve!

Hernando clears his throat—louder this time.

"Lady Gabrielle," Gonzalo says, leaning around Zoh, "when you've finished discussing the unfortunate events that have befallen your brother, I would like to revisit the subject of Perdita."

With considerable effort, I drag my eyes away from Thomas and Zoh.

"Let's settle on a price," Gonzalo says. "What say you to *seventy* marks?"

Zoh's moan tests the limit of my patience. I tug on the barmaid's shoulder. "I order you to stop this display."

Zoh straightens and wipes her swollen lips. "Zee red hair ees jealous, no?"

"I'm *not* jealous," I insist, "but your conduct sickens me."

Zoh slides off Thomas' lap and scoops up her knife. She places her sandalled foot on his thigh, and drawing up her skirt, returns the stiletto to its sheath.

"If these two lovelies are to fight, allow me to place the first wager." Gonzalo clasps his palms. "Hernando? Molly? What do you say?"

Hernando frowns and shakes his head. Molly smacks Gonzalo's arm.

Thomas stands. "There'll be no fight. Come with me, lass."

"Lass." Zoh's violet eyes are steamy. "Very familiar, eh? Zoh deedn't know Smeethson like zee red hair."

Thomas ignores Zoh. "I thank you for your assistance, Molly. Now if you'll excuse me, I'll see that Lady Gabrielle is tucked in for the night. She'll take my quarters."

Zoh snickers.

I back away from Thomas. "I want to be a part of the plan to rescue Damon."

"Not a chance," Thomas says. "You're lucky I let you stay this long."

Molly looks thoughtful. "Lady Gabrielle has a point. March is her brother. I say you take her along to the Levers."

"She's little more than a child," Thomas says.

"I'm not a child!" I resist the temptation to stamp my foot.

Gonzalo laughs. "There are waifs less than half her age picking pockets."

"I demand to go to the soap shop." Before Thomas can disagree, I turn to Hernando. "And about those diamonds."

Hernando spreads his arms. "I wish I could help you, milady, but my services do not come cheap. I have struck a deal with the rebels, and I shall keep my word." He bows. "I'm a man of honour."

"Honour?" I fume. "You're no better than your uncle!"

When Hernando straightens, he looks hurt. So does Gonzalo. I instantly regret my words.

"I'm sorry," I say quickly. "You've all been so kind to me. I didn't mean that."

Thomas steers me towards the door. "Say goodnight, milady." He whisks me out of the cabin before I can utter another word.

I'm thrilled a plan has taken root to rescue my brother, but I'm frustrated I'm not to be a part of it. And I can't even begin to deal with how infuriating it was to watch Zoh kiss Thomas like that. Did he enjoy it as much as he appeared to?

Thomas' cabin turns out to be so small that I can touch the walls on both sides. A narrow bunk beneath the window and a small sea chest are the only furnishings. Thomas stoops beneath the low roof.

"But where will *you* sleep?" I ask.

"There's plenty of hammocks below deck. Are you hungry?" he asks.

"No," I lie.

"Well, I'm famished. I'll see if I can find something in the galley."

"Before you go, I have a question," I say quickly.

He sighs. "Haven't you said enough for one night?"

"I want to know about you and Zoh. Are you . . . fond of her?"

He shakes his head. "Not in the way you think."

"But you kissed her." I sit on the bunk and tuck my hands beneath my thighs. "Is she your sweetheart?"

"At one time." Thomas opens the sea chest and removes a coarse blanket. "I'll see you in the morning, milady." He throws the blanket over his shoulder and exits.

Thankfully, he doesn't lock me in.

I climb on the bunk and gaze out the porthole. A ghost with bangs and dark circles for eyes floats in front of the city walls and the lighthouse.

What will the next two days bring? Will Damon be free by Saturday night, or will we all be dead?

I look at the moon, which I now know to be a sphere, just like the earth, instead of the wheel of the Goddess' chariot. Is the Goddess even real? Is there any point in praying to Her? Still, I climb off the bunk and onto my knees.

"Please save my brother," I whisper. "And please don't let Margaret or any of the rebels or Thomas be harmed."

With a jolt, I realize I never told Thomas or the others about the rebels' plans to attack the prison instead of the courthouse. But tomorrow, I will.

32

THE SOAP MAKERS' SHOP

A knuckle raps impatiently at my door. "You are awake, eh?"

I crawl out of the bunk and wrap a blanket around my waist. I wear only my chemise.

When I open the door, Zoh breezes in, arms laden with clothing. "Zoh breeng dresses for zee soap shop."

"But I'm not going," I say sourly. "Thomas said so."

"I've changed my mind, lass." Thomas leans in the door.

I jerk the blanket higher. I must look a fright with my hair sticking in every direction. If Thomas is embarrassed to see me in such a state, he gives no indication. Still, his unexpected decision to forfeit makes me suspicious.

"I thought you didn't want me anywhere near the soap shop," I remind him.

"I don't trust you, so I'll keep you within arm's reach," he replies. "Dress quick. Molly thinks you could pass as a merchant's daughter, but I have serious doubts." He leaves.

How peculiar.

Zoh gives me a sideways glance while she arranges the dresses on my bunk. "A shopping treep. How romanteeque."

I close the door. "Where did you get these?"

"Hernando's last prize was a Berengarian merchant sheep," she says breezily.

"S*hip*," I correct.

I paw through the dresses, trying to find something suitable. I'm delighted that I'm to go to the soap shop after all, but Zoh's presence is a bitter reminder of the kiss she and Thomas shared last night. What *else* did they share after he left my cabin?

"Do not worry about Zoh, eh?" the barmaid says, as if reading my mind.

"I don't know what you're talking about." I avoid looking at her.

"He not kees Zoh last night. Oh, his leeps on Zoh all right. But eet was your leeps he want."

Her assertion both pleases and confuses me.

"But he said I'm a child," I protest.

"You not a child to heem, even though he not want to admit eet." Zoh fishes a gold dress out of the pile and holds it up. "You theenk on eet. You know Zoh ees right." She looks critically at the dress. "Thees look nice with those green eyes."

"My eyes are hazel," I tell her.

"Zey green right now," Zoh says, eyebrow arched. "Green like jealous."

"But *you* want him." I toss the blanket on the bed and reach for the dress. "Why did you kiss him if you don't?"

"Zoh luff Hernando," Zoh replies. "Zoh make *heem* jealous."

Recalling Hernando's reaction to the kiss, I decide it hadn't perturbed him.

The barmaid grins wickedly. "Zoh have no idea she make *you* jealous too."

I cover my mouth to conceal my dismay.

"Don't try to hide eet now." Zoh smiles. "We all saw eet."

She helps me into the gold dress. Though it's the proper length, the bodice gapes.

Zoh looks down my bosom. "Zoh can see the floor, eh? Not good."

I let the gown drop to my ankles and choose a light grey riding habit. It has a short coat and long, loose fitting trouser legs, giving the semblance of a skirt.

"This is more practical," I tell Zoh while she buttons my coat. "I wish I had a mirror."

She pins my hair beneath a peaked crimson hat and applies powder and rouge to my cheeks. She arranges a grey silk cape over my shoulders and attaches a small handbag to my wrist.

"What's the need for the *paste?*" Thomas growls when I emerge from the cabin.

"Zoh says it makes me look older," I remark primly.

Zoh arranges the hat's red veil over my eyes. "Meestress Lever sneef out a fake. Eet take a woman to know zees."

Thomas turns his broad shoulders away from us. "Let's be on our way then."

I stare between Minx's brown ears as Thomas and I ride through the soap and perfume district, but this street smells no better than the others. And once again—like the day Papa died—I've hardly seen a soul. It's eerie.

"Where is everyone?" I wonder.

Thomas grunts. Apart from stopping to ask directions, he's hardly spoken since we picked up Minx and Damon's white gelding at the Black Bull. Thomas didn't even explain how the horse managed to get there from the Red Nag. I don't hold a candle to Thomas when it comes to secrets. Maybe a little gratitude will loosen his tongue.

"Thank you for letting me come along," I offer meekly.

"You know more about the Levers than I do," he replies. "It makes sense to bring you. But when we're done, you'll go back to the ship."

"I think not," I reply.

"And I say you will."

We argue the rest of the way to the tiny shop marked "Levers' Soaps."

Thomas dismounts and secures the reins for both horses. "While I persuade Mister Lever to sell me his mule and cart, go inside and keep the wife occupied. Speak to her of nothing but soap. Understood?"

"Perfectly." I slide off Minx's back.

Thomas digs in his pocket. "Use this to distract her. From what Zoh says, you could buy her soul with it." He presses a few marks in my hand and disappears around the back of the shop.

A bell tinkles above the door as I enter.

"We're closed!" a voice says sharply.

Mistress Lever, wearing her white bonnet and an apron, glowers at me from behind the counter.

I close the door. "But I need soap, and I'll pay you well."

She wrinkles her pointed nose. I'd forgotten how much she resembles a rat. I place my coins on the counter.

Her gaze fixes first on the money, then travels to my hand. "You don't have the skin of a lady." Her beady eyes try to search beneath my veil. "I've never seen you in my shop before, but you seem familiar."

Does she remember me from the constabulary?

"Who did you say your father was?" she asks.

"I didn't say." I turn away from her and walk to a shelf

laden with clay jars. "But he is rich and has considerable influence with the Council of Merchants."

I select a jar and open it. While pretending to examine its grey, unremarkable contents, I glance out the rear window. I see only a mule in a stall and the blackened stonework of a kiln. No sign of Thomas or skinny Mister Lever. "Do you have anything scented with hyacinth?"

"I don't make scented soaps. *This* is what you need for your rough skin." I face Mistress Lever as she removes a jar from behind the counter. "It's made with a very special ingredient." She lowers her voice. "The fat of a *hanged* man."

I shudder.

"That's why we're closed today. Because of the hangings," she announces.

I feel as if the room has been tilted on its side. Today?

"Last night, the Watch arrested some rebels for pulling down the Duke's statue—the big one in the Temple square."

By the Goddess' eyes. Margaret.

Mistress Lever seems delighted to share more information. "Then—under *torture*—one of the rebels confessed to plotting to attack the prison tomorrow. Can you imagine such foolery?" She leans on the counter. "The Governor's going to execute them this afternoon—along with the one sentenced earlier this week."

Damon.

"I know this because I have connections to the prison." The soap maker's eyes glitter. "My husband's brother is a sentry there. Still, it's a big inconvenience for *us*. We've scarcely had time to incinerate last week's bodies."

My concern for Damon, Margaret, and the others shoves aside that grisly picture.

"Do you know if they arrested a young woman?" I ask.

"They did indeed," she replies suspiciously. "How did you know?"

I can't bear the thought of Margaret being tortured.

"Why do you find this news upsetting?" she presses me.

"I don't," I lie. "I just feel . . . dizzy. Do you have some smelling salts?"

"I'm not an alchemist," she snaps.

Is there time to return to the ship and tell Hernando about the arrests? And if there isn't, what can be accomplished without the Redemption's cannons?

"However, I might have something else that will work." Mistress Lever steps from behind the counter and uses a key to unlock a large wall cabinet.

As if in a dream, I move towards her.

She opens the cabinet, then freezes. "I remember where I saw you now." When she faces me, her eyes are narrow slits. "You were at the constabulary. Perhaps you'd like to explain why your father—who was dead as a doornail—is now rich and *alive*."

I shove her into the cabinet and slam the door, turning the key in the lock.

The door rattles. "Let me out!"

I bar the shop's entrance and close the shutters. I hope the Levers' neighbours have gone to watch the hangings and won't hear her banging and shouting.

"Open this door immediately! Help!" the woman cries.

I fear her pounding will tear the cabinet door from its hinges, but I have to tell Thomas what I've learned.

Behind the shop, the mule is still tied to the manger. The Levers' cart is parked next to the limestone kiln. Bile rises in my throat as I notice a pair of boots poking out from under the cart.

"Thomas!"

To my relief, the young blacksmith steps out of a shed, a harness slung over his shoulder.

I point at the boots. "Is that Mister Lever? Did you—"

"Of course I didn't kill him," Thomas interrupts. "Do you think I'm a beast? But he's trussed up like a chicken, and he'll have a sore head tomorrow."

"Well, I locked Mistress Lever in a cabinet," I inform him.

Thomas looks impressed.

"Did Mister Lever tell you about the arrests last night?" I ask. "And the executions being moved to today?"

"He did." Thomas drapes the harness over the side of the cart and begins to untangle the long reins. "But we didn't have much time for conversation. What did the wife say about it?"

When I'm done explaining, Thomas shakes his head. "Did those dimwits pull down the statue because they thought George needed the lead?"

"I don't know," I reply, "but it's possible."

"And when did they decide to launch an attack on the prison? They were to start a riot at the courthouse—to distract the guards on the walls."

Ram's bollocks.

"I might have suggested the prison was a better target," I admit. "Does it matter now?"

He looks at the sky and curses. "Well, thanks to their idiocy, they won't be creating *any* kind of diversion. Can you handle the mule, lass?"

The mule wheezes in protest as I back it out of the stall.

"How will we get the cart into the prison without the Levers?" I keep a firm grip on the mule's head while Thomas arranges the harness on its back.

"Zoh will drive it and tell the sentries that the Levers can't come today." Thomas lifts Mr. Lever's heels and drags him behind the shed.

I back the mule between the cart shafts. "Hopefully, the sentries believe her. Apparently one of them is related to Mister Lever."

"Zoh can be very convincing. All she has to do is flash those violet eyes of hers and—never mind." Thomas secures the harness to the shafts. "I'll return to the Black Bull and tell Molly and the others—and hopefully get word to Hernando. Half his crew are on shore leave."

"I'll go to the Temple and try to get word to Mother Celine," I offer. "Maybe she can help Margaret."

Thomas looks relieved. "The Temple would be a good place for you as long as it's no longer under siege. Now bring the horses."

By the time I return on Minx, the mule is ready.

Thomas ties Damon's horse to the cart, then removes two pistols from his saddlebag. "Use them if you must to defend yourself. You already know how to load and fire."

"But don't you need protection?" I ask, pulse skipping.

"Don't worry about me, lass." His dark gaze makes my pulse skip faster. "Now keep those pistols close."

I thrust the weapons in my waistband and draw my cape over them. "Will you give me some ammunition then?"

Thomas opens the handbag dangling from my wrist and inserts two bottles of black powder and a pair of lead balls. When he places a palm atop my rein hand, my fingers tremble.

"Go straight to the Temple. I'll bring Damon and the others there—if I'm able." His eyes and tone are insistent.

I smile at him with a confidence I do not feel, for I'm not going to the Temple—at least not right away.

33

CHANGE IN PLANS

The doors and shutters of the shops are closed. Minx starts when the breeze blows a crumpled paper—one of Margaret's pamphlets—between her hooves. Full of dire thoughts, I urge my mare to a canter.

The guardsman seated on a bench outside the Red Nag heightens my concern. The door behind him hangs from its hinges and creaks in the wind. Has George been arrested too? I'd hoped he would be able to tell me what happened last night.

The guardsman swaggers into the street as I pull up.

"What do you want here, miss?" he demands.

He looks young despite his scowl and his long black beard. Can I weasel information from him?

"I brought my horse for shoeing. Is the blacksmith here?"

"He's been arrested," the guardsman says, confirming my fears. He stares at Minx's hooves and strokes his beard. "Your horse isn't shod."

"That's why I brought her!" I stretch out the hand bearing the gold signet ring. "I'm Katarina Visser."

As the guardsman examines the ring, his insolence fades. "My apologies, Miss Visser."

I press my advantage. "Why did you arrest my blacksmith?"

"I didn't. I'm here to keep an eye out for trouble." He rests a hand on his baton for emphasis. "The blacksmith was harbouring rebels."

"Rebels?" I ask, feigning ignorance.

The guardsman sneers and rubs a knuckle under his nose. "Scholars with high ideals. What's wrong with the way things are, Miss Visser?"

"My father would agree with you." It isn't exactly a lie. "How many were arrested?"

"Five—including the girl. They arrested the blacksmith just this morning. We found some of these inside the shop." The guardsman removes a pamphlet from inside his coat. "'Tis treason, Miss Visser."

I mask my despair. Still, which of the rebels escaped?

Also, the guardsman has made no reference to the pistols. Did the City Guard discover them, or did George conceal them in time? And what of Papa's sword? I don't dare go hunting for it inside the shop now.

The bells at the courthouse toll. With growing trepidation, I count each peal.

Eleven o'clock.

"Two hours till the executions," the guardsman observes. "Will you put in a good word with your father about me, Miss Visser? My name's Fredrick."

I tip the beak of my hat. "I'm grateful, Fredrick, for your efforts to rid the city of these dangerous people."

"Thank you!" He waves as I rein Minx away. "Good day to you, miss!"

I wish there was a way I could tell Thomas that George has also been arrested.

Maybe there is.

The Temple square crawls with citizens heading north. Does everyone intend to watch the hangings? I search the crowd for Rolf or his guardsmen, but see neither. I wonder if they've been deployed to the prison. The Temple steps are deserted, and the doors are closed—and likely barred from the inside.

The Duke's statue, however, has been toppled and smashed. The red stains on the pedestal and cobblestones are dried blood, not paint—evidence of the rebels' violent capture. I pray Margaret wasn't hurt.

A hand tugs at my skirt, and I look down at a freckled face.

"Sam! I'm glad to see you. I need you to get a message to Mother Celine. If I tell you, can you write it out for her?"

Sam salutes me with his stump and presses against my calf as I lean over to whisper in his ear. He grins and darts into the street behind the Temple. I turn Minx's head and follow the crowd.

34

THE GOVERNOR'S PERCH

The drummers on the prison wall beat an ominous cadence as I navigate the masses flowing towards the gates.

My nerves are on edge. How conspicuous I feel on Minx.

Two men walk together on my left. The taller one knots furry eyebrows as he calls to me, "Not your kind of crowd, miss?"

I look straight ahead and pretend I didn't hear him.

"Maybe she doesn't know they're going to hang a wench today." His companion cranes his thin neck to see above the crowd. "Hopefully, we get close to the front."

Poor Margaret.

When I reach the gate, I recognize Grey Mustache, the sentry I wanted to bribe on the day of Damon's trial. Will he recognize me? I'm acutely aware of the weapons nestled against my ribs.

Grey Mustache steps in front of Minx. "You can't bring the horse in!"

I'm determined not to back down this time. I'll brazen my way into the prison yard one way or another.

I thrust the signet ring under his nose. "I'm Katarina Visser. Surely you knew I would be here."

He fingers his mustache as he studies the ring. "My apologies, Miss Visser. Where's your escort?"

"I don't need one!" I bluster.

Grey Mustache beckons to the younger sentry—the one with the pudgy face. He shoulders his way through the crowd towards us.

"The Governor won't approve of you mingling with the populace. For your own safety, Miss Visser, you must do as we tell you," Grey Mustache explains.

Why are men determined to thrust themselves between me and my goals?

One of my pistols might persuade him to let me and Minx by.

"Take her to the Governor's Perch!" Grey Mustache tells Pudgy Face.

What? This isn't part of my plan.

"Is the Governor here?" I ask.

"Not yet." Grey Mustache stares into the crowd behind me. "You there! No weapons of any kind!"

"It's not a weapon! It's my rolling pin!" a familiar voice argues.

The baker's wife again.

The young sentry tugs on Minx's reins and leads me into the yard. I look immediately towards the gallows. The six ropes are a grim reminder of why I'm here. I know three nooses are intended for Margaret, George, and my brother. What of the other three?

Red and gold banners drape the Governor's Perch. What will I do when Visser arrives and finds me up there? I search the yard for the Levers' cart, Thomas, and Zoh, but I don't see them.

Pudgy Face halts at the bottom of the staircase and holds out his hand to me. "This is where you get off, Miss Visser. I'll return your horse after the executions. We've orders not to afford any opportunities to the rebels."

"But the Night Watch surely captured all of them." I ignore his hand and dismount, taking care not to jar the pistols.

"Some rebels managed to escape, so they might attempt a rescue. We must keep you out of harm's way. Now go on up." He sounds impatient.

He waits while I climb the dozen stairs to the landing. I wave at him from the top, and he leads Minx away, the crowd folding around them. I hope this isn't the last time I'll see my horse.

I open the door. The Governor's Perch has a wide opening, bordered by gold curtains, that faces the gallows. A chair piled with red cushions sits on a dais in the middle of the room. The grapes, meat, and cheeses arranged on a table don't tempt my churning stomach.

I recall Grey Mustache's words:

"The Governor likes to watch. I hear the sight of young rebels swinging gives him an appetite."

I close the door and move to the opening. As the prison yard swells with citizens, cold despair creeps into my bones. I search the crowd for a familiar face, but I see only men and women hungry for spectacle.

May the Goddess protect all of us.

I unpin my hat and set it on the table. Next I load and prime the pistols, grateful I don't blow off my foot. I place the weapons on the table and conceal them with a cloth napkin.

When Visser arrives, I'll hold him hostage and demand the release and safe exit of the rebels. After that, I don't care what happens to me.

When I look to the gates again, a black-haired woman

drives a mule and cart past the sentries. Zoh! The knowledge that she has arrived gives me greater confidence.

I unfasten my cape and lay it on the back of the chair. Where should I stand when the Governor enters? I move the pistols to the opposite end of the table and cover them again.

A commotion at the gates draws me back to the window. Magnus is hitched to a wagon loaded with ale kegs and driven by Molly. She waves her white arms in displeasure as Grey Mustache blocks her way.

What if he won't let her in?

Behind the ale wagon, a retinue in red and gold has amassed. Governor Visser, resplendent in his crimson coat, reins his black horse alongside Magnus.

I take a deep breath to calm my galloping nerves.

Molly steps down from the wagon to confront Grey Mustache while four servants carrying a litter add to the bottleneck behind her.

Katarina is here *too*? Of all the foul luck.

I'm so absorbed by the events at the gate that I nearly jump out of my skin when the door behind me creaks.

"Miss Katarina, I didn't expect to find you here."

By the Goddess' eyes.

Rolf closes the door before facing me. He cocks his head and smiles, revealing his broken tooth.

"Lady Gabrielle." He slides the bolt into place. "What a welcome surprise. You have chosen a convenient location for our meeting. It affords a measure of . . . privacy."

I realize I've been holding my breath, and I let it out in a rush as I take a step towards the pistols. Rolf lunges and grasps my left wrist. Pain stabs my shoulder as he twists my arm behind my back.

"Be still now," he whispers. "I've been hunting you all week. We've much to discuss."

His voice is mesmerizing and the pain in my left arm is excruciating. I obey him, legs trembling.

"I want to show you something." His hands hovers in front of me. Silver glints in a sunbeam. "Recognize this?"

"It's my father's ring," I say. "You stole it."

"My old friend Simon Rouge was a surprisingly easy target. He had no idea how much I hated him."

"You betrayed him."

"I gave him what he deserved. He had all the honours—this ring, a fine fief, a pretty wife, children. Do you know what I got for all my years of service?"

I bite my lip. I refuse to participate in this despicable conversation.

Rolf twists my wrist until I whimper.

"I got *nothing*. But the tables have turned. Fortune no longer smiles on Simon Rouge—or you, milady."

Do I have the nerve to reach for the knife in my boot? The table is close. Should I try for a pistol?

"You're a monster," I hiss at him. "I should have killed you when I had the chance."

He jerks my wrist again. Still, the pain sharpens my resolve.

"What a joyous reunion you shall have with your father," he threatens. "And your brother won't be far behind."

"Please. I feel faint." I try to sound frightened and helpless.

I sag in his arms, and he lets me drop to one knee. I fumble for Papa's knife and wrap my palm around the handle. I rotate my wrist.

"Katarina's not clever like you." Rolf hovers over my left shoulder. "It was easy to trick her into telling me where your brother was though she begged me not to harm him." The stench of his rotten tooth nauseates me. "Now. Where are the diamonds?"

"Let me go first. Please," I say weakly.

He relaxes his grip. I whirl and drive at his gut. He screams. I wrench the blade upwards before yanking it out. Rolf staggers and slumps against the wall, cradling his belly. Red gushes between his fingers.

"I'll kill you," he gasps. "I'll kill you ten times over."

I ignore my throbbing shoulder as I wipe my bloody hands on the napkin and trade the knife for a pistol. I want to say something clever, since he thinks me so, but nothing comes to mind.

Cocking the pistol, I back towards the window, looking down to see if Rolf's outcry alerted anyone. Pudgy Face stares up at me, and I smile to reassure him that all is well up here. He turns his attention to the gallows. Obviously, he hasn't noticed Katarina yet.

The blood throbbing in my temples echoes the drums on the walls. I position myself so I can see the gallows and keep an eye on Rolf. The executioner now stands behind the first noose. He looks inhuman in his black mask and cowl. The drums quicken as six prisoners, wrists bound, trudge out of the stone tower. George is first, followed by Margaret, the Heron, and Firebrand.

Goddess help them.

Hammer of Justice limps a few paces behind. I assume he's the one who confessed under torture. My heart sinks when I see that the final prisoner is Damon. He surveys the crowd as if searching for someone. I long to cry out to him, but what would I say?

Rolf groans. "I've never seen a weapon like that. Where did you get it?"

It takes me a moment to realize he refers to my pistol.

"Never mind," I say impatiently.

The prisoners mount the gallows, where the executioner secures a noose around each neck. The prison walls block my view of the sea, so I can't tell if the Redemption has left the harbour. Because of my interference, there won't be a disturbance from the courthouse either.

"I take it back. I won't kill you," Rolf rasps. "I want you to help me."

I realize the drums have stopped.

Arms folded over his chest, the executioner waits at the gallows' edge. Visser is directly below.

Now is the time to act.

Rolf's face is grey. His breeches and shirt are drenched in blood. He's no threat.

"I'll help you if you help me," I tell him.

He blinks.

"I can get away two shots," I point the pistol at him. "I have the advantage of surprise, but when I fire, the sentries will respond. Do I take Visser first—or the executioner?"

"Which shot is clearer?" Rolf asks, wincing.

I look down. Visser's retinue surrounds him as he dismounts.

"The executioner," I reply.

Rolf nods. "Then you have your answer."

Though I'm doubtful I can hit my target from this distance, I turn towards the gallows, kneel, and and brace my right wrist on the ledge.

35

HIS GREATEST PERFORMANCE

"Governor Visser!" Mounted on a white horse, a grey-haired man in a blue surcoat and plumed hat weaves through the crowd.

I withdraw the pistol.

"Who's here?" Rolf demands.

The Governor turns to face the Great Gonzalo. "Your Grace?"

I cannot see Visser's expression, but his voice sounds incredulous.

"Out of my way! Let me through!" Gonzalo smacks those on either side of him with the ends of his reins.

The guardsmen push back the crowd to give him room.

"I was not expecting you, Duke Edmond!" Visser calls.

Why has Gonzalo arrived without an escort?

I already know the answer. With the executions moved up a day, he didn't have time to assemble one. So, here he is. Alone.

"Hound's spit," I mutter.

"What's happening?" Rolf asks.

"Hush," I say.

Gonzalo stands in his stirrups. "Governor Visser, show proper respect for your liege lord!"

Visser walks past Katarina's litter. He doesn't bend a knee or kiss Gonzalo's outstretched hand.

"It's a pleasure to serve you, your Grace," Visser bows his head slightly. "To what do we owe this unexpected honour?"

I don't like the way the Governor draws out each syllable. Has he already seen through Gonzalo's disguise?

"Governor, did you not receive the missive informing you of my intention to visit Andwarf?" Gonzalo demands.

"I did not. How unfortunate." Visser definitely sounds suspicious.

I fear for Gonzalo.

"I am highly displeased," Gonzalo continues. "I have just learned of the murder of Lord Simon March. He was my loyal vassal, and may he rest in peace." He waves an arm towards the gallows. "Are those prisoners responsible for his death?"

Visser folds his arms. "They are not. They are rebels, your Grace."

"One of them is Lord Simon's son!" Katarina clambers out of the litter.

"Gadzooks!" Gonzalo splays a hand on his chest. "This cannot be so!"

"Katarina!" Visser grasps his daughter's arm. "Get back in the litter!" He turns to Gonzalo. "I apologize, your Grace. My daughter is under the young man's spell."

The pudgy-faced sentry stares up at me. I can guess the source of his confusion: why are there *two* Katarinas? He disappears under the platform. Is he headed for the stairs? I should check the bolt on the door, but I don't want to miss the drama unfolding below.

Katarina breaks away from her father, leaving her veil

behind. Her brown hair is dishevelled as she grasps Gonzalo's right stirrup. "Duke Edmond, save Damon March!"

"Pay no attention to her," Visser says. "March has chosen to align himself with a poisonous nest of insurgents." He gestures at a pair of guardsmen, who close in on Katarina.

"No! He's honourable and kind, your Grace!" Katarina protests. "I beg you to take us to Marianas!"

As I feared, footsteps ascend the stairs.

"Who's coming?" Rolf groans and slides sideways.

Gonzalo now cups Katarina's chin, and I fear for both of them. This masquerade cannot end well.

"Of course you may come with me, my child." Gonzalo raises his eyes to Visser. "I demand that you free Lord Damon—and the others. Immediately."

The door rattles. Pudgy Face must be on the other side.

"Guards, take my daughter to my perch," Visser says calmly.

Katarina screams as the guardsmen drag her away from Gonzalo.

I don't want Katarina up here. She'll be safer in her litter.

"Tell me, *Duke* Edmond, where is your retinue?" Visser's voice drips with scorn.

He is moments away from exposing Gonzalo as a fake. What will Visser do? Hang him with the others? Where in the name of the Goddess is *Thomas*?

"They were delayed by the crowds. I rode ahead." Gonzalo looks nervously over his shoulder as if eyeing an escape route.

"Let me in!" Pudgy Face demands. "You are *not* Katarina Visser!"

"Caught like a rat in a trap," Rolf mocks me.

I pray the locked door will keep the sentry out a little longer.

"This man is not the Duke! Seize the imposter!" Visser commands. "Take him to the gallows!"

By the Goddess' eyes.

Gonzalo draws his sword and flails it as guardsmen try to drag him from the saddle. The white horse rears, hooves lashing.

"Close the gates!" Visser orders.

"Open this door!" Pudgy Face demands.

Gonzalo turns his horse and gallops towards the gates while citizens, screaming, throw themselves out of his path.

Please Goddess. Let him escape!

"Good people of Andwarf, listen to us!" a familiar voice cries.

It's my brother!

I look to the gallows—where Firebrand, Margaret, and Damon stand, arms linked.

How did they get free of their bonds and nooses?

The other prisoners and the executioner have vanished.

What's happened?

"Why are you taxed unto *death?*" Margaret demands.

"Why indeed?" a man in the crowd responds.

"Meanwhile the merchants grow rich!" Damon declares.

"And fat!" a woman adds.

Firebrand shakes his fist above his head. "And the worst of the merchants is Conrad Visser!" he rails. "He kills the innocent to hide his crimes!"

"Silence!" Visser orders.

"Down with Visser!" a man hollers.

"Down with Visser!" A chorus of voices cry. "Down with the Governor!"

Visser waves his arms at the sentries on the walls. "Shoot the prisoners!"

Goddess. No.

Crossbow bolts rain, and the crowd panics.

"Stay! Fight!" Firebrand pleads, extending his hands to the people.

Some seek cover under the gallows while others stream towards the gates. My poor brother staggers, clutching his chest, then plummets from the platform and falls into the milling crowd.

"Damon!"

I've failed him.

"Let me go to him!" Katarina shrieks below me.

A bolt strikes Firebrand in the eye. Another pierces Margaret's throat as she reaches for him. She crumples on top of him on the gallows.

I've failed them all.

A body slams against the door, splintering the wood around the hinges. More shouts and feet on the stairs confuse me.

What do I do?

"Now you've cooked your goose," Rolf says.

A memory returns of Papa staring down the guardsman, and I make my decision. "Not my goose. Visser's."

I aim my pistol at the Governor's bald head and pull the trigger.

36

RETRIBUTION

The concussion blows me off my feet.

Why didn't I use two hands?

Katarina shrieks. I peer over the sill. Visser sprawls on the ground, blood puddling beneath his shattered skull. So much blood.

And silence.

The crowd stares at the body of the Governor while Katarina, still held by two guardsmen, whimpers. Even Pudgy Face has stopped pounding on the door. Does he know what I've done?

"Did you kill him?" Rolf demands.

I nod.

"Didn't I say, 'apple trees make apples?'" he asks.

I shut my eyes and open them slowly, but the Governor's body is still there.

A crossbow bolt hisses past my ear and smacks the wall behind me. I jump, tripping over the pistol at my feet. I don't recall dropping it. I pick it up and shove it in my waistband. An explosion shakes the platform, and I cling to the casement.

"What was *that*?" Rolf asks.

White billows mask the prison gates. As the wind disperses the smoke, a gap in the wall appears. Citizens race towards it.

Two young men armed with pistols run up the steps to the parapet.

"Huzzah!" Red Cap shouts.

"To freedom!" Tricorn Hat cries. He fires, bringing down a sentry.

Red Cap whoops and shoots another.

They're too late. Far too late.

"Death to the Governor!" a woman cries. "Death to his family!"

Katarina sobs.

Below me, a dozen folk have formed a circle around Katarina. The guardsmen are nowhere to be seen.

Goddess help her.

"Death to his daughter!" the baker's wife cries, brandishing her rolling pin.

In the blinking of an eye, the dozen is transformed into a mob eager for retribution. Sobbing, Katarina kneels while they close in around her.

I back away and cover my ears to shut out the horror. But I already know I will never stop hearing Katarina's screams.

"Gabrielle," someone groans. "Gabrielle, listen to me."

It's Rolf.

"I'm dying. My hands alone prevent my guts from spilling on the floor. A quick end would be welcome. Remember, we made a bargain."

Yes. Death is what he deserves.

I kneel before Rolf and reach for his bloody hand. "But first, you have something of mine."

"The spoils of victory," Rolf says when I tug Papa's ring from his finger.

But I feel empty, rather than victorious, as I slide the ring on my thumb. I've lost both Papa and Damon.

"A quick death," Rolf reminds me.

"Quick enough. The mob can finish you," I tell him.

"As you wish, Gabrielle Rouge." The corner of his mouth lifts in an admiring smile.

I retrieve the loaded pistol and cocking it in one hand, unbar and open the door with the other. Pudgy Face grapples with two men on the landing while others ascend the stairs. The pair hurl Pudgy Face over the railing, and he hits the ground with a sickening crunch.

I fire my pistol in the air. The men on the landing and staircase freeze.

"Down with Visser!" I shout.

"Down with Visser!" a young man waves a baton above his head.

I gesture to the open door. "Help yourselves to one of his lackeys!"

The men push past me in their eagerness.

Shouts travel from the dungeon. I watch from the landing as ragged prisoners armed with swords stream out of the tower. They clash with the stunned members of the Guard. Zoh whips her mule, driving the cart towards the gates.

When I reach the yard, I avoid the bloody, broken bodies of Katarina and her father, and run straight for the gallows, intending to find my brother. Hooves thunder. Someone shouts my name.

Minx gallops towards me with the executioner on her back. He extends an arm, and I turn to flee, but he grabs me about the waist and lifts me off my feet.

I flail at him with the pistol. "Let me go!"

"It's me, lass!"

"Thomas?" I wrap my free arm around his neck then slide my leg over Minx's back.

Settling behind Thomas, I cling to his waist. The crowd obstructs the soap makers' cart, which lies just ahead. Thomas turns the mare towards it.

I press my mouth against Thomas's ear. "I won't leave without Damon!"

Without his body.

"We've got him!" Thomas shouts.

My relief is short-lived. Another concussion rumbles the ground beneath us. Though I can't see the Redemption, I know its cannons must be aimed at the prison. Hernando said the walls would crumble like biscuits. I hope he is right.

The next volley detonates stone and lumber. Ahead of us, the mob clamours to squeeze through the gap in the wall. Someone claws my leg, and I smack the man between the eyes with my pistol. He howls and clutches his face.

I steal a glance over my shoulder as a fourth explosion topples the tower. When panicked citizens try to climb onto the back of the Levers' cart, Zoh strikes them with her whip. The cart bounces through the gap in the wall. A guardsman drives a supply wagon across our path before we can follow.

"Hold on!" Thomas shouts.

Minx coils and leaps the wagon tongue, landing lightly on the other side. She gallops through the hole in the wall and gains on the soap makers' cart. The odour of yeast hangs in the air. Molly must have had both ale and black powder on her cart.

We hurtle through the square and into the street, heading south. Rioters are already breaking shop windows and looting. Is this the better world the rebels envisioned?

Magnus, bellowing, trots ahead of us. Molly and Gonzalo have disappeared. While the Levers' cart bounces away over the cobblestones, Thomas reins Minx to a stop. I give him both of my pistols.

"Damon, Margaret, and Firebrand are in the cart," he tells me. "Zoh will take them to the Temple."

"Are any of them alive?" I ask fearfully.

"I don't know. But I'm taking you to the Black Bull." Thomas gathers up the reins and turns Minx's head. "You can meet Molly and Gonzalo there and go to the Redemption when it returns to the harbour. That's the safest place for you."

"No! I must see Damon first. I've come this far, Thomas. Please."

Thomas surveys the madness that engulfs us. "This isn't the place for an argument. I'll do as you wish, milady. For now."

We gallop towards the Temple.

37

SANCTUARY

Explosions and screams dog us. When I look over my shoulder, smoke obscures the violence and terror.

Thomas guides Minx into the square between the Temple and the university. Ahead of us, the Heron pokes his head from under the tarp covering the back of the Levers' cart and looks around as if considering his options. I don't care about him. I both long and dread to see my brother's body.

Mother Celine leans over the parapet and points. "Enter through the south gate!"

An alton holds open the solid metal gate, which is scarcely wide enough for Zoh's cart. Thomas and I follow on Minx. Sophie emerges from the Temple and hurries down the steps, the hem of her kirtle bunched in her hands.

"Mister Smithson, did you bring Margaret?" Tears stream down the vestal's face.

I don't wait for Thomas' reply. I slide off Minx and run to the cart where Zoh helps me roll back the tarp.

The Heron, who appears unscathed by the riot, crouches beside three blood-soaked bodies. My poor brother lies on his side, but I cannot see his face. A bolt protrudes from Firebrand's right eye. Blood trickles from the corner of Margaret's mouth and pools around the bolt through her throat.

They're all dead. I can't bear it.

"Oh Margaret," Sophie sobs.

"A sad harvest," the Heron says, closing Firebrand's left eye. "From the moment we met, we were rivals, but I never wished for this."

"And where were *you* when they rallied the crowd?" I shout at him. "Hiding under the gallows?"

The Heron gapes at me.

I pound my fist on the wheel, and the pain is surprisingly satisfying. "My brother is dead because of your stupid ideals!"

The rebel cocks his head. "Are you *Will?*"

"Never mind!" My rage blinds me. "Where did you desert George? And Hammer of Justice?"

"They disappeared into the crowd after they helped us load the cart. Hopefully they got away." He rubs his eye through the gap left by a missing lens. So—not entirely unscathed. "Am I to understand you are Swordthrust's *sister?*"

Damon moans and twitches.

Praise the Goddess. Did I imagine he moved?

He moans again and tries to roll onto his back, then cries out in anguish. I start to climb onto the wheel, but Thomas pulls me down.

"We must get Lord Damon inside, milady. Step aside." Thomas gestures at the Heron. "Help me lift him."

Zoh's arm encircles my shoulders as the rebel and the blacksmith, still wearing his mask, ease my brother from the cart. The bolt pierced his shoulder, not his heart. I smear away tears of relief.

"So, the leetle prince is steel alive, eh?" Zoh shakes her dark head. "Zoh weesh she could say zee same for zee others."

I open my mouth, but no words come.

She squeezes me closer. "Zoh will go to zee sheep now. You and Smeethson come too, eh?"

I'm overwhelmed by joy and grief. "I won't leave Damon. But thank you for your help today. You've no idea what it means to me."

She smiles. "You weel do zee same for me one day, eh? Zoh have brother too, but he ees no preence."

She releases me and mounts the cart to help with Margaret and Firebrand.

An ashen-faced Sister Agnes emerges from the Temple. She's aged ten years since I saw her last. "Mister Smithson, is that man *alive?*"

"He is," Thomas affirms. "And he's Lady Gabrielle's brother."

The old woman braces her shoulders. "Then bring the son of Simon March inside."

"Please be careful," I beg Thomas.

With Damon strung between them, Thomas and the Heron move him step by shuffling step towards the Temple. At the bottom of the stairs, Thomas lifts my brother into his arms. Damon groans and faints.

Sister Agnes totters down the steps. "Mother Celine will attend to your brother, Lady Gabrielle. Sophie, help me prepare the others for their death rites."

Sophie stifles a sob and nods.

More vestals emerge from the Temple, and the sad news about Margaret and Firebrand is passed from one to the next. I leave behind their sorrowful litany and enter the sanctuary, where Damon is still draped across Thomas. Children huddle, eyes fearful and mouths agape, at the foot of the Goddess statue. Con stands apart from the others. Part of me longs to comfort her, but Damon comes first.

Mother Celine sweeps up. "Please take him to the infirmary, Mister Smithson. Anne awaits you there." Her blue gaze drifts to my blood-stained clothing.

"I'm sorry about M-Margaret," I stammer. "When I followed her to the Red N-Nag last night, I had no idea—"

"You cannot blame yourself for the dangerous path Margaret and Henri chose," Mother Celine interrupts. "You may come to the infirmary, Lady Gabrielle. But you must keep your emotions under control. Right now, we must attend to your brother." With a swish of her robe, she turns to follow Thomas.

Henri must be Firebrand's real name. I'd forgotten Mother Celine knew him. Recalling her admonition about self-control, I hasten after her.

When I enter the infirmary, the first thing I see is the bloody barb and a finger-length of iron jutting from Damon's shoulder. He lies on his side on a wooden table. Thomas stands beside him, holding him steady. Anne is gathering clean bandages while Mother Celine selects a pair of shears.

When I move to the other side of the table, Damon's face is a mask of pain. I place my hand over his, and he opens his eyes. "Gabby, is that you?"

"Yes, Damon."

"You were outside the courthouse after the trial." His lips are tinged with blue, his skin is cool and clammy, and his pulse is far too fast. "What happened to your hair?"

"I—I—never mind that now. Shouldn't he have a blanket?" I ask.

"Yes, of course," Mother Celine says. "Anne, get him one."

As I arrange a blanket over Damon, he says, "I saw Maggie and Henri fall. Are they dead then?"

"We'll speak of it later. For now, it's enough that you're safe," I assure him.

He frowns as his gaze moves to Thomas. "And you, my childhood friend. Always here for me."

"Stop talking," Thomas growls. "You Marches are never short on words."

"Lord Damon, you're fortunate the bolt went through your shoulder and isn't still buried inside." Mother Celine extends a cup. "Have a few sips of brandy for the pain."

Groaning, Damon props himself on his elbow and pulls the cup to his lips while I support him. He coughs as brandy spills down his chin and wets his shirt. When the cup is empty, he wheezes, "Hopefully it takes effect soon."

Following Mother Celine's calm instructions, Thomas and Anne soak their hands in brandy before severing the crossbow bolt. Damon cries out and slumps against me when they tug the bolt from his shoulder. After Mother Celine stitches Damon's wounds, she presses cloths soaked in brandy and honey against them.

"Not too snug," Mother Celine says gently as Anne wraps his chest and shoulder with a long bandage. "That's better. Now place him on his side, Lady Gabrielle. Thomas, help her. Just so."

Mother Celine pins the end of the bandage while Anne props pillows under Damon's head and behind his back and hips. Mother Celine tucks yet another pillow under his feet. I pull the blanket over him again and watch his chest rise and fall.

"Mister Smithson, this is not the usual conduct of an executioner," Mother Celine observes.

"I suppose not." Thomas dips his hands in a basin and dries them before untying his mask. "I'll change if you have anything that will fit."

"We still have the uniforms of our Temple Guard." Mother Celine says as she washes her own hands. "Anne can show you where they are kept. Lady Gabrielle, you'll want to change as well." When I protest, she raises a tiny palm. "I'll remain here to care for your brother. All you can do now is wait and pray."

As I precede Thomas out of the infirmary, the realization that I aimed a pistol at him this afternoon turns my legs to water.

"What's wrong?" Thomas grips my elbow. "Are you hurt?"

I shake my head as shame washes over me. Now that Damon's been treated, memories surface of Visser's shattered skull and Katarina's screams. My teeth chatter.

Thomas leads me into the garden, where I sink down on a bench.

Thomas drops on one knee. "Milady, what are you thinking about?"

"I saw you in the warden's office a few days ago," I tell him, shivering. "You were dressed as an executioner—though I didn't know it was you at the time."

"How did you manage that?" he marvels.

I stifle a sob. "With the Temple telescope."

Thomas unbuttons his coat and shrugs it off. "I should have guessed." He folds his coat and places it on the bench. "Rest your head, lass."

The quiet garden is lovely, and it feels wonderful to lie down. I'm so tired. "How did you convince the warden that you were the executioner?"

Thomas loosens his collar. "The Governor's hangman met with misfortune when he set to drinking with Gonzalo and me. We stowed him in the Redemption's brig, and I paid a visit to the warden, who was eager to acquire my services since I told him I was the Emperor's former executioner. He didn't even ask why the Emperor sent me packing."

I try to focus on the sound of his voice. It helps to keep the monsters at bay. "But if Gonzalo hadn't arrived when he did, I could have *shot* you."

Thomas pats my hand. "There now. You didn't kill me, much as you'd like to. It's a terrible strain you've been under. Tell me. Why didn't you stay at the Temple as you said you would?"

I massage the knot between my brows. "You should have known I wouldn't."

"I suppose." Thomas sighs. "Rest easy in this, milady. Because of you, we found a way to rescue Damon."

I take a deep breath and slowly release it. "But our work isn't done. We have to get him out of the city."

Thomas turns my hand over and fingers my blood-stained sleeve. "This could be your brother's blood, but I seem to recall your clothes were bloody long before you touched him." He looks at me expectantly.

I've no intention of telling him what happened with Rolf in the Governor's Perch. I want to banish those events from my memory. "I'm too tired to talk. I'll try to get some rest. Maybe you should too."

His dark eyes are suspicious as he rises. "I'll leave you in peace then. Or as much peace as anyone can muster in times like these."

A scream beyond the walls confirms this sentiment.

Once he's gone, my thoughts drift to Henri—the Temple orphan who called himself Firebrand—and Margaret, his sweetheart. How I already miss her sharp tongue.

I nestle my head against Thomas' coat and give way to grief.

38

FROM THE ASHES

"Close your eyes," Con says.

I squeeze them shut as she pours hot water over my head.

"Where did you go last night?" When I don't answer, she sets aside the pitcher and rubs a bar of soap against my scalp. "And how did your clothes get all bloody?"

Her questions make me want to stuff my fingers in my ears. "It would take too long to explain. Ask me another day. Please."

Con rubs harder. "Can I call you Gabby—since you're a girl after all?"

I nod and surrender to the fingers massaging my skull. It's ages since I properly washed my hair—red or black. I wish Con could scrub away every vestige of Gabrielle Rouge.

When Con's finished, she sits cross-legged on my bed and watches me towel and comb out my hair. "Sister Agnes says the man in the infirmary is your brother," she announces, adding, "I wish I had a brother."

I pull a strand into my range of vision. My hair's still dark, but I can see the red at least. I reach for the clean shirt on the bed.

"Everyone's upset about Margaret. But I'm not. She didn't like me." Con points at the grey riding habit pooled on the planks. "Why don't you wear that, Gabby?"

How can I tell her it's the costume of a murderess?

AT TWILIGHT, Sister Agnes comes to the infirmary to give me a break from watching over Damon. I've stayed at his side since sharing the dire news about Margaret and Henri. After I force down some supper, I decide to check on the state of the city.

I'm surprised that the door to the observatory has been left unlocked. On the roof, I discover the Heron leaning against the parapet, staring at dozens of fires. As I join him, screams, shouts, and shattering glass drift on the wind.

"Have you come to watch a better age rise from the ashes?" The rebel sounds more cynical than inspired.

I shake my head and rub my chilled forearms.

"The mob is a powerful instrument for change. It only requires a strong voice to lead it," he observes.

"Your voice?"

"Why not?" He faces me. "And if the mob listens, I'll finish what the others started."

Has he changed his mind about violence?

I tuck my cold hands under my arms. "You'll die if you go out there."

"No. I'll die if I remain *here*," he says slowly. "The mob will turn on the Temple when they run out of merchants and remember the High Fabricator is Duke Edmond's sister."

"Why do you call her that?" The events at the prison seem to have hardened him. I liked him better back at the Red Nag.

"Because of the great lie she tells." He wrinkles his thin nose in distaste. "The promise of an afterlife is the tool of despots, and the gods are dead."

His ideas are even more heretical than Mother Celine's.

"Perhaps you merely fail to see the blessings of the Goddess in your life," I counter.

He gives me a look of pity. "All my life, I have been reminded that I fail to deserve them." He grasps my sleeve. "You should come with me."

I resist the urge to tear free. "No. I'll remain here. With my brother."

"*My* brothers are the ones who share my vision." His tone is condescending. "Even so, I'll have none of that Fierelli claptrap of roads and quests and paradise. There is only this world, which is brief, dark, and cruel."

I shrug him off and take a step backwards. "Then you won't attend the death rites for Margaret and Firebrand?"

He shakes his head. "Meaningless ritual." His features soften. "It's strange that you are not a boy, Gabrielle March."

Now he looks more like the young man I remember. "I'm sorry I deceived you." I hold out a hand to him. "If we meet again one day, I hope you'll tell me your real name."

He shakes my hand and says, "And I dearly hope I shall never have to."

Con darts onto the roof from the observatory.

"Your brother's in a rage, Gabby!" she gasps. "Sister Agnes says you must come quick!"

WHEN I REACH THE INFIRMARY, Damon sways beside his bed, waving a sharp instrument. Anne and Sister Agnes try to reason with him.

"Don't touch me, you old witch!" Damon's eyes are wild.

"Damon, calm down," I urge.

"Thank the Goddess you're here, milady!" Anne gasps.

"When I left, you were sleeping. What's happened?" I ask Damon.

He thrusts a bloody finger in my face. "The young witch cut me!"

"I'm not a witch! I just need some of his blood for the microscope—to see if there's infection." Anne holds up a small clay disk. "I use this to capture the drops. If there's an infection, it will appear in the sample long before he fevers."

Sister Agnes' rheumy eyes squint at him. "If you ask me, the infection is in his *brain*."

"Damon, give me the instrument." I extend a hand. "These women mean you no harm."

Damon stares at me uncertainly. His behaviour is so unlike him, and I'm alarmed by the blood soaking his dressing.

"This is science, not witchcraft," I assure him.

He lets me take the instrument, and I return it to Anne. "What do you call this?"

"A scalpel." Anne doesn't take her eyes off my brother. "Please lie on the bed, Lord Damon."

"For the last time, I'm not *Lord* Damon!" he shouts at her.

I press a hand on his bare arm. "Don't be such a bully. Lie down please."

His skin feels hot. Could he already be running a fever?

Once I have him settled, Anne swipes his bloody finger against the clay disk. "I'll take this to the laboratory." She whisks out of the room.

I sit on the edge of the bed and sponge Damon's face with a cloth.

"There'll be no more objectionable behaviour from you, Lord—er—Mister March," Sister Agnes says firmly. "We're doing our best to help you. Now get some rest."

Damon turns his face towards me. "Stay with me while I sleep, Gabby. I have such terrible dreams."

I brush the damp hair from his forehead. "I'll stay. You go, Sister Agnes."

Once she's gone, I hum one of Papa's songs and watch the tension ease around his mouth. He closes his eyes.

"Gabby, promise to tell Maman that I love her," he murmurs. "Tell her I never wanted to hurt her or Papa."

"Maman already knows this," I murmur back. "And you'll tell her yourself when you see her."

His breathing slows and deepens. In sleep, he looks even more like Maman. Once again I feel like I'm the older sibling.

I'll do whatever I must to protect him.

39

FORGIVENESS

The moon peers between cloud wisps when I enter the garden. Riotous sounds, a reminder of mayhem, drift over the walls. Arrayed in spotless white robes, the bodies of Margaret and Firebrand are arranged on two pyres.

The children, wrapped in blankets, watch with round eyes as Anne pours resin on the pyres. One by one, the residents of the Temple come to pay their respects. I line up behind Sophie.

She turns to me and blinks large brown eyes. "I never knew her meetings with Henri would lead to this. I was excited to be a small part of the movement though I was afraid to climb over the wall and dash about the city with her. I should have talked her out of it."

Does Sophie suspect how guilty *I* feel? Why did I let Margaret leave the Red Nag with the others? Why didn't I make her come with Thomas and me to the ship?

"You didn't know it would end like this," I say instead.

Sobbing, the vestal tucks a sprig of goldenrod behind Margaret's ear and caresses her neat brown braid. "Sleep well, dear friend," she whispers.

When it's my turn, I kiss Margaret's icy cheek. A cloth conceals her neck wound. "I wish we'd had more time together. I learned so much from you. I'll never forget you."

On the other side of the pyre, Firebrand's smooth chin and cheekbones gleam like marble. Bandages conceal the right side of his face. His still lips once stirred the resolve of his companions and the citizens of Andwarf.

How quickly lives change—and end.

"'For I discern the way to freedom lies above,'" I murmur in his cold ear. "'Pluck up your courage, Comrade; let it fly like a dove.'"

When I rejoin the other vestals, a small hand touches mine. I look down into Con's solemn eyes and draw her against my hip. She clings, but no sobs wrack her skinny body.

Mother Celine takes the torch from Sister Agnes and positions herself between the pyres. "Night brings darkness but also dreams. Dreams of freedom, equity, and justice. I consign this righteous young man and woman to the flame. May it purify them and make them acceptable in the eyes of the Goddess. May they enjoy the fruits of Paradise. Better should we die in the endeavour, than chart an easier course, and freedom find never. Sela."

"Sela," we repeat.

I think about my meeting with the Heron and his radical notions about religion. What made him so bitter and cynical?

Mother Celine places the torch against Margaret's pyre, then Firebrand's. Con's grip tightens on my hip as the resin ignites. Is she thinking about her mother and the workhouse fire? The flames snake across the wood and lap at the still bodies. I notice Thomas, who wears a Temple Guard uniform, standing in the shadows. I wish I could see his face.

My sorrow rises with the smoke that billows against the

night sky. Margaret and the lad she loved will never grow old together.

A hand touches my arm.

"Come to my chamber," Mother Celine says.

I brush the Goddess' globe and send it spinning. I wish there was a place where I could hide.

Mother Celine washes her hands in a basin and dries them on a cloth. "As soon as order is restored, I'll send word to Margaret's family. Poor Henri had none."

I swallow the lump in my throat. "Will there ever be order again?"

"This isn't the first time the city has known violence, and it won't be the last," Mother Celine replies as she gestures to her chairs. "Rest. I'll light the hearth and prepare some tea."

I'm grateful for the warmth once a fire crackles. I sit and spread my fingers on my thighs. Papa's silver ring and Katarina's gold one sparkle.

Should I keep them as reminders of what happened? Is that why Papa wore the Duke's ring but never spoke of war?

Mother Celine hangs a copper kettle over the flames and sits next to me, extending her small feet towards the fire. "I heard the altercation between the rebels and Von Haugen's guards in the wee hours of the morning. At sunrise, I learned you and Margaret were missing. Next—that more rebels had been arrested. I feared the worst."

I cover my face with my hands. "I'm sorry, Mother Celine."

"Save your apologies, Lady Gabrielle," she says quietly. "I went to the Governor's residence to plead for your lives."

"You left the Temple?" I look at her, but she stares into the fire.

"Yes—though Governor Visser would not speak to me.

Instead he sent out his mercenary." She interlaces tiny fingers on her abdomen. "Mister Von Haugen was delighted to tell me that Visser wanted to wipe out the rebel chapter once and for all. That he would tear down the Temple stone by stone and kill each person inside unless I gave *you* to him. I knew then that *you* had not been arrested."

"What did you tell Rolf?" I ask.

"It's best you don't know the language I used." Mother Celine smiles to herself. "When I returned to the Temple, Sam was waiting with your message. I went to the roof to see what was happening at the prison. The telescope was already aimed there, and I used it to watch you enter and climb up to the Governor's Perch. When I saw Rolf do the same, I feared for you."

"I stabbed him," I blurt. "And I shot Governor Visser."

When Mother Celine turns her face towards me, her blue eyes are wide. "Tell me how this came to pass."

"It's too awful."

She reaches over and rests her tiny palm on my forearm. "You'll do more harm than good if you build a wall around yourself, my child. Start at the beginning. Leave out nothing."

The fire has burned low, and my tea is cold by the time I finish.

"I'm sorry my actions hurt Katarina, Margaret, Henri, and Damon," I conclude. "But I feel no remorse for what I did to the Governor or Rolf. Does that make sense?"

Mother Celine rises and stands before me. "Though those men deserved their fates, you must ask the Goddess' forgiveness." She cups my skull in her hands. "Furthermore, for each life you have taken, you must salvage another, even if that person is your mortal enemy. Only then shall you know peace. Now. Let us pray together."

. . .

AFTER I LEAVE Mother Celine's study, I pass through the corridor connecting the children's rooms. The little ones sleep, curled like kittens, in their beds. Con whimpers and clutches her blanket. What horrors has she known in her short life? And what others lie in store?

I shake off dire thoughts and go to my own room, where I light a candle to chase away the shadows. *Everyman's Journey* lies on my table. I strip to my chemise and wash my hands and face. I lie down, and cushioning my head on my arm, open the volume.

The candle flickers as I read, this time perceiving things I missed. Fierelli's words give me a lens— like a telescope—to view Everyman when he meets a Stranger at a fork in the road to the Celestial City.

Everyman: Are there not digressions or short cuts by which a person can lose his way?

Stranger: Some side paths diverge from this narrow trail, but they are wide and meandering, tortuous and steep. You must walk the path which is straight and true.

Everyman: But how shall I discern right path from wrong?

Stranger: You shan't. You must make your best choice and live with the consequence.

I recall Firebrand's words:

"*One sentence at a time, Fierelli revolutionizes our world.*"

The light of purpose within the Temple Guardian shines in a book written to transform the minds of all who read it. Warmth suffuses my veins and ignites a spark of hope for my future.

Maybe we are more than we can imagine.

40

BITTER FRUIT

Sophie and I dig two holes beneath the walnut tree and place Margaret's and Firebrand's urns inside them. After we finish patting the soil over the small graves, I turn to find Thomas watching us.

"I'd like a word with you, milady." He nods at Sophie. "Will you give us some privacy, lass?"

Sophie nods and disappears inside the Temple.

I don't like him calling her "lass."

Thomas cuts into an apple with a small knife. He holds out the slice, and I take it. The flavour is both sweet and tart.

Thomas gestures to the stone bench. "Rest a while, milady."

Curious, I sit. When I open my mouth to ask what he wants, he hands me another apple slice and cuts one for himself. I surmise he won't speak his mind until he's ready. The minutes drag while we share the apple in silence. At last Thomas tosses the core in the bushes and returns his knife to his belt.

"I want to speak to you of Rolf Von Haugen," be begins.

My spine stiffens.

"Mother Celine told me that—in order to defend yourself—you stabbed him," he says with an undertone of reproach.

I push aside my irritation with Mother Celine for sharing this information.

He rests his hands on his hips. "I'm sorry for that. Truly. But why didn't you tell me he was hunting you?"

"I was afraid of what you or Damon would do." I wipe my hands on my breeches. "If you'd known, what *would* you have done?"

"I'd have killed him."

I shudder.

"And you shot the Governor as well?" Thomas shakes his head. "I thought I knew you, lass, but you've plenty of secrets. Tell me how it happened."

The story unfolds easier this time though surprise, revulsion, and rage steal across Thomas' handsome face. When I'm finished, his dark eyes hold mine for a long moment.

"I wish you'd trusted me enough to tell me all this," he says.

"But I do trust you." The words come out in a rush. "You've no idea." I stop myself before I start babbling like a ninny. "Can we speak of Lille instead?"

He nods.

I compose myself. "Here are the facts. Damon doesn't want to be Lord of Lille. He wants to study at the university in Marianas."

Thomas whistles. "That's a daft notion."

"You altered *your* destiny by leaving the fief," I argue. "Why can't Damon do the same?"

He shakes his head. "But if your brother sails to Anglia, who takes charge of your father's lands?"

I clear my throat. "I will."

Thomas cocks an eyebrow.

"Damon may not want Lille, but I do. And I'll fight for it if I have to." I realize my hands have formed into fists.

The corner of his mouth twitches.

"Do I amuse you?" I ask, annoyed.

"No, it's only that you look exactly like your father right now." Thomas sits beside me. "And who had a chance of stopping Simon March when his mind was made up?"

Relieved, I continue. "I want you to go to Marianas with Damon to keep an eye on him. Intercede with the Duke on his behalf. We have no money, so—"

"Do you think the Duke and I are on speaking terms?" Thomas interrupts.

I try to remember what Papa said about Thomas' time in Marianas. "But you worked in the Duke's foundry, didn't you?"

"I did. For Mister Leopold," Thomas says. "But that's water under an old bridge, milady. And I never met the Duke."

"Oh." I wish I had a year to learn all there is to know about Thomas. "So, why *did* you come back from Marianas?"

"That's a story I'd prefer to forget," Thomas replies. "I don't think I'll be returning there anytime soon."

His refusal frustrates all my plans. I can't send Damon—weak and injured—to Marianas alone.

"But I'll come with you to Lille," he says. "I haven't been home since before my mam passed. My da—" He pauses and shakes his head. "It's never been easy between us. To tell you the truth, Lord Simon was more of a father to me than my own." He rests his elbows on his knees. "And though I loved Damon like a little brother, my days of looking out for him are over. He's got to make his own way. As for you, milady, I remember how proud Lord Simon was that you learned to ride before you could walk."

Will I always be a child in his eyes?

He smiles. "And now the girl from Lille has become a woman."

Life is short. Didn't I just inter Margaret's ashes? I will myself the courage to speak.

"Ever since I kissed you, I feel like we—I mean I—" I take a breath and place my hand on his.

He jerks away as if I scorched him. His horrified expression quashes any hope I had.

I shouldn't have listened to Zoh's teasing or dreamed Thomas has feelings for me. When he called Sophie "lass," I should have realized that it's a word. Nothing more.

"I'm sorry. I misspoke. I don't know what came over me." As I rise, I keep my eyes averted—to hide my humiliation. "I'll go check on my brother."

Thomas stretches the muscles in his lower back. Is he oblivious to the emotions roiling within me? "If you need me, I'll be here."

I know he will—but only because I'm Lord Simon's daughter.

Concern knots Sister Agnes' brow. "He's got a powerful fever, Lady Gabrielle."

I place a hand on Damon's forehead. His skin is hot.

"I've given him a cold sponge bath and some willow bark tea," Sister Agnes continues.

I'm relieved to hear this since Maman also uses willow bark for fevers.

I check Damon's dressings. The pads are stained with pus. "Is there nothing more we can do for him?"

"We could apply some of Anne's bread mold to his wounds." The old woman fiddles with the cloth covering a small basket. "Anne believes the spores will attack the animalcules causing the corruption."

"It sounds like an unorthodox treatment," I say doubtfully.

Sister Agnes removes a slice of moldy bread from the basket. "Perhaps it's a risk worth taking since he hasn't yet responded to traditional remedies. Would you rather he die of a fever?"

"Of course not."

She crooks a bony finger at me. "Then wash your hands and help me remove his bandages."

After we're done applying the bread and redressing Damon's wounds, Sister Agnes tells me to wash my hands again. "Mother Celine tells me you'll return to Lille as soon as your brother is well enough to travel," Sister Agnes says as she offers me a towel.

I nod. I'm perturbed that Thomas and Mother Celine share so much information with one another but so very little with me.

Sister Agnes dips a cloth in a water basin and dabs Damon's forehead. "Will you tell your mother what happened at the prison?"

Does she mean—will I tell her that I killed two men?

I swallow. "I'm not sure."

Sister Agnes folds the cloth and sets it aside. "Did you know your mother was a vestal here?"

"She was?" I sink onto a chair behind Damon's bed.

Sister Agnes' wrinkled lips expand in a wistful smile. "Violet came to us when she was eight."

"But her family perished in a fire," I say quickly. "She was raised in the household of her great uncle, who died not long after she married my father."

Sister Agnes shakes her head ever so slightly.

How much of what I've believed most of my life is a lie?

"When your mother was in her sixteenth year, Lord Simon passed through Andwarf on the way to his new fief. He stopped at an apothecary shop to ask about a remedy for an old wound. Your mother and I were there, purchasing rare herbs. When she offered him advice, he never took his eyes from her face. And I knew."

Bitterness creeps over me. Why did Maman keep her own connection to the Temple a secret all these years? And why did she send me here—and consign me to a fate that *she* was able to avoid? It is thoroughly unfair and smacks of betrayal.

"Later that day, he came to the Temple and asked for Violet's hand in marriage," Sister Agnes continues, oblivious to my warring emotions. "The former Guardian was delighted to ally herself with one of the Duke's most decorated warriors." The old woman sighs. "This was long ago, of course."

Nearly twenty years, I would guess. How strange it is that I had to come all the way to Andwarf to hear this tale.

"A wonderful story," I conclude, but my tone rings harsh.

"Despite our best laid plans, the Goddess opens hidden doors for us." Sister Agnes adjusts Damon's blanket. "Why do you wish to send your brother to Marianas?"

As if he heard her, Damon moans.

I stroke his forehead to calm him. "It's what he wants. If he survives this fever."

"Oh, he'll survive." The old woman places her gnarled hand on mine and squeezes. "Now, if you'll excuse me, I'll crawl into my bed. Do you mind keeping an eye on your brother?"

"Not at all. Thank you for your care and attention."

"You must have faith that this will pass, my dear," she says, pausing in the doorway. "Faith is all we have when the road ahead is uncertain."

After she's gone, I kneel beside the bed, resting my cheek on my forearms, and listen to Damon's ragged breaths. I consider what I have learned—specifically about Maman's past. Just who was her family?

41

THE MOB

A DOOR SLAMS.

Groggily I sit up and look about, uncertain of my surroundings. It's fully dark, and moonlight touches Damon's face, slack and innocent as a child's.

I'm still in the infirmary.

I touch his cheek, then his forehead and neck. His skin is cool and dry. His fever has broken!

I open the door to call for Sister Agnes and find myself looking into Thomas' startled face. Anne and Sophie are behind him.

"How's Damon?" Thomas asks.

"Much better, thank you," I tell him.

A boom and angry shouts reverberate throughout the Temple.

"Pack your things. Best be quick," Thomas says. "The mob's here."

Fear spurs me up the stairs to my room. Through my window, firelight glows beyond the Temple walls and highlights the branches of the walnut tree. I gather my few possessions, including Anne's copy of *Everyman's Journey*. When I make my way back downstairs, I smell smoke.

Can the Temple burn?

In the sanctuary, the children are awake and rubbing their eyes. Mother Celine wanders amongst them, offering words of comfort. Sam sits at the foot of the Goddess. Where has he been the last few days? Thomas leans against a pillar, reading a note.

"Sam brought us word from Hernando." Thomas folds the note and applies it to a torch flame. "The Black Bull has been ransacked and burnt to the ground, along with most of the ale houses in the district. Molly, Zoh, and Gonzalo sail tonight on the Redemption. The ship is Damon's last chance for a safe and speedy exit." He stares at me. "You also might like to know the rebels have taken over the Governor's residence."

I picture the Heron seated behind Visser's desk. Will he be more generous than his predecessor? Are Red Cap and Tricorn Hat with him? How could those young men possibly govern a city?

Anne and Sophie enter, supporting Damon between them. He now wears a Temple Guard uniform. His legs wobble, and he looks pale and weak. I fear we have moved him too soon.

"Thomas, please help him," I ask.

Thomas takes Sophie's place and drapes Damon's arm over his own shoulder.

"Is it true we're leaving?" Damon asks.

"Send out the witches!" a woman shouts outside the Temple.

"Yes, Lord Damon, and not a moment too soon," Mother Celine says.

"Mother Celine, you can't remain here," I tell her. "As the Duke's sister, you'll be the mob's next target."

She stiffens. "My life's work is nurturing the orphans of this city. I won't desert them."

"But what if the mob storms the Temple?" I ask.

Sister Agnes shuffles in with a basket. "Just let them try. We've thunder balls aplenty."

"Can you ride?" Thomas asks Damon.

Damon nods.

"He's still very weak," I point out.

Anne opens Damon's yellow tunic to check the dressing. "His wounds are far from healed."

"We'll have to take the risk," Thomas says. "Sam, get our mounts."

The boy darts from the sanctuary. Thomas helps Damon stagger to the statue of the Goddess.

I set my belongings next to Damon. "How will we get past the mob?"

"Wrap yourselves with these bandages." Sister Agnes grabs a handful from her basket. "Tell the fools outside we have a pestilence in the Temple. That'll make them think twice."

Anne and I swathe Damon's head until only his eyes show. The vestal helps me wrap a bandage around my own forehead and another from crown to chin.

Yet another disguise.

When I offer to return her copy of *Everyman's Journey*, Anne smiles wistfully. "Keep it—till I see you again."

I squeeze her hand. I hate to leave her and Sophie behind.

Thomas, his own head swathed in bandages, turns to Mother Celine. "I thank you for your kindness. I'll repay you one day."

"You already have. Ten-fold." Mother Celine looks so tiny next to him. "Please take good care of Lady Gabrielle. I've grown fond of her."

I kneel at her feet and look into her kind blue eyes. "One

day I'd like to return to help Sophie and Anne with their missions. Not just because it's what my father wished. It's what *I* want."

"We'll be waiting." Mother Celine adjusts one of the bandages concealing my face. "Farewell, my child. I hope our paths cross under better circumstances."

I rise and, stooping, wrap my arms around her. "Goodbye Mister Fierelli," I whisper in her ear.

When I draw back, Mother Celine looks startled.

A hand tugs my breeches, and I look down into Con's sad, wet face.

Her lower lip quivers. "Are you leaving me behind?"

"I'll come back, Con. I promise." With my thumbs, I wipe the tears from her cheeks. "In the meantime, you must do your best in your lessons, and behave yourself for Sister Agnes."

"*That* would be a miracle," the old woman observes.

Sam re-enters with Minx, who prances on the slippery marble. Her neighs echo in the sanctuary.

"Lady Gabrielle, you and Damon take the mare," Thomas instructs.

"What about you?" I tuck my things in my saddlebag. "What in the world—" Papa's sword hangs from my saddle. "How did you get this?"

"George wanted you to have it," Thomas replies.

Before I can ask how he managed this, a bellow reverberates from deep within the Temple. Snorting and farting, Magnus trots into the sanctuary. He wears a crude red harness and bridle. The children scream in fear and delight.

"How do you think Sam got here safely from the tavern?" Thomas strokes the bull's nose.

Magnus snorts again and shoves his head into Thomas' chest, nearly toppling him.

I mount Minx and guide her to the statue. As Anne and

Sophie help Damon settle behind me, I hope he has the strength to hang on.

Thomas gives me a pistol. "It's loaded. If you need it, don't be shy."

I want to refuse, but I must protect my brother at all costs. The weight of the weapon in my hand brings little assurance that I'll know where and when to use it.

"Anne! Sophie! Join the others on the roof!" Mother Celine calls. "You know what to do!"

As the two vestals sprint from the sanctuary, Thomas vaults onto the bull. Two altons help Sister Agnes unbar and open the huge doors.

Outside, torchlight reveals a sea of leering faces, wreathed in smoke. Two men lunge forward, then quickly retreat when they see Magnus. Thomas guides the bull onto the terrace, and I follow, but the mob blocks our access to the stairs.

"Let us pass!" Thomas' voice echoes beneath the Temple roof.

Magnus bellows and paws the stone flags while Minx neighs and prances. Those closest to us back away.

"For the love of the Goddess, let these men through! They have the plague!" Sister Agnes cries behind us.

"You're lying!" Mistress Lever shouts.

I should have known the soap makers would be here.

"We've burned two bodies already! You must have seen the fires!" Mother Celine calls. "This party must leave the Temple and city—lest contagion spread!"

The Temple doors bang shut.

"She's a witch!" Mistress Lever accuses. "They're all witches!"

"If there's been witchcraft, it hasn't cured us of the plague!" I assert. "Would any of you like to come close to be sure?" I point my pistol at Mister Lever. "How about you, sir?"

The skinny man ducks behind his wife.

Mistress Lever thrusts out her chin and glares. "I say we kill them!"

The mob stretches down the Temple steps and spills into the square. Damon's grip tightens on my waist. Remembering Katarina's fate, I'd prefer to turn the pistol on him rather than allow him to fall into their hands.

"Look at the sky!" an old woman cries.

The crowd turns away from us, looking south. A huge ball floats above the city walls. Damon's thighs clench beneath mine.

I've never seen the like of it. Am I dreaming?

"What in the name of the Goddess is that?" Damon breathes in my ear.

A crone in a tattered blanket shuffles out of the crowd. She looks familiar though I'm not sure where I've seen her.

"Fire, blood, and plague! The signs are everywhere!" She points a crooked finger at the ball, which now blocks the lighthouse from view. "Be you ready!" she shrieks. "The time of Great Destruction has come!"

Now I remember. She railed at me in the street just before I discovered Papa's body at the Crossed Keys.

The crowd panics. Screams and shouts reverberate against the Temple as the citizens of Andwarf turn their backs and flee. Mistress Lever shoves her husband aside in her haste to reach the steps.

"Let's get to the ship!" Thomas calls, sliding off Magnus. "If this is the end of the world, the timing couldn't be better!"

As he leads the bull down the broad steps, sure-footed Minx follows. I lean back in the saddle and press the pistol into my brother's hand, so I can grip both the reins and pommel.

"Safe journey!" Sophie cries from the rooftop.

"The Goddess go with you!" Anne shouts.

Once we reach the square, Thomas remounts, and we set out for the harbour at a reckless pace.

Andwarf is a nightmare. We ride past the blackened skeletons of shops. Corpses float in canals. The bodies of Night Watchmen and merchants hang from lamp posts. We come upon a party of looters, but they give us a wide berth. Our plague bandages and Magnus' threatening bellows must make them think twice about accosting us.

As we cross a canal, a riderless horse trots out of the gloom, throws up its head, and neighs. Minx whinnies in reply. The stray horse angles towards us, coming close enough for me to grab his reins.

Thomas slides off Magnus's back and slaps the bull's rump, sending him ahead. He strokes the neck of the agitated horse until it calms and nestles its head against Minx.

The blacksmith checks the girth before springing into the saddle. "Can you manage a gallop, Damon?" he asks, sawing the reins as the skittish creature threatens to bolt.

"I'm all right," my brother asserts. "Let's get to the ship before this city kills us."

Thomas' new mount races down the street. Minx and I take up pursuit while Damon hangs on for all he's worth.

42

PARTING

The moon paints the Redemption's sails with silver. Thomas fires his pistol in the air, sending his skittish mount into a fit. The ship answers with a volley, and a longboat disembarks. From the sunken fishing boats, charred remains of the docks, and the deserted, broken buildings lining the esplanade, I deduce the mob has already been here.

Thomas and I ease Damon from the saddle and sit him on the flagstones. I shift my brother's tunic to check his wounds.

"Quit fussing, Gabby." Damon claws at the bandages swathing his face. "I'm fine."

"You won't be able to climb the ladder to get into the ship," I tell him.

"Just see if I can't," Damon replies.

"They'll raise him in the boat," Thomas says, as he unwinds his own bandages. "We lost Magnus somewhere. Maybe he went to the Black Bull. What's left of it."

As we watch the longboat draw closer, I untie the cloths concealing my face.

"Milady, you never said what happened to the lass in your brother's tale," Thomas says. "I'd like to know."

The last thing on my mind is storytelling. "I can't remember where I left off."

"The lad fell from the Goddess' cart and became a shooting star," Thomas prods. "And the lass?"

"She dove after her brother and died with him," Damon answers. "The Goddess put them in the sky as the morning and evening stars. Isn't that the way I told it, Gabby?"

"I believe it is."

"Not a romantic ending. Is it possible the evening and morning stars are one and the same?" Thomas gestures at the night sky.

My thoughts turn to the great telescope and Margaret's patient instructions on how to use it. She never had a chance to teach me about the stars.

How hard it is to make a friend and then lose her.

I clear my throat. "The truth might spoil the ending."

The longboat is closer now. Hernando and Gonzalo row while Zoh kneels in the prow, holding up a lantern. Molly's bulk fills the middle.

"Tell Maman I'm sorry I'm not the son she and Papa wanted me to be," Damon murmurs.

"We are what we are," I say to comfort him. "Maman understands that."

"Are you so certain?" Damon asks.

In truth, I am not. In the last week, our whole world has been turned upside down.

I slide the gold ring from my finger. "Katarina wanted you to have this, though I didn't have the chance to give it to you. I know you didn't return her affection, but she loved you deeply and defended you more than once. Now that she's gone, you must wear this to remember her."

"If you wish me to," Damon says.

I place the ring on his little finger.

"And I want you to have Papa's as well." I tug at the silver ring on my thumb.

"No, Gabby." Damon kisses my forehead and whispers, "Papa's lands were yours all along. In your heart, you know he'd prefer it this way."

I recall Papa's words to me back at the Garland Inn:

"The Goddess alone understands why you were born second—and a girl. You are more suited to overseeing a fief than any man I know."

The longboat bumps the esplanade, and Hernando and Gonzalo toss ropes to Thomas.

"A sad state of affairs," Hernando observes as he helps Thomas secure the boat. "There won't be anything left of the city for the Duke to reclaim."

"What do you mean?" I ask the privateer.

"The Duke will send men and ships to take back what's his. He won't let Andwarf remain in rebel hands," Hernando explains.

"The mob won't stand a chance against an armed invasion," Thomas concurs.

His words remind me of what Damon said during his trial regarding Governor Visser and Emperor Maximillian. Twenty years ago, the Duke of Anglia presented Papa with Lille as a buffer to prevent the Imperial army from marching overland and retaking Andwarf. With Papa dead and the city in chaos, what will stop the Emperor now?

"How are you, Lady Gabrielle?" Molly calls from the longboat, disturbing my speculations. "I feared for you!"

"I'm fine, but my brother's hurt. You'll make sure he's cared for, won't you?" I reply.

Hernando's pointed teeth glisten in the moonlight. "On the

lips of Munificus, I make this vow, milady. The Duke's own physicians shall attend him."

The privateer and Gonzalo climb out while the women remain seated. When the men transfer my brother to the boat, Damon rests against Molly's knees, and Zoh tucks a blanket around him. I'm grateful for the lantern, which allows me to see Damon's face.

"I won't let him out of my sight." Molly places a white hand on Damon's uninjured shoulder. "He owes me two weeks rent."

"Speaking of that." Hernando pulls a pouch from his coat and bows. "I'm returning two of your diamonds, Lady Gabrielle. I'll not leave you destitute."

I am moved by the gesture. "Thank you, but give them to my brother. He needs them more than I do."

"As you wish, milady." Hernando extends his arm to Thomas. "Until we meet again."

Thomas clasps his hand. "Safe travels."

"The tide's going out," Molly says. "And there's dry throats waiting in Marianas. Gonzalo, what shall we call our new tavern?"

"My Lady of the Horse?" Gonzalo suggests.

"That has a nice sound," Molly agrees.

Gonzalo raises a skinny finger. "Will anyone wager that Lady Gabrielle *won't* make an appearance in Marianas one day soon?"

Hernando takes up the oars. "Not I, uncle. The Goddess favours her, and who bets against the gods?"

After all that Molly and the others have done for me, I hate to bid them farewell.

A loud snort startles the horses. Magnus trots out of the gloom, his crimson saddle dangling beneath his belly.

"Magnus!" Molly exclaims. "Oh, my beautiful boy!"

"Rest easy, Molly. We'll take him back to Lille if he'll let us," Thomas promises.

As the longboat re-enters the harbour, Magnus' mournful bellow echoes my own sadness.

Dear Goddess, please let Damon be all right, I pray as I wave goodbye.

"You can do nothing more for your brother," Thomas says. "He's a man, and he must chart his own course."

My heart leaps when Thomas drops on one knee and takes my hand. "What are you doing?"

His grip is firm. "Stop wriggling like a fish, and listen." He clears his throat. "I've told you I owe your father a great deal, and so I'll repay that debt by serving you as my da served Lord Simon." His dark eyes glitter. "I pledge myself to you, Lady Gabrielle March."

His words are a bitter reminder of the futility of my attraction for him, feelings I've carried for a long time like a silly maid's folly. But since Thomas thinks I'm a woman now, and Damon views me as the future Lady of Lille, perhaps it's time I acted accordingly.

"I thank you for that pledge, Mister Smithson, and I expect your skills and advice will prove invaluable." I take back my hand.

Thomas gives me a pensive look, as if my response is not the one he anticipated. Then his face relaxes, and he rises.

"Let's mount up, milady. I've no idea what to expect at the city gates. Hopefully Magnus will give any ruffians we encounter something to think about." He turns his broad shoulders to me. "And I must confess I'm more than a little curious about that strange object we saw in the sky. I don't imagine it was the Goddess' chariot."

I watch the longboat grow small as Hernando and Gonzalo

stroke closer to the Redemption. Hernando's voice floats on the waves.

The lass was the fairest
With eyes blue as rain
Her hair tied in a love knot
As she strolled down the lane
Tu lar tu lee
Tu lar lee a lee

My mind drifts back to Papa, singing in his room at the Garland. How I miss him.

Gonzalo sings the next verse.

A great lord came a riding
And the lass he did see
Oh, his poor heart was taken
By one so pretty.

I hum the chorus, feigning a lightness I do not feel.

"That's more like you." Thomas places my mare's reins in my hand before he mounts his skittish horse.

More like me? Do I even know who I'm becoming?

"Try to keep up, Mister Smithson." I swing into the saddle.

If the Imperial army is about to march through Lille, Maman needs to be forewarned. She also has secrets which must be brought to light. It's time I went home.

I turn Minx's head towards the city gates and spur her to a gallop.

If you enjoyed *Gabrielle and the Rebels,* please post a review on Amazon and/or Goodreads. Tell your friends and local librarian about it.

Are you ready to buckle up for more of Gabrielle's adventures in the Winds of Change series? *Gabrielle Rouge, The Outlaw Gabrielle* and Gabrielle and the Emperor are available through Amazon and Kobo.

GLOSSARY OF ARCHAIC AND INVENTED WORDS

- Alms - money or food given to the poor
- Alton - a male youth who lives at the Temple of Andwarf
- Andwarf - coastal city
- Anglia - a large island ruled by Duke Edmond
- Artisan - a skilled worker in a particular trade, especially one that involves making items by hand
- Bactia - goddess of the South Wind; represents fertility
- Bay - a horse with a brown coat and a black mane and tail
- Berengaria - the country ruled by Emperor Maximillian
- Black powder - gun powder
- Bollocks - testicles
- Boon - favour
- Breeches - tight-fitting trousers
- Chamberlain - head servant
- Colognia - capital of the Berengarian Empire

GLOSSARY OF ARCHAIC AND INVENTED WORDS

- Consumption - tuberculosis
- Crofter - similar to a tenant farmer; permitted by a landowner to live on and farm a small portion of land
- Deity - god or goddess
- Fealty - a vassal's oath of loyalty to his overlord
- Ferring - a coin of with a very small denomination; similar to a penny
- Fief - land granted by an overlord to a vassal who holds it in return for allegiance and service
- Fortnight - two weeks
- Frock - dress
- Gunner - a person who operates a cannon
- Hie - hasten
- Imperial War - fought twenty years earlier between Emperor Maximillian and Duke Edmond; both sides claimed victory; Duke Edmond claimed territory on the continent (Andwarf and surrounding lands) as a result
- Inesol - god of the East Wind; represents law and order
- Kirtle - a loose-fitting gown with long sleeves
- League - a distance of approximately three miles
- Lille - Lord Simon March's fief; south of Andwarf
- Litter - a portable bed or couch carried on two poles
- Marianas - the capital of Anglia
- Mark - a coin with a larger denomination, similar to a dollar
- Munificus - god of the West Wind; represents friendship
- Portcullis - a heavy iron gate that can be lowered to block access to a bridge or castle
- Rechter—the head of the Council of Merchants

GLOSSARY OF ARCHAIC AND INVENTED WORDS

- Score - twenty
- Shite - manure
- Stone - a unit of measurement equal to fourteen pounds
- Talen - a gold coin of considerable value; originally minted by the Emperor, but defaced and re-minted by the Duke of Anglia
- Vassal - a holder of land
- Vestal - a young woman who serves at the Temple
- Zephrum - god of the North Wind; represents war and aggression

DISCUSSION QUESTIONS

1. Why does Gabrielle accompany her father Simon March to Andwarf? What emotions is Gabrielle experiencing?

2. Consider Simon's view of his daughter: "You are too tall, too outspoken, and too rough around the edges... The Goddess alone understands why you were born second—and a girl. You are more suited to overseeing a fief than any man I know." Is this accurate? Does Simon deserve Gabrielle's hero worship?

3. What events set in motion Gabrielle's progression from a "country mouse" growing up in the shadow of her father to a young woman prepared to act on her own intuition and take risks?

4. Who are some of supporting characters Gabrielle encounters? Did you have any favourites? Who are the book's villains? What motivates them? Do they deserve the fates they receive?

5. After Gabrielle's arrival at the Temple of the Goddess, Mother Celine tells her, "While you are here, we shall try to discover the gaps in your education. Your father's letters indi-

cated there are several." What "gaps" does Gabrielle have? What does she discover about life at the Temple and its missions? What does Gabrielle learn about her mother?

6. What role do these inventions (microscope, printing press, telescope, pistols) play in advancing Gabrielle's quest to save her brother? What do you think about the author's use of technology, instead of magic?

7. What do you think of the book's treatment of organized religion? Respond to this quotation: "Mother Celine's face shines with purpose as she looks up at me. 'Of course I believe in Her (the Goddess). But I don't believe She resembles the statues erected in her honour, and I don't believe She is wholly female. Instead, I worship the beauty and the logic of Her creation.'"

8. Do you agree with Molly's assessment of the rebels: "You should have heard their wild notions. Bactia's buttocks, what a world we'd have with those schoolboys running it"?

9. *Everyman's Journey* is based on John Bunyan's *Pilgrim's Progress*. What interpretations do these characters have of *Everyman's Journey*: Simon, Anne, and Damon? Who is its author?

10. Would you classify *Gabrielle and the Rebels* as fantasy, historical fiction, alternative history, or romance? The book is directed at a Young Adult audience (ages 12-17). Do you think it's appropriate for young adult readers? Why or why not? What do you think might happen in the sequel *Gabrielle Rouge*?

ACKNOWLEDGMENTS

As always, I'm grateful to those who have weathered the many zig zags and revisions to this manuscript and offered encouragement and advice along the way: the Estevan Writers Group, Marie Powell, and Sharon Plumb. Thanks especially to Randy, Robin, and Blaire—my finest critics.

ABOUT THE AUTHOR

Maureen Ulrich is an award-winning author and playwright and a retired teacher from southeast Saskatchewan. When she isn't writing, Maureen enjoys attending football, baseball and hockey games, reading, and riding her motorcycle. Please follow her at https://maureenulrich.ca

ALSO BY MAUREEN ULRICH

Power Plays

Face Off

Breakaway

Shootout

The award-winning #jessiemachockeyseries can be purchased in eBook and paperback formats.

"***Power Plays*** is a wonderful title for a novel which has as its focus not only the sport of hockey but the ways we all tend to seek what we want in our various relationships. Ulrich demonstrates that there are many ways to succeed in relationships without resorting to any sort of bullying. She stresses the importance of accepting and celebrating the differences between people rather than using them as an excuse for malicious behaviour. This is an excellent novel which provides lots of action, a little romance, and a great deal to think about. Highly Recommended." **Canadian Review of Materials**

Why not read Maureen's first **poetry collection**?

Something's Different: A COVID Journal in Verse

Read about a Maasi boy's quest to find a baby elephant in Kimeto's Journey, a book designed for **Middle Grade** (ages 8-11) readers.

Picture Books (available in print only)

Sam and the Big Bridge

A Home for Hairy

www.ingramcontent.com/pod-product-compliance
Lightning Source LLC
LaVergne TN
LVHW021655060526
838200LV00050B/2356